About the Author

A visit to the town of Oradour-Sur-Glane in 2019, combined with a deep passion for history, compelled the author to create this, his first written work. A second visit to Oradour-Sur-Glane in May 2023, plus further research into the events there, have prompted extensive rewriting of the original manuscript to more accurately and faithfully portray the horror of that day. Born in New Zealand and living most of his life in Australia, the author now lives in a picturesque village in the South-East Queensland hinterland with his delightfully eccentric French wife, cats, dog and guitars.

Oradour

Revised Edition

Robert Brooke

Oradour

Revised Edition

Vanguard Press

VANGUARD PAPERBACK

© Copyright 2024
Robert Brooke

The right of Robert Brooke to be identified as author of
this work has been asserted by him in accordance with the
Copyright, Designs and Patents Act 1988.

All Rights Reserved

No reproduction, copy or transmission of this publication
may be made without written permission.
No paragraph of this publication may be reproduced,
copied or transmitted save with the written permission of the publisher, or
in accordance with the provisions
of the Copyright Act 1956 (as amended).

Any person who commits any unauthorised act in relation to this
publication may be liable to criminal prosecution and civil claims for
damages.

A CIP catalogue record for this title is available from the British Library.

ISBN 978-1-83794-288-6

This is a work of fiction. Names, characters, businesses, places, events
and incidents are either the products of the author's imagination or used in
a fictitious manner. Any resemblance to actual persons, living or dead, or
actual events is purely coincidental.

Vanguard Press is an imprint of
Pegasus Elliot Mackenzie Publishers Ltd.
www.pegasuspublishers.com

First Published in 2024

Vanguard Press
Sheraton House Castle Park
Cambridge England

Printed & Bound in Great Britain

Dedication

To Patricia

Acknowledgements

I would like to offer my sincere thanks to the following family and friends who happily gave their time to proofread my early efforts and to offer their constructive input. I have no doubt that many of these suggestions have materially improved the final form of this book. Patricia Brooke, Ailsa Brooke, John Ellis, Fiona Brooke, Sally McKaige, John Barrass, Peter Farnbach and Shaun Rogers. Many thanks to you all for the love and support you showed as I navigated my way through the writing process for the first time. Sometimes, it would appear, a second go is needed to finally get it right.

Introduction

The war had begun well for Germany.

Hitler's forces had swept all before them as they moved through Europe in the late months of 1939 and on throughout 1940 and '41.

The only disappointment had been the failure to bring Great Britain to heel!

Somehow, it still held out. Despite the massive campaign of air attacks by the Luftwaffe and the growing presence of the German U-Boat fleet, trying to strangle England's Atlantic Ocean supply lines to the US and Canada.

Despite knowing that an enemy committed to the struggle and rebuilding its strength lay just across the Channel, Hitler set about the continuing development of plans for his most daring and potentially dangerous undertaking yet.

Adolph Hitler's hatred of Soviet Russia ran deep. The overthrow of the socialist giant had always been his ultimate goal. His plans had been years in the making.

He had signed a non-aggression pact with the Soviet Union in 1939, though that was simply a means to an end. It allowed him the freedom to move militarily against Poland and other European nations without fear of Russian retaliation.

At least, not until he felt that he was ready to move first against Stalin's unprepared armies.

On June 22, 1941, he launched his plan to achieve just that.

At first, the massive offensive (named Operation Barbarossa) was unstoppable. The poorly prepared Russians, caught off-guard against the onslaught that befell them, could offer little organised resistance. The might of Nazi Germany swept them aside completely and rolled on remorselessly towards what was, for Hitler, the greatest prize of them all: Moscow.

However, in their stunning early success lay the seeds of their undoing. The Germans advanced so quickly that they eventually outpaced their own supply lines. Furthermore, the fickle Russian winter came early and with a savage intensity. Diesel fuel, vital to the continuance of the advance, was becoming increasingly scarce.

At the same time, the Russian defence was finally becoming more resolute and better led. The new Soviet commander, General Zhukov, was gaining control over his enormous but hitherto poorly organised resources.

Through his tactical and administrative brilliance, he was beginning to coordinate the Russian defences with increasing effectiveness.

The Germans had managed to make it all the way to the outermost suburbs of Moscow.

There, however, they were stopped and would go no further.

In a land used to frigid winters, that of 1941/42 was particularly harsh. Coupled with the growing difficulties in resupply and the stiffening Russian defence, the advancing German armies outside Moscow were finally halted within sight of the city.

In the southern sectors, though, on the front lines of southern Russia and Ukraine, the fortunes of war were still favouring the German armies.

There was hope that they might still be able to get past the Russian defences, holding desperately around Stalingrad, and break through to the Black Sea oil fields. If the German armies could only reach the oil, everything would swing back in their favour.

However, as with the assault on Moscow, this goal too, was to remain elusive.

Stalingrad held out against them in, perhaps, the most terrible siege battle in history.

For the Germans, the war of advance was now slowly, but inexorably, turning into a war of attrition and retreat.

The most decisive turning point in the southern sectors, though, was a campaign known to history as the Battle of Kursk.

Kursk was, and remains, the largest tank battle ever fought. The Germans had brought their much-vaunted Panzer divisions to battle against the lesser-known Russian tank squadrons. The Russian T34 tank, though, soon proved itself a powerful and worthy adversary.

The battle had begun in July 1943 with an initial offensive by the Germans. Their aim was to encircle a Russian army that had advanced into one long sector of their lines, creating a giant bulge—referred to in military terms as a salient—potentially vulnerable to attacks on the flanks.

The Germans seized this opportunity, attacking from both the northern and southern flanks simultaneously.

Both advances were trying to join up in a classic pincer movement in order to isolate and trap the Russian army enclosed within.

However, the German advance stalled on the northern side after only a few days, and the Russians counterattacked in vast numbers.

The battle raged throughout July and August of 1943, and when the smoke cleared, any remaining hopes the Germans had for final success in Eastern Europe were over.

The agonising and bloody process of retreating towards Germany was now inevitable.

Chapter 1

Northern Ukraine, Early January 1944

Daylight had not yet begun to show itself. The first salvos of the new day, however, courtesy of the Red Army, were already starting to make life uncomfortable once more. This was the daily routine and it was unrelenting.

This time the artillery shells were pounding emplacements further up the line, but the sounds and the shock waves were still powerful.

The troops of the SS 2nd Panzer "Das Reich" Division were as used to the tumult as anyone could be. They had been on the Eastern Front for well over a year and had experienced some of the toughest fighting any men had ever endured.

It had been relentless, bloody and ultimately, futile.

This barrage though, was mild by comparison. The shells were falling on someone else. Nothing for them to worry about this morning.

They simply got about the business of preparing their food and the filthy muck that passed as coffee from behind the shelter of their tanks, or in their foxholes.

For them, the shellfire was usually less of an issue than the constant, bitter cold. The cold was the killer. The intensity of the shelling might wax and wane, but the cold stayed forever; it settled deep in the bones. No man could ever get used to that.

Diekmann braced himself against that cold as best he could and emerged from his tent. He began to wander over towards the nearest cook's fire to get something hot to eat. It did not matter how bad it was, it just needed to be hot. The same went with the ersatz coffee.

SS Sturmbannfuhrer (Major) Adolf Otto Diekmann commanded the 1st Battalion, Der Fuhrer Regiment of Das Reich Division. Now, a tall and spare man where once he had been athletic, he nonetheless demanded and received absolute respect and total obedience from the troops under his command.

He had been with the battalion since the invasion of France in 1940. Through the heady months of total success that followed, where all opposition simply melted away before them, they had become the one of the best combat units in the German army. They were amongst the elite units of the Waffen-SS.

His men wore the name of their unit on an embroidered cloth band, sewn onto the sleeve of their uniform coats, just above the cuff.

To a man, they wore it with singular pride. In a Nazi ruled Germany, there was little to challenge the status of being a member of one of the elite SS Regiments.

The fighting on the Russian Front, however, had worn them down mercilessly. They were now severely short of replacements for their battle loses, and their equipment was wearing out before their eyes. Near total exhaustion had further compromised their combat readiness.

There was an undeniable risk that at some point soon they would cease to be a viable fighting unit.

Diekmann warmed his hands against the metal sides of his coffee cup.

Full daylight was still over an hour away. It was gloomy and freezing but, at least this time, his small sector of the line was not in the sights of the Russian artillery. His troops were emerging from their perpetually uncomfortable and always temporary dugout sleeping quarters. Their first thoughts were to get their coffee and something to eat. Diekmann smiled ruefully at how poor an assortment of humanity they looked.

All were filthy, most unshaven, with everyone looking gaunt and wasted far beyond the limits of mere exhaustion. Yet still there was no end to their ordeal in sight.

He noted how the men all seemed to wear the same blank and expressionless look as they each sipped at the hot liquid in their tin mugs. They were like automatons, incapable of any action that required independent thought. None of them seemed to have the wit any more to think beyond the next fifteen minutes.

They simply followed their orders, no matter what those might be. Over the last year, those orders had demanded them do some terrible things.

The final nightmare had been the Battle of Kursk, which had left the once mighty German 2nd Panzer Division in tatters. It had also produced a similar effect on the morale of the men of Diekmann's own battalion.

Gaunt and pallid, Diekmann's own mental processes were little better than those of his men. His exhaustion was near total and even the most simple of orders took his mental faculties' time to process.

Before the war, he had been a keen sportsman. Very fit, he had been a lover of life. Married with a young family, he embodied the ideals of youth and racial purity that National Socialist Germany prized so highly.

The war, however, had changed him dramatically.

Today, he could do little more than just lean against a Panzer and allow the coffee cup to warm his hands. Parts of his soul, he was certain, would never be warm again.

The darkness of his reverie, however, was interrupted by the sound of someone calling out his name.

"Major Diekmann?"

It was *Leutenant* (Lieutenant) Barth, an officer of the 3rd Company of the 1st Battalion.

"*Brigadefuhrer* (General) Lammerding is looking for you, sir. It seems we've received orders to move again."

"Now that's a surprise," replied Diekmann, "we've been here nearly a whole two days. It was beginning to feel too much like home. Where to next, I wonder?"

Barth did not respond to the question, thinking it rhetorical.

"The general has asked me to tell you to report to him at once, sir," said Barth.

Diekmann wearily stood up from his recline against the tank. He straightened his cap, and tugged down at the bottom hem of his jacket in a feeble attempt to smarten his appearance.

"Very well. You might start rousing the men and getting them ready to break camp. Have them ready to move within the hour, just in case."

"Yes, sir, *Herr* Major," replied Barth, snapping to attention. "Heil Hitler." Though exhausted himself, he still threw out a perfect salute. To do less was to disrespect the Fuhrer.

Diekmann promptly returned the salute. "Heil Hitler," he responded.

He made his way through the icy mud, to the camp of his commanding officer, General Heinz Lammerding. Lammerding's small compound consisted of his own tent and a communications truck, from which he seldom ventured very far. In situations as fluid as those of the last few months, he felt uncomfortable being too far away from radio contact with Army Group HQ.

Lammerding was sitting at a small desk outside his tent. Sitting alongside him was Diekmann's Regimental Commander *SS Obersturmmbanfuhrer* (Lt Colonel) Sylvester Stadtler. Lammerding saw Diekmann approaching and leant back in his chair until he arrived.

Diekmann stopped at the desk and stood to attention. He raised his arm again in the Nazi salute. "Heil Hitler."

Neither Lammerding nor Stadtler stood up. They both replied with "Heil Hitler" and gave weary salutes in response.

Stadtler half turned in his seat. He called over his shoulder to a nearby orderly to fetch another chair immediately.

The chair arrived promptly and Diekmann sat down.

"I have been told you wished to see me, sir. I presume we are to move again?"

Lammerding paused for a moment before answering.

"We are, Otto, we are." He made eye contact with the Major briefly before glancing over at Stadtler. He finally broke into a weak smile, anticipating the effect his next words would have.

"This time, it appears we are going to France; after a couple of weeks furlough in Germany first of course."

Diekmann sat immobile, eyes wide and staring at the general, his exhausted mind having difficulty in processing the completely unexpected words he had just heard.

Lammerding waited in vain for a response. "Well, don't you have anything to say?"

Eventually, Diekmann stammered, "I… I… can't believe it! I didn't expect to leave here alive."

"You haven't yet!" Despite his own exhaustion, Lammerding managed another smile. "I assure you though, Otto, it's quite true. The orders came through overnight. It appears we are to be relieved. We are being exchanged with units currently serving in the west."

"Group has decided to give us some time to rest and rebuild, and to give our replacements a taste of what it is they signed up for. We can't keep having all the fun ourselves now, can we?"

"So it's true then, sir? We are getting out of here?" queried Diekmann uncertainly, still struggling to accept that this was not a mistake or worse, a cruel joke.

Lammerding glanced at Stadtler, indicating he should take over.

Stadtler leaned forward. "It is absolutely true, Major," he said. "We are to begin moving out immediately. Here, in this envelope is your copy of the orders from Group."

He handed a slim envelope to Diekmann. "I'm sure even you would agree that both you and your men are spent. It is time to get you out of here. We don't think you'll be able to hold the line if the fucking Russians decide to attack again."

Diekmann's brow furrowed at the comment.

"I didn't mean that as a criticism!" responded Stadtler hurriedly. "I do believe it is an accurate summing up, though. You and your men have earned the right to be exhausted."

Diekmann said nothing but he exhaled slowly and his posture relaxed.

Stadtler continued, "Now, you'll have a decent march ahead of you today. It's over thirty kilometres to the nearest rail head."

Diekmann became aware of the fog of exhaustion clearing from his mind. Lucid thoughts and metal sharpness were already returning, for the first time in weeks. "Don't worry about the marching, sir. I have no doubt the men will be up for it."

"I have no doubt either, once you give them the news," said Stadtler, the hint of a rare smile touching the corners of his tired eyes. "Now, to work… you are to prepare an Order of March and get the men moving. Other battalion leaders will be receiving their own orders immediately after you. I want your battalion out first. Once you reach the rail head at…" he checked his map. "Shostka, it would seem, you and your men will be allocated carriages on those trains returning to Germany. There you will all be given two weeks leave. After that, it appears we shall all be meeting again somewhere near Toulouse in southern France I believe. It all sounds rather pleasant in fact. We might even be able to forget there's a war on for a while."

Diekmann rose to his feet and spoke to General Lammerding. "Thank you for this news, sir. I shall inform the men immediately."

"No need to thank me. These are the orders as I have received them. Besides, as Stadtler has said, you and your men have earned it. The last year has been worse than a nightmare, I'm sure you'll agree. We all need it."

Diekmann looked at Lammerding and then at Stadtler. For the first time he began to notice just how tired his own senior officers looked. Lammerding leaned forward and shook Diekmann's hand.

"It won't be all fun in the sun in France, you know," he said, "we'll have to keep control of an area where the French Resistance is operating in strength, and we can't expect too much help from our reluctant allies in the Vichy government. Also, there is always the likelihood that the Invasion will be attempted this coming summer. The men will need their fighting edge more than ever."

"Once they've had the chance to get some rest away from this arsehole of a place, they'll be as good, or better, than ever," replied Diekmann.

"I have no doubt of that," said Lammerding. "Now! Get to it! There's much to be done."

Diekmann gave a perfect Parade Ground salute and a sharp "Heil Hitler" spun around and briskly headed back to his battalion's position.

As soon as he reached his tent, he looked around to find his junior officers. He did not need to look far. Lieutenant Barth was on his way over, having already spotted him on his return walk.

"I've got the men packing and preparing to move, sir. Do you know where we're going now?"

"Yes Lieutenant, as a matter of fact I do. Would you be so kind as to find *Kapitan* (Captain) Kahn and the other company commanders? I want them assembled here within the next fifteen minutes. We have a long day ahead of us and we shall need to get going shortly."

Barth paused. "May I ask where it is we're going, sir?"

Diekmann tried to give away as little as possible. "I'll tell you when we're all together, Lieutenant. Now, please, get the officers together for me."

Barth saluted and went on his way.

Diekmann took a deep breath and slowly exhaled. He had not felt this mentally alert in months. The news of their immediate withdrawal was a powerful tonic. It had completely overwhelmed the exhaustion that he thought had become permanent.

He went over to the cook's fire and poured himself another ersatz coffee. For the first time in ages, its taste actually registered with him.

"Fuck, this is disgusting muck!" he said.

***

Diekmann had sat himself on the ground, his back against one of the wheels of a Mk IV Panzer. He was reading the written orders Stadtler had given him when the group of his officers arrived.

Barth approached with Captain Kahn, his direct senior, and the captains of the other two companies of the battalion.

"Everyone is here, sir."

"Excellent!" replied Diekmann. He got to his feet and composed himself. "Now, gentlemen, I have just been reading through our orders for the third time, just to make sure I wasn't dreaming. I have to inform you now that as of today, we are on our way home!"

There was stunned silence from the group.

"It's true, gentlemen. We are being relieved! We are going back to Germany for two weeks furlough and after that, we are to be redeployed to France."

The effect of his words was electric.

The first to react were several nearby privates who had been quietly, but keenly listening in on the officer's conversation. They started yelping in delight. Others heard their reaction and demanded to know what all the fuss was about. When they in turn found out, their reaction was the same.

The news spread so fast throughout the battalion that by the time the officers could get back to their companies, it had long preceded them.

Ordinarily, Diekmann would not have tolerated such behaviour, even to the point where troops behaving thus might expect to be court marshalled. This time though, he himself was feeling such euphoria that he scarcely even noticed the indiscipline.

They were about to be delivered from the Valley of the Shadow of Death. They were going home.

***

Five days had passed since that heady morning in the Ukraine. Diekmann's battalion had led the march for the rest of the Division as they slowly made their way to the railhead at Shostka. The march took two days, but as they drew further from the front line and the constant shelling, the going became easier. The condition of the road improved and the spirit of the men grew stronger with each kilometre travelled.

Shostka had worn its share of destruction during the many months of intense fighting that had shattered so much of western Ukraine over the preceding two years. Intense efforts by huge gangs of forced labourers, treated as little better than slaves by the Nazis, had restored the rail yards to a functional state again. For the time being, the movement of troops, both into and out of the combat theatre, was reassuringly efficient.

From Shostka, the train took them on to Kiev and from there they began the journey back to Berlin. Frequent stops in sidings to allow trains to pass on their way to the front, meant that it took three full days before they finally reached the capital of the greater German Reich.

Another year of war had changed Berlin dramatically from the city they all remembered!

As the train approached through the outer industrial suburbs, the effects of allied bombing were becoming increasingly evident. The damage to the manufacturing sector was extensive and ruinous. As their train passed factory after shattered factory, the men had little difficulty in telling which ones were the most vital to Germany's war effort.

Many factories were simply left in ruins, unattended and ignored. Others, however, had hives of labourers hard at work in the middle of the night, struggling to restore them to production.

Allied bombing was fast turning Germany's magnificent capital city into a crumbling, shattered ruin. Attacks were now a constant menace, Americans by day and the RAF by night.

Berlin lay far enough away from the English coast to ensure that the raids, while still frequent, exacted a heavy toll on the allied bomber crews who lacked the protection of fighter escorts for much of the trip.

Such though was the growing supremacy of Allied air power that, despite the risks to the aircrews, the German capital had just undergone a brutal campaign of intensive air bombardment that had lasted several months.

Even so, a surprising amount of Berlin's extensive infrastructure remained functional although much reduced. For their part, many businesses were still open and trading. Most though, were finding products to sell increasing hard to come by.

Shortages of goods, even the most basic of food items, were very much an unpleasant fact of life now for citizens of the German capital.

The train carrying Diekmann's men pulled into the Anhalter Bahnoff Railway Station late on one of the rare quiet nights. The allied bombers had other targets to occupy them this evening.

The Station, built nearly a century earlier had, from the day it was opened, been considered one of the grandest in Europe. Now, much of that grandeur lay in ruins. Heavy bombing had destroyed most of its marshalling yards and large sections of the elegant terminal building itself.

None the less, that which remained still impressed the men as they emerged from the train onto the darkened platform. Very few trains used the terminus now. Those that did, could only do so safely on the quiet nights when the allied bombers were busying themselves elsewhere and then, only under the cover of the blackout.

For these exhausted soldiers, emerging onto the soil of their capital once more was a powerful tonic. Despite the devastation that lay around them, they could already feel their sense of purpose becoming re-invigorated. They were highly idealistic men in a storied fighting unit. They knew they would soon be ready once again to return to the great, unfinished struggle.

Unloading the train of their meagre personal possessions and the battalion's light equipment was quickly managed, and with a minimum of difficulty.

Almost all the heavier equipment, including all of the division's tanks and artillery, had been left behind in Ukraine, to be passed on to the troops arriving to replace them. The battalion could expect to be completely re-equipped once their redeployment to southern France was complete.

Diekmann gave orders that the men assemble in the car park outside the Station. Once they were together, he called them all closer. Once they had gathered around, he stepped up onto a nearby bench seat so they could all see him as he spoke.

"Well, men, you now have two weeks at liberty to reacquaint yourselves with your loved ones, or to set about finding some new ones!"

A burst of laughter rippled through the assembled men.

"Today is the 13th of January. You are all to meet here by midday on the 27th. Go now. Recharge your batteries. Recharge your minds. Be proud of what you have achieved for the Fatherland in the last year. There is still much more work to do. The Fuhrer will expect great things of us in the months to come. You know as well as I, his faith could not be in safer hands."

This time there was a loud roar of assent from the entire battalion.

"Now, men, you have been given your travel warrants. Go to your homes, spend time with your families and if you get the chance, fuck yourselves senseless! Go forth and conquer!"

This brought a huge cheer from the assembly as Diekmann stepped down from the seat.

The men began to separate into smaller groups as they said their farewells to their brothers in arms, with whom they had just been through hell. The next task would be turning their minds to finding their separate ways home.

If not home, then perhaps the nearest *Beerhaus* or brothel.

Barth walked over to Diekmann. Despite the difference in rank, the two men had become close through the trials of combat and, when away from the responsibilities of command, would often relax in each other's company. When the opportunities presented themselves, both could be heavy drinkers.

"Do you mind if I ask what your plans are, sir, for your leave?"

"My wife and children are in Magdeburg and I haven't seen them for over a year. First available train tomorrow, I shall be on it. What about you?"

Barth smiled. "I don't have far to go. My parents live just outside Potsdam. I am going to look for a taxi shortly. I may go and find a beer or two first though."

Diekmann looked at him and said, "It distresses me to see an officer of mine having to drink alone. Would you like some company until your taxi is called?"

Barth smiled. "I was just about to ask if you were thirsty."

"Excellent," said Diekmann, "I know just the place. There is a great *Beerhaus* not far from here if the RAF has not already got to it. As your senior officer, I order you to buy the first round!"

"Now I know why they say rank has its privileges," replied Barth, muttering in theatrical jest.

***

The morning of the 2nd February 1944 saw an ancient, weary steam train chugging purposefully through the central regions of France, several hundred kilometres directly south of Paris. Diekmann and his battalion were its only passengers. The train was steadily moving towards what was to be their ultimate destination, a village called Valence d'Agen, which none of them had ever heard of, still further to the south.

Five days of near continuous travel, constantly changing trains, interminable waiting and irregular meals was nearing an end. The men looked out of the windows at the beautiful, green French countryside as it rolled by, marvelling at the change in their circumstances from only a few weeks earlier.

After experiencing the worst place on earth, surely this must be among the best.

The land appeared untouched by war. The early spring saw them passing by fields of wild flowers and daffodils, or cows in small herds standing in lush, grassy paddocks. Sheep and goats also populated many fields, while still others had the first green shoots of the grain or vegetable crops that would be ripe for the picking a few months hence.

This area of France lay under the collaborationist wartime government led by Marshal Philippe Petain. He had been one of France's most loved heroes in the Great War, and it was to him that France turned once again after the German armies had so completely overwhelmed their own and those of their English allies in 1940.

Petain, however, was now an old man. He no longer had the fire in his belly that helped him so successfully inspire his armies a quarter of a century earlier. Negotiating from a position of abject weakness, he could only contrive a solution that saw him lead a government of local administration only, managing the southern Departments of France on behalf of their German overlords, from a makeshift capital in the city of Vichy.

The previous government of France had evacuated Paris in a near panic. They took with them, or destroyed, as many public records that might be useful to the Germans as they were able.

From Paris, most members of the old French government headed south. Some eventually managed to make it across the Channel to the apparent safety of England. Others found their way across the rugged mountains of the Pyrenees into Spain or Portugal. For others still, their escape route took them across the Mediterranean into what was still at that stage, the free French territories of Algeria or Morocco in northern Africa.

Many more simply went to ground and trusted in the bonds of family or friends to keep them hidden from the Nazi conquerors.

Others, however, happily threw in their lot with the new Vichy government.

As well as managing all the functions of normal government, the Vichy administration was expected to do the bidding of Nazi Germany, in terms of controlling the activities of the French Resistance movement, popularly known as the Maquis. The Maquis sought to continue France's war with Germany in a way that their own collaborationist government now simply refused to do.

The Maquis had originally grown out of the French Communist movement. The desire to resist the German occupation was not unique to the Communists though. The Maquis had since grown and now held fighters of all political colours.

They saw in the Vichy government, as much an enemy of France as the Germans themselves. For their part, the more hard-headed, pro-fascist members of the Vichy government saw in the Maquis a political enemy as well as a combative one. The nature of the Vichy government meant that it had drawn into its folds many French men and women who were firmly of a like mind with their fascist German overlords.

In Vichy, the line between conqueror and conquered was often a very blurred one.

Valence d'Agen was a small village in one of the most picturesque regions of France. It seemed as far from the war as any place in Europe could be in 1944.

It was late morning when the old train, belching impressive clouds of steam, pulled into the station at the larger, nearby town of Agen. The men began to disembark and form up into ranks. No orders were required; the men knew what was expected of them. They were no longer the exhausted shadows of the soldiers they were just a mere month earlier.

Now they were rested and on the way to regaining their strength and fitness.

All had shaved, their uniforms cleaned and repaired by wives or mothers or, in some cases, replaced by quartermasters where the old ones were too far-gone. All their weapons and personal kit had been thoroughly cleaned and serviced.

Much still needed replacing outright. That was part of the planning that lay behind the redeployment. The regiment had suffered heavy losses on the Russian Front. This was to be the time to rebuild their numbers and replace tired weapons with new equipment.

The men rated themselves highly and in consequence, demanded the best that Germany could send them. Their role in this war was far from being over. They all knew they would soon be required to re-join the fight.

No one realised this more than Major Adolf Diekmann.

He had already replaced his old, tattered uniform whilst he was on leave. His boots and leather belts he had polished to a smooth gloss. With his back was now firm and straight again, he had regained the mental clarity that complete exhaustion from the last years fighting had done so much to crush. He was still thinner than before, but that was of little concern.

His movement orders had advised that there would be transport arriving to collect the men within the hour. He, however, had decided upon other plans.

Well briefed, he knew it was a twenty-five-kilometre march to the tent barracks that had been assigned to them in the interestingly named village of Valence d'Agen.

There would be no need for transport for the men he had decided, the battalion would march.

He sought out Captain Kahn.

"Ah, Kahn. I need you to assign thirty men to remain behind and see that the battalion's equipment is loaded and accounted for onto the lorries when they arrive. I will be leading the march to the barracks."

Kahn was a steady officer. Not an intellectual, but tough, competent and very thorough when it came to following orders. Those qualities, combined with years of solid service in the SS had seen him reach the rank of captain. It was unlikely though that he would progress much further.

"Yes sir. Heil Hitler," he responded.

"Heil Hitler," replied Diekmann.

Kahn set off immediately.

Diekmann turned back towards his men. He immediately gave orders having the companies fall into rank to commence the march.

The march was easy enough for seasoned troops. The men had only to carry their weapons and a light pack. Their personal kits and battalion equipment were being brought up by the lorries, which overtook the marching column when it was still fifteen kilometres from the village. The road was excellent and the battalion made good time, arriving about seven p.m.

The men who had remained behind to see to the loading of the lorries had ridden in those same vehicles on to the destination.

Once there, they used their time to start setting up the large campsite.

They had begun erecting the tents for the men following on foot and getting the cooking arrangements underway. By the time the first troops of the marching column arrived, the campsite was almost complete.

That night, the entire battalion ate and slept well.

The next day, after completing the setting up the last of the tent barracks, Diekmann granted the men some free time to explore the village and acquaint themselves with the surrounding countryside.

Their new home turned out to be an old and picturesque village set amongst the hills and farmlands of the Garonne River region. The town had little to offer by way of entertainment, but the promise of ample, excellent food and good spring weather certainly helped compensate for that.

The weather was indeed sunny and increasingly warm, the French countryside lush and inviting.

The local villagers, however, nursed grave suspicions concerning the new German arrivals. Most had the good sense to keep their feelings to themselves.

The next few weeks saw changes in the battalion begin in earnest.

The privations and constant nearness of death that had marked their life on the Eastern Front so recently, soon began to fade into the past.

Replacement personnel for their combat losses began to arrive. These new arrivals were soon integrated into the battalion's various companies.

With plenty of good food, the men began to put on weight and fill out their uniforms once more. Plenty of close order drilling and route marches was having the effect of rebuilding their fitness and stamina.

Soon enough, they were starting to look forward to getting back to work. They all realised it might not be too long before the chance arrived.

From General Lammerding on down to the lowest private, everyone believed that this would be the year the Allies would move from the safety of their bases in England. This would be the year they would attempt the invasion of Europe.

No one knew precisely where or when, but most guessed it would be the *Pas de Calais*, where the Channel is at its narrowest. When? Most likely late spring or early summer. That was the gossip.

All had the expectation that the French Resistance, the Maquis would start to become more active in the months prior to the invasion.

It was to be their task to kill or capture these Maquis, wherever they could find them. Any that they captured were turned over to the German State Police, the Gestapo, immediately for interrogation.

The Gestapo had little sympathy for such captives and their methods of interrogation, whilst effective, were usually brutal in the extreme.

Diekmann was pleased with the progress of returning the battalion to full fighting strength. Lorry loads of ammunition and stick grenades, new MG-42 machine guns, replacement rifles and all manner of items of personal kit were now filling the quartermaster's stores.

They were, once again, a formidable fighting force.

The good food, the discipline of the drilling and marches, as well as the addition of hundreds of new replacements had completely restored the *esprit de corps* of the battalion.

Now that it was battle-ready once again, Diekmann's Battalion had as its main objective, combatting the growing activities of the Maquis. This new enemy was despised even more than the Red Army.

At least the Russians fought in uniform. They fought in the open and they died with honour. This new enemy did none of those things.

They skulked about in the night. They wore no uniforms. They pretended to be friendly to the Germans by day, and killed them by night. They engaged in acts of sabotage, murdered senior officers, or committed ambush attacks on small, isolated groups of German soldiers.

However, for the moment, Maquis groups were keeping their activities to a minimum. Beyond nuisance attacks on railway lines and bridges, there was little activity to merit major engagement by the SS. Their attacks were 'hit and run', often opportunistic and with no obvious operational base.

The SS saw these attacks as cowardly acts of terrorism. Frustration at their own inability to effectively strike back, was growing.

Chapter 2

4 May 1944: Outside Flavignac, South-West of Limoges, Central France

Five men carefully positioned themselves around a long, narrow field. Those that wore watches checked them; it had just passed one thirty in the morning. All were dressed in dark colours; all had spread out to pre-selected locations, and all listening intently for the faint sound of a distant aero engine.

Positioned carefully, they could cover all the approaches to the field by road. Should any unexpected vehicles appear, they could quickly alert their companions and quietly melt away into the night.

So far this evening, there had been no road traffic at all. The field was secluded and lay towards the rear of an ancient farmstead, hidden from the nearest roads by dense stands of large evergreen conifers.

The field had been cultivated for many generations, but this year it had been left fallow. Untouched this growing season, its new purpose was quite different from the usual cultivation of crops. Winter rain had helped flatten it out and the early spring sun had gently hardened the surface. It was a now perfect, makeshift airfield.

The first low drone of the approaching aircraft filtered through to their anxious ears and three of the men began to move to new positions in the middle of the field. They set themselves about one hundred metres apart but in a straight north – south line.

As the sound grew louder, the man at the southern end sent out three quick flashes of light from his torch, in the direction of the sound.

Within seconds, the engine note changed as the pilot altered direction to bring the aeroplane around, so that he could commence an approach from the south. After a minute, all three men turned on their own torches and pointed them towards the now approaching aircraft.

They had marked out the landing field for the pilot.

The RAF Lysander was designed for precisely this kind of work. Lightly built with a high wing, it required a minimum of landing field space in which to operate. It was the aircraft of choice by the British Special Operations Executive (SOE) for use in these clandestine runs into occupied France.

The pilot had made this particular run before, and was familiar the approach. Tonight, the near-full moon and light cloud ensured that he had the best conditions possible to make the landing.

The southern approach was one of the sides free from the screen of trees and the Lysander came to a halt within a hundred metres of its wheels touching down.

Immediately, the three darkly dressed men ran up to the aircraft and opened the doors. Quickly and efficiently, they unpacked the cases that the plane had brought from England. There would be weapons and explosives, radio parts and most importantly, updated codebooks. Changing the radio codes regularly was vital. The risk of the Germans breaking them was far too great otherwise.

This time, however, the plane had also brought a passenger, as well as the supplies.

A slim man, slightly taller than average and of youthful appearance. Like the others, he was also darkly clad, carrying a valise and a backpack. He stepped out of the cabin and onto French soil for the first time in nearly four years.

The men on the ground signalled to the pilot that the Lysander was now empty of its cargo. The doors slammed shut and the pilot revved the engine. The plane began to move again. The pilot swung it around to the south and opened the throttle to full. The small aircraft quickly gained speed and left the ground.

Within seconds of becoming airborne, the pilot banked into a graceful right hand turn, setting a return course towards England. The whole exercise had taken less than two minutes.

The last two men, having remained on lookout duty throughout the operation, now came running up to join the others. Everyone, including the new arrival, helped carry the supplies away to the safety of a disused cellar under a seemingly derelict barn, adjacent to the old farm.

After the supplies had been securely stored, the small, low-level hatchway to the cellar was quietly closed again. The men then carefully covered it over with pieces of rusted and useless farm rubbish. Several strands of dangling ivy had been gently pulled aside earlier to allow access.

These were now carefully arranged back into place, totally concealing the discrete entrance.

The men quietly said their farewells and the group broke up. Four of the original five men went off together into the night.

The new arrival remained with the last man and they set off together without a word. Ahead of them lay a two kilometre walk along a backcountry lane to reach the man's house. He had a small farm for raising pigs and goats. There he had lived for almost the entirety of his forty three years.

Only after they were safely inside his house could they begin to relax. The older man drew the curtains securely to ensure no light could escape. He then lit a paraffin lamp and, from its dim light, the two of them could finally see each other properly for the first time.

They embraced in the traditional French manner, kissing each other on each cheek.

"We had been told to expect a passenger this time. My name is Lucien Morin. This is my home."

"It is good to meet you," said the other putting down his bag. "I am Lieutenant Daniel Martin. Free French army. I managed to get to England in 1940. I can't tell you how good it is to be back."

Lucien's face, still handsome but wearing the early middle-aged creases of a hard working life, showed surprise at hearing this.

"You're French! So, the SOE are finally learning. The last one that came across was English. He thought his French would be good enough to let him pass unnoticed. He didn't last three weeks."

Daniel half smiled. "It seems that's a common story, unfortunately. With luck, I may last a bit longer."

A woman's face appeared from around a door.

"Ahh Daniel, this is my wife, Yvette. Yvette, this is Daniel. He will be our guest for a few days."

Yvette pulled her dressing gown tightly around her and stepped into the room.

"*Enchantee, Monsieur,*" she said quietly. She had long since resolved not to get too involved when Lucien brought strangers into their home in the middle of the night.

"*Enchantee, Madame,*" replied Daniel smiling.

He was surprised at how attractive she was. Lucien seemed to have too much roughness about him to be the kind of man that a beautiful, younger woman would naturally gravitate towards.

Yvette looked at him and Daniel thought he saw a flash of unexpected curiosity show in her eyes also.

"Go back to bed, my dear," said Lucien, "we shall try and be quiet. We have work to do."

She looked at her husband and nodded. "Very well then. Good night, *Monsieur*." She smiled shyly and turned back towards the bedroom door.

"Good night, *Madame*," replied Daniel.

The two men sat down at the small dining table in the centre of the front room. Daniel produced a map from an inside pocket of his coat and spread it out on the table between them. It was a map of central and western France.

Putting residual thoughts of the woman to one side, he turned to Lucien, "Now, *Monsieur*! Firstly, my code name is to be 'Kestrel' while I am here."

Lucien nodded in understanding.

"Secondly, as I'm sure you're aware, this coming summer is likely to see some interesting events happening." Lucien looked intently at him, understanding fully the insinuation.

"I have no idea where or when these events might occur, but we have our own small role to play right here."

He tapped the map in the centre of the Limousin region where they currently were.

"It will be our task to gain as much intelligence as we can about where the Germans currently have their men deployed. We need to monitor where they are being sent and in what number. We need to know which units are in this region and especially, the strength of their armour."

"I have been ordered to insist that the Maquis units in this region do not undertake any unnecessary sabotage operations for the time being. We need to keep a low profile and concentrate on gathering intelligence. The time will come soon enough for action. What the Allies need most now is information. That must be the focus."

"My role here is simply to advise the local Maquis groups to ensure that their activities are as well co-ordinated as possible. I'm not here to lead anyone, merely to act as an advisor so that everyone knows what it is the Allies need from us here in the field."

Lucien nodded and stared at the map on the table. He kept his thoughts to himself but it was sounding as though the invasion must be getting close.

"We already have a lot of information about the bastards," he said. "Getting more is not too difficult. It is simply about staying hidden and observing. Are you sure that's all they want us to do?"

"For the moment, yes. Accurate intelligence is the most important service we can provide right now. We will know things are starting to get close, really close, when we begin to get orders about commencing actual operations. Then your men can start to fight back. This time when they do, it'll be part of the real fight to set France free."

Lucien breathed deeply and exhaled slowly. "So, it's nearly here. At last!"

Lucien got up from the table and went over to a large sideboard that was the most prominent piece of furniture in the room. He opened a door and produced a two-thirds full bottle of Armagnac and two glasses. He returned to the table and sat down.

"Well *Monsieur*, I trust that you will join me in a small drink?"

"Only a small one?" replied Daniel.

Lucien chuckled. "Perhaps a medium one then."

Daniel leaned back in his chair. "Do you mind if I ask how it is that you come to be here? I mean, in the sense that the war seems to have passed you by. I know you are active now, but did you not fight in 1940?"

Lucien leaned back also. He thought he detected a slight rebuke in Daniel's question. He paused for a minute to settle his temper and gather his thoughts.

"I fought in the last war. I was only sixteen when I went to Verdun. By the time I was seventeen, I had been gassed once and shot twice. They invalided me out before the end of the war, shortly after the Americans arrived in Verdun. Afterwards, I came back here to my parent's farm… this farm." He looked around and gestured, taking in the room.

"I got home to find that my older brother had been killed in the fighting less than a month before. And then, almost no sooner than the war was over, both of my parents died during the Spanish Flu outbreak in 1919."

Daniel sat silently and listened. He himself was only twenty eight, yet here was a man who had lived through more horror than he could comprehend whilst still little more than a child.

He suddenly regretted his last words. He was aware they had sounded more accusatory than was his intention.

"I'm so sorry," he said quietly, "I had no idea. Please forgive me if I offended."

"That's all right," said Lucien, "there are quite a few like me. Veterans of the last war not called upon at the start of this one. In many ways, the worst part has been having to watch old Marshal Petain become a tool of the Boche. We loved him back then, in the last war. Now, he may end his life dangling from a rope. I find it very sad when I allow myself the time to think about such things."

Daniel took another sip of the Armagnac.

Lucien topped up both of their glasses and continued.

"As for my life here, Vichy has determined that all able-bodied men must do some form of service on behalf of our beloved Boche masters. As I am no longer in the most robust health after being gassed and shot, I am simply allowed to generously donate a proportion of my animal stock to the mighty German war effort."

"The Boche have called around every spring since they've been here. They help themselves to as many of my baby goats and pigs as they wish. This year they took all the offspring and a couple of the adult sows. They have left me with barely enough to breed from next year, and nothing to sell at market. They have been doing this to all the farmers that I know of in the Limousin. Probably throughout the rest of France as well."

Daniel mulled over Lucien's words.

"There may well be a positive side to that. The Russians are giving them hell on the Eastern Front. The food they've been relying on from the east is drying up. It's why they're taking so much from here. Between the Russians and the Allied bombing in Germany, France must now be supplying a huge part of what the Germans need for food."

"France is supplying all their food? Why is that a positive thing?"

"Because it means that their own country can't support them. When the invasion comes, it will stop their supplies of food from France. Once that happens, the Germans are likely to collapse quickly."

Lucien thought about what Daniel had just said. Clearly, the young man did not have the same experiences of the Germans that he had.

"I suspect you are too optimistic. They will not go down without a fight. The ones around here are mostly Waffen-SS. Those are tough bastards. Nazi fanatics the whole fucking lot of them!"

He took another swallow of the Armagnac.

"How much of them have you seen, Lieutenant? When did you get to England?"

Daniel leaned forward and put his glass on the table.

"My unit was one of hundreds that were forced into retreat after the Germans broke through at Sedan. The entire front then started to collapse all the way to the Channel coast."

"We wound up well south of the main evacuation port at Dunkirk. We ended up trapped at Calais with several British units. Completely cut off. They were just going to leave us behind, to either surrender or die. The evacuation ships could not reach us. I was one of only a few hundred who managed to get out and eventually find a way across the Channel."

"I was smuggled across to Jersey on a Breton fishing boat along with seven others. After Calais, we had to make our way down the coast as best we could once we got through the German lines. It took us a few weeks and some very close scrapes, but eventually we got as far as Brittany. There were many of us who were not so lucky. In the end, the British got us back to England before the Germans captured the Channel Islands."

They both sat silently for another minute as they finished their drinks. Lucien decided the conversation needed to end for the night.

"We have a small, hidden niche down in the cellar with a bed," he said.

"I'll show you the way. I must get a couple of hours sleep before the animals start demanding my attention in the morning."

The 'hidden niche' turned out to a tiny but well-crafted room, the entrance to which was inconspicuously located behind the stairs that led down into the cellar.

With the staircase hinged at the top, it was easy to lift out of the way, allowing access to what appeared to be a blank wall behind it. That wall was really a carefully fitted, discrete section of removable timber panelling. It pulled away, revealing a small doorway, perhaps a metre high, leading into a tiny room. Daniel slid in his bag, and then crouched down low and squeezed through himself.

"We call it the Mouse Hole," said Lucien.

Once inside, the ceiling was higher but still too low to allow him to stand. The furniture was sparse, just the bed, a small table and a simple wooden chair. On the table was a pitcher of water, a glass and a candle in a holder, along with some matches. The water though, was fresh, and the sheets were clean. Clearly, the room had been prepared for him earlier.

Lucien bade him goodnight and set about replacing the panel to hide the entrance. With the timber panel and stairs back in place, the tiny room became virtually invisible.

Daniel lit the candle and contemplated his little bed chamber; the tiny room appeared to have been a part of the cellar for many years. The bed was long enough, but narrow. He took off his shoes and socks and lay down. It was more comfortable than he had expected. Leaning closer to the little table, he blew out the candle, laid back, and fell asleep almost immediately.

He awoke to the sound of feet coming down the stairs into the cellar. There was a knock on the timber outside his room.

"Are you awake? I have some food for you," a woman's voice.

Daniel shook his head to try to rouse his senses.

"I'm just going to open up the door. It's quite safe, no else is here."

"OK, thanks," replied Daniel.

The timber panel came away and Yvette stood there, stooped over and looking in on him, still lying on the bed.

"You can't stay in there all day you know, it's nearly ten," said Yvette with a laugh.

"My God," said Daniel looking startled, "is it really? I shouldn't have slept that long."

Yvette laughed again. She seemed much more at ease now that there was day light outside.

"It's easy to do so down here in the Mouse Hole. There is no light to let you know that it's daytime. Anyway, you would have needed the sleep. I have something for you to eat. You must be hungry by now."

Daniel swung his legs over the side of the bed and sat up promptly at the mention of food. She was right. He was very hungry. It had been nearly a full day since he last had a meal.

"Do you mind if I come upstairs to eat. It feels a bit like a prison cell in here."

"Please do," Yvette replied, "I can make some tea as well if you like."

"Thanks, I'll just be a minute."

He emerged from the cellar shortly after. He had put his shoes and socks back on and combed his hair but still looked as though he had not fully woken up yet.

"Welcome to the world," said Yvette, "Lucien is out with the goats at the moment. He should be back soon."

Daniel sat down at the same table where he and Lucien had talked the previous evening. The room looked very different in daylight. There were decorations and colours he had not seen in the weak light of the paraffin lamps.

Yvette had set the table with home baked bread, dried sausage, and a few cheeses. There were some home pickled *cornichons* on a plate as well.

"Now I know I'm home in France," he said, "I've missed this so much…"

He started to carve off a few thin slices of sausage and wedges of the cheeses. Yvette poured him a cup of tea.

"I'm sorry there is no coffee. It's impossible to come by now. I haven't had any in over a year. Even tea is nearly impossible to get now. The Germans take everything."

"Well, I may be able to repay some of your hospitality there, at least," said Daniel, "I have a packet of tea in my bag. I brought it with me as a peace offering to whoever was given the task of keeping me hidden."

"Real tea?" exclaimed Yvette, "we have so little that we mix what we have with herbs to make it go further. Thank you for thinking of it."

"*Mon plaisir*. I would have preferred to bring coffee, but it's just as hard to get in England as it is here, I suspect."

Yvette poured a cup of tea for herself and they sat in silence as Daniel ate. He was aware that the food on the table was likely to represent a large part of what Lucien and Yvette had, so he was careful not to eat too much.

Yvette noticed this also and was silently grateful. The last Germans to call had not left them with much to feed themselves.

Daniel looked up from his food and noticed Yvette quickly look away from him. She had been gazing at him while he ate. He noticed again how attractive she was. Slim with dark hair and blue eyes. Again, he thought what an unlikely couple she and Lucien made. He was in his early forties and she, from all appearances, still in her twenties.

He could not help but wonder where the attraction between them lay.

No sooner had that thought crossed his mind than he could hear the sound of footsteps approaching from outside the house. Yvette looked towards the door as it opened and Lucien walked in.

"Glad you could join us," he said wryly, "I've been up since six. Farm animals don't like to be kept waiting."

It was now Daniel's turn to feel rebuked, but tactfully, he let it slide.

Instead, he said, "Is there anything that I can be helping you with? I grew up on a farm in the Bourgogne. I wasn't really cut out to be a farmer but I still remember a lot."

He laughed, almost involuntarily. "After all, it's supposed to be my cover if I get questioned. I'm a simple farm worker."

Lucien shrugged at the notion. "You don't look too much like a farm worker. Too much of the military about you. You might try slouching a bit more and talking rougher."

"Anyway, there isn't as much to do as there should be. We have so few animals left I can manage most things easily enough myself." Lucien thought for a moment before he spoke again. "I do have a few jobs that you could help me with though, if you know how to use a hammer. There are some repairs to the barn and a couple of outbuildings that I've had to put off because I can't do them on my own."

"I'd be glad to help anyway I can," said Daniel.

"Good!" said Lucien, sounding cheerier. "Anyway, there is much to do in regard to the real purpose of you being here. That must come first."

"Absolutely," replied Daniel, "when are we able to arrange a meeting with the local Maquis leaders? I have instructions from the SOE that I need to make known to the Resistance. Essentially, what I outlined to you last night. What it is the Allies need specifically by way of intelligence about German troop movements and dispositions. They are trying to put together the most complete picture they can of the current situation in all of occupied Western Europe."

"I've already sent out messages that we are to meet tomorrow night nearby," said Lucien, "I sent out word as soon as we were advised that the SOE was sending you. We are to meet at the farm where your plane landed last night."

"Excellent!" replied Daniel, "so there's not too much we can do in the meantime then?"

"Not really, no," said Lucien.

"In that case, after you've had something to eat, why don't you take me out and show me around your farm. Perhaps we can make a start on some of those repairs you wanted to do?"

Lucien seemed to cheer up even further at the thought.

"All right then. Sounds like a good idea."

***

The following evening was overcast and dull, with a light, drizzly rain falling.

The two men and, to Daniel's surprise, Yvette had made their way back to the old farm where the Lysander had landed two nights earlier. Daniel had not expected Yvette to be a part of the operation, but she was dressed in the dark clothes, had her hair tied back and seemed completely comfortable with the damp walk.

When they reached the main household building of the old farm, Lucien approached alone at first, but once he was content that all was secure, motioned for Daniel and Yvette to come in from their place of cover.

They entered, via the kitchen, into a large and well-furnished room. The comfortable homeliness and the quality of the furnishings took Daniel by surprise.

From the outside, the house looked quite care-worn. Not run down, but much in need of maintenance that was clearly well overdue.

Inside though, it still held up well, conveying the atmosphere of an earlier and less austere time. The furnishings and fittings were of a superior quality, but now starting to show their age. The old, heavy curtains were carefully drawn to prevent any light from escaping to the outside.

After his initial surprise had passed, Daniel noted how well filled the room seemed. There were many more people than he was expecting. Clearly, the Maquis network was extensive.

Lucien was making his way around the room, happily reacquainting himself with friends and fellow Maquis comrades.

One woman in particular, dark haired, attractive and of similar age, held him in conversation for several minutes before he moved on.

The number of women present surprised Daniel. Many quite young, though several were approaching middle age. Most of the men were Lucien's age or older.

Sitting apart from this group were an elderly couple. Daniel guessed them as both being in their eighties, the likely owners of the house. It was to this couple that Yvette immediately gravitated.

The elderly couple both stood up and embraced her with an obvious, deep love.

They held each other in an embrace for a long moment and then they sat down again with Yvette in between them on a beautiful, but ageing sofa.

Lucien spoke to the group, "This is our guest just arrived from England. This time the SOE have finally had the good sense to send us a Frenchman!"

This brought a ripple of laughter.

Lucien continued, "We will know him as 'Kestrel'. He is here to brief us on what the Allies will need from us over the next few weeks. Apparently, the timeline is getting tight!"

The inference of this last sentence brought several sharp inhales of breath from around the room.

Daniel stepped forward.

"Thank you all for coming. I am told that most of you have travelled many kilometres to get here. I know that has its special challenges these days."

Another ripple of laughter, this time more nervous.

"Basically, I am instructed to tell you that what the Allies really need most right now is good, solid intelligence. They ask that you reign in your enthusiasm for sabotage operations for the moment. Accurate intelligence is more important right now. They need to know what units are stationed where, what their strength is and whether there are any signs of impending redisposition. As complete and as accurate as we can make it."

Daniel explained at length what he had already told Lucien and Yvette earlier.

Each of the local Maquis groups had their own methods of reporting their information back to England. Any fresh intelligence they could gather was to be forwarded to the SOE as soon as possible. Generally, each group had radio transmitters securely hidden away, from which they would make their reports.

One of the men who had been at the airfield when Daniel arrived came forward. They both shook hands and the man finally introduced himself.

"I am known as *Ecureuil* (Squirrel), Kestrel. I have brought out the new code books that came with you the other night. They have been passed around."

"Excellent, thanks," said Daniel. He turned back to the assembled group. "I also came with a good supply of spare radio valves if any of you need more. I suggest you all take a couple. We must ensure that our ability to communicate is not compromised in the slightest. The next few months are likely to be important ones. I have no idea of dates or locations. I can only guess that France is going to be free again sooner rather than later."

At these words, the room went completely silent. Tears, driven by powerful emotions, began to glisten in the eyes of a number of the Maquis.

"These are momentous times," said Daniel, "we need to be discreet for the time being. Intelligence gathering only! The time will come soon enough when we will be able to get our weapons out and use them in anger. But for now, discretion please."

Daniel stepped back and the assembly immediately began to break into smaller groups. Obviously, those who knew each other well and wanted to discuss the news they had just received. There was now serious planning to do.

Daniel looked around and saw that Lucien had gone to join Yvette with the elderly couple. He walked over to join them.

Yvette stood up and spoke quietly so that no one else could hear his real name. "Daniel, may I introduce my grandparents. Bernard and Delphine Briand."

"*Bonne soir, Madame et Monsieur,*" said Daniel, "I didn't realise that this would be a family gathering as well."

"There are many families here this evening, *Monsieur,*" said Bernard, "There are several sets of brothers and sisters here. Several cousins. Also a few complete strangers, just to mix it up!" He smiled. "In France, Resistance to the Boche is a family affair!"

Daniel took an instant liking to him.

"It is very brave of you to host gatherings such as this," said Daniel, "if the Boche were to find out, I don't want to think what might be in store for you. They're not known for their subtlety when it comes to interrogation."

Bernard threw his head back and laughed loudly. Several people in the room stopped talking and looked at him.

Bernard then leaned forward and became serious.

"I am way past the point where I worry too much about what the Boche may do to me. Even if they were to take me alive, I am quite confident that my old heart would give out before I gave up information about Delphine or our darling Yvette."

"My only concern is that I live long enough to see France be rid of these murderous bastards once and for all. Has humanity ever sunk so low as these Nazi swine before? For the life of me, I can't think of an instance."

Daniel was deeply moved by the passion of the old man.

Bernard continued, "I am eighty two years old, *Monsieur*. In my lifetime, France has been invaded twice by the Germans, and once more not long before I was born.

"They are now the true enemy of my country. They have cost my family dearly in the last war. If it pleases God, let them be kicked out and never trouble our country again."

Daniel stood silently before the old man. Bernard was still shaking with emotion. He looked at Yvette and noticed that both she and Delphine were weeping. Daniel could not help but wonder what magnitude of loss the Germans had caused them in the past.

He reached out and grasped Bernard's hand.

"France will be free again," he said, "and soon! I have never had such confidence in anything in my life. I have seen the forces building in England. English, American, Canadian, Free French. So many other countries have their forces there, all keen to cross the Channel and put these Boche bastards to the sword! Have faith. We shall all get to see a free France once again!"

Even though Daniel had only been speaking to Bernard, his words had captured the attention of the others in the room. Someone in the room started singing the *Marseillaise* and in an instant, everyone else joined in.

The isolation of the farm ensured that there were no prying ears to take note of the enthusiastic rendering of the National Anthem.

Chapter 3

10 May 1944: Oradour-Sur-Veyres, West Limousin Region

Daniel had spent most of the last week based near the village of Oradour-Sur-Veyres, about thirty km to the west of his base with Lucien and Yvette. There had been increasing German activity in the area, which the Maquis were monitoring. He had gone to offer what help he could and to see for himself the qualities of the Maquis operatives in the field.

The local Resistance leaders name was Thomas Renand, known to the Maquis by his code-name 'Reynard'. He had proven himself in the field to be both resourceful and discrete. His sector had been quiet over the time of the occupation because he had made sure not to draw unwanted attention to his group. They had always travelled to other regions to help those groups in their Resistance activities.

As a result, the few German troops who were on station there were generally more relaxed in their attitude. This easy relationship they had with the locals would occasionally lead them to say more than they should.

Thomas was also a veteran of the previous war and spoke passable German. He had developed a technique of engaging German soldiers in conversation in their own language.

This would frequently lead to him telling them stories of his time in the trenches around Verdun. He always managed to make the Germans he was fighting at the time, seem like honourable fellow soldiers.

Once the soldiers were relaxed enough and involved in the conversation, it was usually easy to get them to offer small, but occasionally important tit-bits of information that could then be passed on to the SOE back in England.

Daniel's youth stood out. It meant that he needed to keep a very low profile whenever there were any Germans passing through. Daytime became his time to sleep. The night was for joining in on observation journeys around the region to gather intelligence. He learned that when the

Maquis were active in the field, they would never sleep in the same building twice. They taught him the skills of staying concealed and motionless for hours on end, while counting vehicles and recording the insignia of the different units as they passed.

It was obvious that the Germans were becoming more active. To the Maquis observers, it looked as though they were practicing the skills of battlefield mobility, to be ready and able to move *en masse* when the call came. They were clearly rehearsing their responses for when the invasion finally arrived.

Oradour-Sur-Veyres lay towards the western extreme of the larger region that came under Daniel's remit. He felt cut off from the rest of the network and was growing impatient to return to Lucien's farm.

It would not have taken long to get there in a car, but with the amount of German activity on the roads, the risk of being stopped and searched was simply too great. Similarly, using that most common form of transport in France, a bicycle, would also likely draw attention to him. He decided he would walk back, travelling at night.

The weather was not good and he would need to stay away from roads as much as possible. He anticipated the thirty-kilometre walk would take him two nights.

The rain and the waning moon would ensure a minimum of light to contend with as he travelled. It would also slow him down, but that was a small price to pay.

Thomas and his wife Marie had prepared him a small hamper of bread, dried sausage and other foods to take with him. These and other supplies he secured in a small backpack, which he wore underneath a long waterproof coat. He had studied the map and knew the roads well enough now not to need a guide.

Thomas took him aside before he set off.

"Don't take the risk of going up to houses to seek shelter during the day. There are families in the region who have become rather too close to the Germans. When you need to sleep, you should be able to find an old disused farm shed. There are any number of them along the way between here and Flavignac."

Daniel clasped his shoulders and they embraced.

"*Bonne chance,* Kestrel."

Daniel took his leave and disappeared into the night.

He had been on the road less than two hours when the weather, already unpleasant, became even worse. Even though it was now well into spring, there were still days when the long tail of winter, wagged.

Daniel had dressed for the rain as best he could, but his clothes were fast becoming heavier on him. Water was finding its way in, despite the waxed oilskin coat he was wearing. His boots were sodden and caked in mud. Each step was laborious as he struggled his way through churned up fields rather than running the risk of being spotted on the roads. He checked his watch. It was nearly twelve thirty in the morning and his progress was too slow. He realised that he had little choice. He simply had to run the risk of following a road if he was to make better time.

Finding such a road was easy enough, but it almost led to his immediate discovery.

He been making faster time on the solid surface for only about five minutes when a vehicle suddenly turned onto the road about a hundred metres in front of him. He had not heard the sound of the engine over the steady drum of the rain.

The loom of the car's headlamps was still swinging around as it made its turn. Just before it straightened up and the lights found him, he dived into the deep, grassy culvert at the side of the road. The car passed by without showing any sign of having seen him. The culvert though was deep with rainwater.

Daniel stood up and ruefully examined himself. He was now completely soaked. He stepped back up on to the road. At least the water had washed most of the caked mud off his boots!

He shook his head and smiled wryly to himself, before setting off along the road again.

There were no further vehicles that night and he managed to cover an additional ten deeply uncomfortable kilometres before he began to detect a slight lightening of the sky in the east. This first hint of the approaching dawn told him that it was time to start looking for shelter for the day. He left the road and began to head towards a large, dense stand of unkempt woodland at the far end of a more recently cultivated field. The fresh mud clogged up his boots again, but he continued on his way.

Once inside the cover of the trees, he could finally begin to relax. The denseness of the undergrowth indicated that the local residents seldom ventured into this copse, at least not on any kind of a regular basis.

He looked around to see if there was anything he could use to make a shelter to rest in for the day. He moved deeper into the woods and after a while, came upon what was clearly once a small path. It was heavily overgrown now. More likely used by deer and badgers rather than humans, he still decided to follow it.

Finally, his luck changed. The path led him towards a small, obviously long abandoned stone and timber building, almost lost amongst the dense foliage of the woods.

The door was slightly ajar and proved difficult to move, the hinges rusted almost solid. The door itself, entangled with years of plant growth. Despite his best efforts, he could only manage to open it less than half way. Still, that was enough to allow him to squeeze in.

Once inside, he found the room was almost perfect for what he needed. While the roof had noticeably sagged, it was still intact. It was, at least, still effective in keeping the water out, and that was all that mattered right now. There was little remaining furniture, only an old wooden table with rotting legs and the rusting metal frame and sprung base of a single bed. There was no mattress, only the broken remains of the wire spring meshing. A stone fireplace dominated the room and it still seemed solid, even though there was no way of telling if the chimney itself was blocked.

He sat on the iron perimeter frame of the old bed. Now that he could finally rest, his body soon began to shake at the onset of a damp, creeping chill that the last night of constant motion had held at bay.

He had been soaked to the skin for hours. Daniel was well aware of how serious that could be if he was not able to dry out and get warm soon. He had to take the risk and try to get a fire going.

He could only hope that the combination of heavy rain and the obscurity of the small shack hidden, as it was, in the dense woods would keep anyone from noticing the smoke.

There were matches, still mercifully dry, in his backpack and the small building afforded plenty of available timber. He found some floorboards were lifting in one corner of the room. These, he could pull up and burn. The old table itself could be broken up for firewood. There was even a supply of actual cut firewood, which had been prepared many years before and never used.

Mice now lived among the logs and Daniel promptly dispossessed them of their home.

He managed to get a fire going easily enough and, to his relief, the smoke went up the chimney rather than billowing through the room. Once it had settled down and he was content that it was not drawing curious visitors, he began to take off his sodden clothes and drape them over the frame of the bed, which he had moved closer to the fire.

He took out the food, which Thomas' wife had packed for him. The bread was soggy but he forced himself to eat it. The dried sausage was unaffected by the drenching and he ate it, hungrily. Best of all, he found she had packed a small jar of preserved apricots. The food restored him and he soon began to feel a warmth flow through him again. Now, he needed to sleep.

He had broken off all the table legs to use as firewood. That left the table top itself, which he placed on the rectangular frame of the bed, in place of a mattress. It would not be the most comfortable bed he had ever slept on but it would have to do.

The temperature in the room was becoming more comfortable now as the fire radiated its warmth from the hearth and through the adjacent, old stone walls. The sodden clothes, which he had spread out, began steaming as the moisture evaporated.

The last item in his backpack was a small thin blanket, which, though slightly damp, had somehow avoided becoming completely soaked. Daniel held it towards the fire until it was warm and then he wrapped it around himself. He had even taken off his wet underclothes and put them to dry by the hearth as well.

He placed a few more pieces of wood on the fire and lay down on the tabletop. He was far from comfortable, but that did not matter. He went to sleep almost immediately.

He awoke with the unsettling sense that someone was looking at him. He had brought with him a loaded pistol, but that was still in the pocket of the oilskin overcoat, hanging from a nail in the wall, more than a metre away. Not knowing what to expect, he slowly began to turn his head in the direction of the door. To his immense relief, the intruder was nothing but a deer, gazing at him curiously from the partly open doorway.

He smiled and spoke softly to the animal.

"*Bonjour, Mademoiselle!*"

The deer twitched its right ear and, in a very calm and unhurried manner, slowly backed away from the door, to wander off again into the safety of the woods.

Daniel sat up. His heart was gradually returning to its normal beat as the surprise of his awakening passed.

The fire had died down considerably; mostly just glowing embers were all that remained. He checked his watch again. He had slept for over five hours. He put some more wood on the fire and blew on it gently. The new wood caught, and soon the fire was burning comfortably again.

Checking his clothes, he was happy to find they were drying nicely. His underclothes were now dry again so he put them back on. Even though they now felt warm, his outer clothes were still too damp to wear. He left them draped over the frame of the bed.

Outside, it was still raining. Not as heavily as during the previous night, but still enough to keep all but the hardiest souls indoors. For Daniel, its continuing cascade was a comfort. It meant that he was likely to remain undisturbed in his derelict hovel until the night fell.

He walked over to the door and looked out. The deer had long disappeared back into the woods. There was no sign of anyone and no noise other than the steady drum of the rain. He tried pulling the door further closed but it sprang back to its old, rusted-in position every time. He gave up trying.

He took off his watch and wound it up again. Not for the first time he was grateful for the screw down crown of his Rolex. The rain and his dive into the flooded ditch had not affected it in the slightest.

It was barely midday and far too dangerous to go anywhere at this time, so he added some extra wood to the fire and lay down again, to try going back to sleep. As before, that sleep came easily.

He awoke this time, consumed by a fit of coughing. He sat up but continued to cough for another minute. His head was feeling stuffy and his chest was tight.

Checking his clothes again, they were now feeling dry and warm. Once he was fully dressed, it immediately improved his mood. Best of all, his socks had been closest to the fire and they were now wonderfully dry and warm. Their warmth brought further relief.

He added a few more pieces of cut wood from the pile that had once been home to the resident mice, and began to set about scraping the mud from his boots.

They too had dried out well. Now that he was fully dressed, he began to consider the remainder of his journey.

He had slept for a further five hours. It was now late afternoon, still too early to get underway again. Despite the rain, there was too much likelihood of encountering others. The roads that lay ahead would, likely, still be busy at this hour. He took comfort from knowing he had safely waited out the day. Only a few more hours and it would be safe to venture out again into the deep night.

Hungry again, he now regretted eating all of his available food that morning. There was nothing left.

His water flask was also empty, so he went outside and held it under a steady flow of rainwater, pouring out of the remains of a gutter suspended under the roof. He drank the entire flask and then refilled it.

The rain was noticeably easing now and, if that continued, he would have a much easier time of things on the second half of his walk. At least, he had that thought to cheer him.

By now, he was not feeling at all well. His head ached and his chest felt as though it were full of molasses. Mostly, he just wanted to be back with Lucien and Yvette. Most particularly, Yvette.

He angered himself at that thought. She was married and not interested in him. Besides, romantic considerations were the last thing that he should be contemplating right now. That was not why he was here.

He went back inside the shack and prepared himself to wait out the evening until it was late enough to set off safely.

By the time he felt confident enough to be on his way again, the rain had all but stopped.

There was still plenty of water dripping on him from the leaf canopy though, as he carefully made his way through the woods. He was retracing his path from the previous night.

This time, he skirted the large, ploughed field rather than walk across it. He was not going to allow the mud to build up under his boots as it had before.

Back on the road once again, he turned east and started walking. His head and chest were feeling even more congested, and it was obvious now that he had picked up what could be a serious chill or worse. Still, his circumstance gave him no choice, he pressed on.

When the need to cough came over him, he hid behind whatever cover there was and used his blanket to try to muffle the noise.

He continued his trek along the road in near complete darkness. Tonight thankfully, other than his own footfall, there was no activity on the roads. He walked on in discomfort and silence.

He had memorised the names of the tiny hamlets and villages along the way. He carefully skirted his way around the little towns of Le Temple, La Grange Neuve and La Rebeyrolle until he knew he was getting close to Lucien's small farm, south-west of Flavignac.

He checked his watch again. It was only just after four a.m. Despite his rapidly deteriorating health, he had made better time that he dared hope.

He finally found the laneway that led to their house and, fifteen minutes later, he was at the door.

No light showing from the house; all was completely silent. Daniel listened to see if he could catch the sound of Lucien snoring. He heard nothing.

He was wondering if he should simply go up and knock on the door when another fit of coughing caught him. He tried to muffle the sound as best he could, but in the quiet of the night, it cut through the air like a gunshot.

Bare moments later, the door opened slightly. Yvette appeared holding a lamp.

"Who's there? Is it you, Lucien?"

"No, it's me, Daniel," he gasped through stifled coughs.

"Good heavens!" exclaimed Yvette. "How did you get here? Quickly, come inside at once."

He did not need to be asked twice.

He sat down on the same chair he had used on his first night there. Yvette could see that he was far from well.

"Did you walk all the way from Oradour-Sur-Veyres? In the rain? Just look at you. My God, you're as pale as death!"

"I don't feel very well," said Daniel weakly, in agreement. "Where is Lucien? Are you here on your own?"

"Lucien is away with his group doing some observations of German movements to the south. There is a Waffen-SS Division down there that he's trying to find more information about. I don't expect him back until at least the day after tomorrow."

"I hope you don't mind," said Daniel. "Is it all right if I stay here until I get over this cold? I'm starting to feel rather wretched."

"Of course!" replied Yvette, emphatically, "I absolutely insist! You look half-starved as well. Wait here please and I'll fetch you something to eat."

Daniel finally felt himself able to relax.

Yvette returned with some bread and cheeses.

"Here, have some of this. I have a soup which I'm heating for you now."

Despite his hunger, Daniel felt less like eating than talking. He had never really been alone with Yvette before. Lucien had always been nearby.

His head filled with the many questions he wanted to ask her; *why was she with such an older man? What had she and her grandparents been through that had made them so emotional when he met them at the meeting at their house?*

Daniel said nothing though. He knew his questions were impertinent so he held his silence.

Presently, Yvette brought a bowl of hot vegetable soup for him.

"There is no meat, I'm afraid," she said.

"That's quite all right," said Daniel, "I completely understand. Soon enough, even vegetables might be hard to come by. Things are likely to get worse before they begin to get better."

He ate some of the soup.

"Anyway, it's delicious," he said.

Yvette smiled.

"You're very kind. It's not as good as I used to be able to make, but ingredients are more difficult to come by now. Even salt!"

"No, I meant it!" insisted Daniel. "But then perhaps I'm beginning to suffer from hallucinations!" he said smiling.

"Taste bud hallucinations?" said Yvette, joining in the joke.

"Well, you said it yourself. I am very sick." Daniel tried to laugh.

The effort simply set him off on another coughing fit. This time it was worse than the earlier one.

Yvette got to her feet and came around by his side. She put her hand on his forehead.

"You're burning up! You have a real fever here!" she said, suddenly concerned at realising just how sick he actually was.

"You need to get to bed and get warm. I have some spare blankets."

Daniel's coughing settled down.

"Please may I finish the soup first? I need it more than I need to go to bed right now," he implored.

Yvette sat back down on her chair but leaned in closer to the table.

When you have finished, I'll get a spare pair of Lucien's pyjamas. He's not as tall as you and a bit stockier, but they are all I have.'

"I do have some night clothes, but I haven't washed them since I arrived and they may still be a bit wet after the rain. I shall take you up on the offer. Many thanks."

As he continue to eat the soup, Yvette got up and went into the bedroom. She emerged a few moments later with a pair of plain, dark blue men's pyjamas and two plain, grey woollen blankets. She placed them on the table.

"Not the most stylish you've ever seen I suppose, but Lucien isn't known for his fashion flair," said Yvette, looking at the small pile, "but they will keep you warm."

Daniel had just finished his last spoonful and pushed the bowl to one side.

"Once again, thank you. You've been very kind to me. I do realise the potential position my being here has put you in…"

"Don't be silly! You will have to go back into the Mouse Hole down in the cellar. Not in my bed!" said Yvette with a coy grin.

Daniel almost began to laugh again but Yvette quickly reached across the table and put her finger against his lips.

"Don't laugh! You know what happened last time. You're sick enough to have me worried. We cannot have you getting worse and developing pneumonia. The nearest doctor is in Flavignac. He is not well disposed towards the Maquis. Most people believe he is a supporter of Vichy. I would rather not have to call him."

Daniel's face showed his concern at her words.

"I don't think he'd give any of us up to the Germans," she continued, "but it would be better not to take the chance."

"We only ever have to see him when Lucien gets sick. Every now and then, his injuries from the last war start to flare up. I wouldn't want to involve him here."

Daniel knew she was showing good sense. She and Lucien had been living with the occupation for four years. They were far more familiar with the risks than he. He would simply have to do as he was told. Besides, he knew full well that he was sick. He felt utterly wretched.

Slowly, he got up from the table.

"Would you mind turning around while I get into these wondrous garments, please."

Yvette smiled and made a big show of turning her chair around so she could sit with her back to him.

As he took his shirt off, he noticed that it was quite damp, this time with perspiration. He must indeed be running a fever!

Yvette led him down into the cellar and opened the Mouse Hole. She went in first, laid the extra blankets on the bed and turned it down, ready for Daniel to climb in.

She came out and Daniel bent over and went in. Once he had himself settled, Yvette came in once more, sat on the chair near the bed and lit the candle on the tiny table.

"You must be prepared to stay in here as much as possible. You need to rest and to keep warm. We're not likely to see anyone until Lucien gets back, but it's best not to take the chance. He's going to be at least another day. Anyway, it's far better if you can remain unseen, so please stay down here out of sight. Unless it's urgent, of course. OK?"

"OK! By urgent, I presume you mean, if nature calls?" asked Daniel with a weak smile.

"Precisely," said Yvette, a coy grin playing with the corners of her mouth. "Now you must try and get some sleep. You must be exhausted. I have to go back to bed too if I expect to get anything done in the morning. If you do need anything, just knock on the ceiling above you. I'll hear it."

"Thanks, Yvette, for everything," said Daniel.

Yvette leaned forward and kissed him on the forehead. She let the kiss linger for a moment longer than Daniel thought she might. He relished the sensation.

"Good night," she said softly, and left the tiny room.

Daniel luxuriated in the memory of the feel of her lips on his forehead. He fell asleep with the thought still whirling in his mind.

He woke mid-morning with Yvette sitting beside him holding his hand. She appeared to be dozing herself so she must have been there for some time.

"Good morning," said Daniel sleepily.

Yvette immediately released his hand and looked away from him guiltily.

"I came to see if you wanted something to eat but you were sleeping so soundly, I didn't want to wake you," she said in a nervous voice.

"That's very kind of you. I had no idea just how tired I was," he said, trying to act as though he was unaware of her earlier intimacy.

"I have baked some fresh bread and there's some cheese and sausage as well." Yvette said, now trying to sound bright. "Also, some tea."

"Wonderful!" replied Daniel as he started trying to lift himself up. Almost immediately, he felt a wave of nausea wash over him and he collapsed back into the bed.

Yvette quickly leaned forward and grasped his hand again.

Daniel lay there for half a minute with his eyes closed and waited while his head cleared. After a few more moments, he became aware of her hand on his and he responded by turning his hand towards hers and returning the gesture.

There they remained, locked in the intimacy of the moment, not moving, and simply gazing at each other.

"What is happening here?" said Daniel eventually. "This can't be right…" He paused again but the two kept their eyes locked each other, their gazes unbroken.

"There is clearly a lot more going on here that I don't understand."

Eventually, Yvette broke her gaze but she did not release his hand.

She tried to speak but broke into a stammering cascade of words, and stopped herself.

She held her thoughts for a few moments to compose herself. There was clearly trying to control some very deep emotion.

"I understand that Lucien told you about how he lost his brother in the war and his parents and a sister in the epidemic that followed."

"The Spanish Flu," said Daniel.

"Yes," replied Yvette, "well, my family suffered something similar. Many families did. Especially around here. The Flu was a scourge around here."

She gathered herself and began to seem slightly more at ease.

"I lost my father and his brother in the war. Also my older sister. She was a nurse and was killed during an artillery barrage near Verdun."

She paused for a moment as she continued to gather her thoughts.

"My mother and I were all my grandparents had left. Then she too, died in the epidemic. I was very young. I barely remember her and I have no memory of my father or my sister at all. My grandparents brought me up in the old house that you've seen. That was my home for many years."

Daniel listened without a word, taking it all in. Yvette continued, "My grandparents were wonderful to me. I love them more than life itself, but they just grow more and more bitter as the years pass. They hate all Germans with a venom I have never seen in any one else. They believe that the Germans have robbed them of everything that they loved in their lives, even me in a way."

Daniel looked surprised at this last point.

"In what way is this?" he asked.

"They blame the Germans for me having to marry Lucien," she said simply.

Daniel looked even more surprised.

"After the war and the Flu had finally passed, our little region had lost most of its younger men. Lucien was one of very few left in the area. Many other young girls left to go to Paris or some other city to try to find husbands. I didn't want to leave my grandparents. They were all I had."

"Did they not approve of Lucien?" asked Daniel.

"No, not really," said Yvette, "not because he was a bad man or anything like that. He isn't. He's not an angel or some kind of paragon, but he is a very decent man."

She picked up the cup of tea she had made and brought down for Daniel and had a sip herself.

"They believe the Germans created the world that left me with no other choice for a husband. Perhaps they are right. Do you remember he told you he was shot and gassed in the last war? Well, those injuries have left him… badly damaged."

"He has terrible trouble with his lungs because of the gas. There are occasional days when he can hardly breathe. One of his bullet wounds was in the lower abdomen and because of that, well… he frequently has… other problems…"

She paused and gathered her thoughts again.

"He doesn't deserve any of these things, but it is the reality. In the end, I married him because he was available and he lived so close to my grandparents. Also because as I said, he is a very kind man."

Daniel nodded. "He is also quite a few years older than you. I couldn't help but notice."

"That too has been a problem at times," said Yvette sadly. "We see many things differently. He is a much more committed Communist than I am. I look at Stalin and just see Hitler wearing another coat. One may be Right, one may be Left, but their methods are similar. I try not to talk of such things with Lucien any more."

"So you aren't a Communist like the others then?" asked Daniel.

"I don't know what I am. I believe in many of the goals of Communism, but not all. Most of all, I hate the constant demands for violence! This belief that change can only come through violent revolution. I believe there must be a better way."

Daniel thought about her words and said, "Maybe one thing that might come out of this war is that people will start to realise that violence is no longer the acceptable way to bring about change. It certainly isn't working very well right now."

Yvette looked sad. "Nothing much is working well right now. Especially now."

"What do you mean?"

"You! Look at you! You are sick, and in bed… And me! For the first time, I want to be free! I want to be free to look after you, but I can't. Not the way I want."

She let go of his hand and left the little room hurriedly, before he saw her cry.

Chapter 4

16 May 1944: Morin Farm, Outside Flavignac

Lucien had been away on his reconnaissance mission for eight days now. His group had travelled further south, and stayed longer than they had intended. The size and scale of the SS activity they were seeing had compelled them to investigate as fully as they dared.

Careful scrutiny had determined that they were "*Das Reich*". Lucien's group understood this to be a Panzer Division. However, there appeared few by way of any tanks with them. These troops looked to be mostly motorised infantry battalions. The absence of heavy armour made them no less dangerous.

They were battle hardened Waffen-SS troops. Dangerous men indeed.

All the information they had gathered had to be encoded and radioed on to England as soon as possible. It could only be done safely in short bursts, with the radio sets then being moved to new locations after each broadcast. All to try to make the whereabouts of the radio operator more difficult for the listening Germans to track down. The Germans used vans with radio detection equipment that could triangulate, and thus pinpoint, the locations of the individual radio sets.

This had led to the capture and interrogation of several radio operators in the past. The Maquis had learned the lessons from these incidents. They were now far more adept at moving the sets from place to place, and not staying on the air for too long.

For their part, the British would use nightly broadcasts on normal BBC radio to send out coded messages to the various Maquis and Resistance groups across occupied France and the Low Countries. The Maquis would listen to the broadcasts and when they heard the code word for their own group, would copy down the message that followed. Then came the relatively simple process of de-coding. In this area, to the south and west of Limoges they were now using the new codebooks that Daniel had brought with him.

It was a system which worked very well, even though the Germans had now cracked down heavily on anyone with even a simple radio set. Most people who owned them kept them well hidden, and only brought them out when they were confident there would be no unexpected visitors.

Lucien arrived home mid-morning, driven in a small farm vehicle owned by one of his near neighbours. They had met, quite by accident at a *boulangerie* in Flavignac after Lucien had returned from the intelligence-gathering trip a day later than expected. Each were buying a few the favoured rural food staple, dried sausages, and other groceries. The neighbour was happy to offer Lucien a ride home. He accepted gratefully.

A visit into town to buy household goods was wonderful cover, especially as it was well known that this neighbour was anti-Communist and not remotely involved with the Maquis.

Lucien had become skilled at keeping his own views on politics hidden from those he knew he could not trust.

He walked the two kilometres metres from the road down to his house. He was greeted at the door by Yvette.

"Daniel is back!" she said excitedly, "he's down in the Mouse Hole. He seems very sick. I think he might have pneumonia."

Lucien looked shocked. "When did he get here?"

"Three nights ago. He walked back from Oradour-Sur-Veyres over the nights when the weather was terrible. He was sick when he got here and he hasn't improved."

Yvette stood aside and Lucien entered the house. He was weary after the last week's activities and could have well done without an unexpected guest. Still, if he were as sick as Yvette believed, he would never have turned him away either.

Lucien took off the small backpack he was wearing and put it on the table. He opened it and took out the groceries he had bought. Yvette packed them away.

"I should go down and see him shortly. How is everything else? Are the animals all right? Did we have any Boche come by and take more?"

"Everything is fine," replied Yvette, "the animals stayed mostly in the barn during the rain but they've been out for the last day. No Boche came by. It was very quiet really. I was quite glad when Daniel came back. At least I had someone to talk to."

Lucien looked at her. A slight hint of anxious jealousy seemed to flash across his face.

"So, he was well enough to be a conversation companion was he?"

Yvette's eyes flashed at him angrily.

"Are you implying something? Are you? He is a sick man certainly, but not so sick that he is incapable of speech! He has slept a lot but still needs to eat and use the lavatory! He has simply been telling me about his life and what it's like in England at the moment. He has done nothing more!"

Despite her anger at Lucien's instant suspicion, she still felt an uncomfortable twinge of guilt at what she had just said. Nothing physical had happened between her and Daniel, but she was well aware of the fact that they were both strongly attracted towards each other. She must never let Lucien find out.

"I'm sorry…" Lucien replied, his posture sagging. "I didn't mean to sound like I was accusing you. It just came out wrong. I hadn't expected that there would be anyone else here while I was gone."

Yvette relaxed slightly. "I do understand. I'm sorry too. Don't forget that you are a day later than you said you would be. I have been worried about you myself. I had heard nothing."

Lucien went over to her and hugged her. He kissed her on the forehead.

"Again, I am sorry. There was more going on than we thought there might be. There is a large SS presence down south. We needed an extra day to learn as much as we could. *'Ecureuil'* is working to prepare a message to send to England tonight."

"Good!" said Yvette, nodding in relief as the tension between the two of them quickly passed. She was curious to know more but knew that the safety of the whole Maquis network relied on the ignorance of each individual regarding matters that fell outside their own responsibilities. The less one knew about what each of the others was doing, the better for everyone.

"They are far stronger in the south than we thought they were," said Lucien.

"The units we saw are all returned from the Russian Front. They'll be hard and ruthless bastards if they are ever given an excuse. It's probably been a good thing that we've not been as active in the field lately. I've heard stories of what these types got up to In Russia if they suspected civilians of fighting back... Murderous bastards..."

Yvette could not suppress an involuntary shiver. She knew as well as Lucien that once the Invasion was finally underway, local Resistance groups everywhere would start to rise up. *How would the Germans respond? Would they undertake reprisals against the local civilians?* SS troops such as these almost certainly would. It was an uncomfortable thought.

The sound of movement from down in the cellar snapped them both out of these pensive thoughts. Daniel was making his way up the stairs to join them.

"Welcome back, Lucien! I thought I could hear your voice. I am so sorry to have found myself like this. I hope you don't mind my intruding on you again?"

Lucien smiled. "That is perfectly fine, Daniel. Yvette has told me that you're too sick to be going anywhere for a while."

"So, it would seem I'm afraid. At least I don't seem to be getting any worse. Yvette has plied me with hot soup and I'm feeling quite at home now down in the Mouse Hole."

"Good," said Lucien, "at least it appears we don't have to add claustrophobia to your list of illnesses!"

Yvette and Daniel both laughed. For once he did not go straight into a coughing fit.

Yvette noticed the change. "You seem to be a bit better today. You're not coughing so much."

"I must say that I am feeling slightly better. I certainly slept better last night. Perhaps the soup is finally working its miracles."

Daniels improved health and mood had a positive effect on both Yvette and Lucien. They both started to relax more.

Daniel turned to Lucien. "Did I hear you say that there is a stronger Boche presence down south than we thought?"

"Unfortunately, yes. We stayed longer and managed to get close enough to try to find out which unit they are. We've worked out that they are a part of '*Das Reich*' Division. Waffen-SS. At least a full battalion, probably more. Well equipped. They are probably rebuilding after being withdrawn from the Russian Front. They are certainly mobile and they're practicing combat manoeuvers on an almost daily basis."

Daniel thought for a short while. "They've probably been reinforced and they're trying to get the new troops up to speed with the veterans. If they've come back from Russia, there would have been a good few holes in their man power."

"That's exactly what we thought too," replied Lucien. "How are we going to approach having these bastards at our back door once the invasion happens?"

"That may depend on where the invasion takes place," said Daniel.

"If it's up north towards Calais, then they will probably be moved up there quickly and won't really be our problem. Has London been told about them yet?

"That should be happening tonight," said Lucien.

"Ahh, excellent," said Daniel, "that should give the SOE something to ponder. They always knew there would have to be a decent number of Germans stationed around the Limousin. It's too central and too important to simply be left to Vichy. I don't think that they realised there would be units like this for us to have to deal with. I think they might even advise us to sit tight and let them pass through."

Lucien was looking at him. "Are you suggesting that when the time comes to fight, we do nothing? Just let them go past and wave them goodbye?"

Daniel sat down at the table. Despite his slight improvement, he was still sick and weak.

"No, not necessarily, but we will need to plan well and we will need to be careful. These guys are Nazi fanatics mostly. They'll be more than happy to line up a few dozen civilians against a wall and machine gun them, just to teach the Maquis a lesson. If we go in with all guns blazing, there will almost certainly be serious reprisals against the nearest town. We will need to keep that in mind and plan sensibly."

Lucien thought for a moment and sat down too.

"Of course you're right, but we can't just sit back and do nothing. The other groups will never agree to that. They have all been living under these bastards for too long. They will take some sort of action. You can count on it."

Daniel nodded in agreement. "Who can blame them? I want to as much as anyone, and I haven't been through anything like what you have. It's vital though, that all the other groups know about the risk of serious reprisals if they push too hard. They have to know that these bastards are nothing but murderers."

He leaned forward and looked intensely at Lucien. "Would you be able to get a message to the other groups in the region? Can you tell them of these concerns? Is it worth trying to arrange another meeting, like the last one at Yvette's grand-parent's house, one night soon?"

Lucien thought about it for a minute. "I doubt they would be too happy about another such meeting. They place us all at the greatest risk. Getting them all to agree to the last one was hard enough. If we were found out, the Maquis would risk losing all of its local leadership. There may be another option. It might be safer if one or two of us went around the region and spoke directly to the groups. Much less risk for the organisation as a whole."

"But more time consuming," replied Daniel.

"Perhaps, but not too much. I have many contacts who have cars. They can ferry me around in discretely," said Lucien.

"So you're suggesting you go yourself?" said Daniel.

"Well, you're in no condition to do this! It has to be me," said Lucien, suddenly sitting upright. "I can't say that I want to, but I can't think of anyone else. I'm the logical choice."

Daniel sat back and pondered the thought.

Yvette had been sitting on the small, worn sofa near the fire listening to their conversation. She could hold her mind no longer.

"Why don't I go? I'm just as capable of passing on messages as you, Lucien. I've done it for you in the past, you know."

The two men immediately stopped talking and looked at her.

"Out of the question!" exclaimed Lucien, "it has to be me. Not many Maquis, especially in any of the more distant groups, know you. I know you've run messages in the past, but only locally, never like this. If the groups don't know you, they simply will not take directives from you. It's that simple. In addition, if the Boche pick you up on any sort of suspicion…"

He left that last point hanging.

"No, it has to be me. I know the entire region well; they all know me and I can move about more readily. That's an end of it!"

Daniel and Yvette looked at each other and then both looked at Lucien. It was obviously decided.

"So what now then? Are you leaving again? You've just got here!" said Yvette.

"I'm not planning on leaving this very minute," said Lucien with a smile returning to his lips.

"I have work to do around here on the farm and I also need to be seen so that no tongues can start wagging. I've been away for a week. If I go away again, you may find that word gets through to Vichy or the Germans. My leaving will have to wait for at least four of five days."

"The next full moon is on the 5th and 6th of June," said Daniel. "It's very possible that the Invasion could be set for around that time. Will that leave you enough time to get around all the different Maquis cells before then?"

"I'll have over a week. I won't stay too long in any one place. I should be fine. Besides, there is no guarantee that the Invasion will happen then. Perhaps they want a new moon. Complete darkness. Perhaps they're invading tonight."

"In that case," said Daniel, "we might as well go into Flavignac and buy several bottles of wine and enjoy the evening when it comes."

"I completely endorse the sentiment," said Lucien "but that would require rather more money than I have right now."

"Well then," replied Daniel with a smile, "let the night be on me! The SOE make sure that we come to France with all the resources we might need, including adequate money!"

He got up slowly. The conversation was clearly tiring him.

"Please stay seated!" said Yvette. "Let me go. What do you need?"

"Can you please bring me the overcoat I was wearing the night I arrived from England?"

Yvette left the room and went down the stairs into the cellar. She returned less than a minute later carrying the overcoat. She handed the garment to Daniel.

"Do you have a small pair of scissors or perhaps a small knife?" asked Daniel.

Yvette went over to the sideboard and returned with a little pair of scissors she had taken from her sewing kit.

Daniel took them and felt around within the folds of the coat for a moment. He turned the inner lining side of the coat outwards and gently set about snipping away the stitching along a seam. After a few minutes he passed the scissors back to Yvette and carefully reached into the opened he had created.

He withdrew a quantity of French five, ten and twenty franc notes. He separated several of them and passed them to Lucien.

"There are three hundred francs here, Lucien. I'm sure that if you select wisely, you might be able to secure us the makings of an enjoyable evening. And it should also leave you with plenty spare for your travels."

"*Merci beaucoup,* Daniel!" said Lucien, shocked at the unexpected windfall. "I shall walk up to see Bernard. He will let me borrow his van to go into Flavignac. I should be no more than four hours or so."

Daniel then handed the rest of the money over to Yvette.

"Please use these to pay for whatever I might cost you. It was never my desire to see the two of you having to spend what little the Germans leave you with, in order to look after me."

Yvette quickly counted the money. There was a further two hundred francs. A not insubstantial amount in rural France at this time.

"My goodness!" exclaimed Yvette. "I haven't held this much money in years."

Daniel smiled. "It's easy for me to give it away, you know. It's not my money!"

All three of them laughed. Then Daniel started coughing and clutching his chest again.

Chapter 5

24 May 1944: Limoges

Lucien had been waiting in the bar for nearly an hour. He had arranged to meet up with the local Maquis leader but clearly, something was holding her up. Usually, a small delay was no cause for concern. Free movement around cities in France was no longer something anyone could take for granted. German soldiers or even French *Gendarmes* could stop travellers at any time on the flimsiest of pretexts. Not police as such, the *Gendarmes* were a national, military force, who were now acting under the orders of Vichy.

Knowing this, Lucien was not getting too worried, but the delay was certainly longer than usual.

He had been in Limoges for less than a day and had immediately set about making contact with the town's main Resistance cell. He had no doubt they would not like hearing his message, but his conscience dictated he must pass it on. All of the likely points of invasion by the Allies lay to the north or north-west. The SS would certainly be coming through their region in order to take part in the overall German response.

His message was simple, be mindful of likely extreme SS retaliation to any Maquis attacks.

At last, an attractive, neatly dressed woman with dark hair came into the bar, not from the street, but from a side door that went through to an adjacent café.

Lucien stood up when he saw her. She recognised him immediately and went over. They made a show of greeting each other like long lost friends. In fact, they were. They had known each other for years. It was she, who had held Lucien's attention at the meeting in Flavignac earlier in the month.

Lucien caught the attention of a waiter and ordered two glasses of Armagnac.

"How are you, Angeline?" asked Lucien. "I'm sorry we weren't able to speak much the last time I saw you." Lucien did not want to say too much in such a public place.

"I am very well, thank you. I apologise for being so late. I had several clients who were demanding to say the least. I didn't think they would ever leave!" came her lilting reply.

Angeline Blanchard was a seamstress by profession. She had, over the course of several years, managed to quietly ingratiate herself with some of the local German officer coterie. She had once repaired the uniforms of several senior officers; they had recommended her to others and her contacts grew from there.

As she had performed these repairs and alterations reliably and efficiently, many of her officer customers had become quite familiar and comfortable in her presence. She was amazed at some of the indiscrete slips they would make when discussing matters of intelligence with each other while she simply worked away in the background, pinning seams or stitching. She had become a very good and attentive listener.

"What brings you into Limoges, Lucien? I haven't seen you here for a quite a while."

"I need some machine parts for the farm. I can't get them in Flavignac without having to wait so I thought I'd do the trip and buy them here, myself. Yvette can manage on her own until I return."

"Very trusting of you, Lucien," said Angeline with a suggestive half-smile.

Lucien returned the look. "Very trusting of her, more likely!"

They both laughed. The flirting was as much for show as it was real. If they looked like a couple on a tryst, it would soon allow any interested eavesdroppers to make their own conclusions and move on.

They both made small talk until their drinks were finished. Then Angeline stood up, took Lucien by the arm and they left the bar.

Lucien took out a packet of cigarettes and offered one to Angeline before taking one himself. They moved close as he lit them. It was an intimate moment that reminded them both of the relationship they had once nearly shared.

There was a time, twenty years earlier, when Angeline had also lived in Flavignac. She was young and very pretty then. Brunette hair and large brown eyes, with a trim and athletic figure, born of her teenage years spent as an aspiring ballet dancer.

Lucien was one of a number of young men who had eyes for her. She liked him too. He was a handsome man in his youth. However, his injuries from the war had left him with a damaged bladder. That, in turn, left him with difficulty in controlling his urinating. It resulted in his deep humiliation on several occasions and shattered his confidence around women.

Angeline had been aware of this and tried to be supportive. Lucien though, was unable to overcome his anxiety and take the steps to initiate the relationship that they both desired.

For her part, Angeline had other men paying her attention and eventually she found a man, several years older than her who owned a clothing shop in Limoges. She had married him and moved away from Flavignac. Cancer had since taken him, but she had kept the business and had concentrated on growing the repairs and alterations side of it.

In the years since, Lucien had seen several doctors and, with a regime of special exercises, over that time he had regained much of the bladder control that the bullet wound had taken from him. Now also, he had Yvette.

Angeline stepped back from Lucien and drew deeply on the cigarette. She looked up at his face and smiled.

"Come with me," she said, "I have arranged a small meeting with some colleagues. It is only a short walk from here. You can tell me what you've been up to over the last few years as a gentleman farmer!"

"A gentleman farmer? You know I'm a Communist."

Angeline laughed. "Of course, I know you are. But I'm not!"

They were joined by three others, all of them sitting around a table in an anonymous, sparsely furnished room in an otherwise unoccupied house.

Lucien had spoken to them about the SS units to the south, and everything he had seen down there. He had explained who these units were and what he knew of their background. The others listened carefully and respectfully remained silent while he spoke.

Angeline had not told Lucien any of their names, nor had she told them his. He was simply a Comrade from another Resistance cell.

After he finished, there were a few moments of silence as the others considered their thoughts.

"So then, are you suggesting that we do nothing?" said one man in a slightly agitated voice. "Are you suggesting that we just sit on our hands and let them pass?"

"No, not at all!" said Lucien emphatically. "I am not a part of your cell. I can't, and won't make decisions for you. I simply wish to let you know what I have found out so that if you are planning anything, you can take into account the possible consequences. Be aware, this is a dangerous wasp's nest that we might be prodding."

"We all understand that," the man replied, "but if we concern ourselves with how the Boche will respond, we'll never do anything! This is war! We have lived under these bastards for four years now! They are our enemy! These Fascist arseholes are the enemy of France. They are the enemies of all workers everywhere. Don't try and have us double guessing. If they retaliate against civilians, we'll attack them again, harder!"

Another man spoke up. "I agree with my comrade. The more we can tie them up around here, the longer it will take them to get to wherever the invasion may be. That gives the Allies more time to establish the beachhead. We need to take these bastards head on!"

Lucien could see their point but he still felt deep disquiet at what might happen by way of reprisals. However, it seems these men had their minds made up.

He turned to Angeline. "And your thoughts, please?"

Angeline sat staring at him for a moment.

Then she leaned forward and said, "I have to agree with my colleagues. If we can tie the Boche to this area, even for just a few days, it may prove priceless to the Allies. I have no doubt that they will target some civilians for reprisals, but we have to take that risk. Wars have casualties. They just do. You, of all people should know that, my old friend."

Lucien sat blankly for a long moment. "You're absolutely right of course. Wars have casualties..." He dwelt on the thought, but could not shake his fears.

Everyone at the table was looking at him intently.

After a few moments, he gathered his thoughts and said, "Thank you, everyone. I have no doubt about your conviction to seeing this through. I just wanted to let you all know what it is we are facing. Plan well, please. Above all else, plan well..."

Angeline looked at him kindly and said, "I have always wondered if you might be too kind hearted to truly be a Communist."

Her companions immediately glared at her but she smiled mischievously and laughed. It was obvious that she was simply teasing and they soon joined in the laughter.

Lucien smiled indulgently at the joke made at his expense. He might have felt a mild rebuke in her comment, but he knew she had not meant it as such. He sat back in his chair and let the moment wash over him.

Nevertheless, when the laughter stopped, he remained, still contemplating an unshakeable feeling of deep disquiet.

***

Yvette had managed to snare a hare that morning. She and Lucien had always kept a few snares set around the farm. Only occasionally though, would they have any luck.

She had quickly despatched the animal as soon as she found it, and brought it back to the house. For once, there would be fresh meat to eat that evening.

Daniel was still recovering. It was clear that he had developed a mild pneumonia and it was a long, slow period of convalescence to get over it. While he was at rest, he was beginning to feel quite fine, but even the slightest exertion was apt to bring on a fresh bout of coughing and rapid fatigue.

He was feeling bored and useless. He was in to France to help focus the Maquis resources towards intelligence gathering for the Allied war effort. Thus far, he had not achieved anything like what he had in mind when he volunteered.

At least, he was not dead and he was getting better. He may yet have an active role to play.

Yvette had seen to the animals as she always did. The goats and the pigs were fed, and they appeared to be enjoying the late spring weather. Perhaps there might be a good breeding season yet, to help rebuild the depleted stock numbers after the Germans had helped themselves.

She went back into the house proudly carrying the dead hare. Daniel was still down in the Mouse Hole. It was by far the safest place for him to stay, in case there was an unexpected visit by a passing German patrol.

Nevertheless, he had long since lost his enjoyment in the novelty of this tiny, secluded room. Its restrictive isolation now felt stifling.

Daniel heard Yvette's footsteps on the floor above his head and he decided to join her. He eased himself from the bed and climbed out of the little room. He needed some human company.

Yvette heard him as he was coming up the stairs. She found herself looking forward to his company more than she usually did. They had drawn back from each other after their earlier moment of intimacy. Both had tried hard to rebalance the relationship on a less charged level.

Thus far, they even believed they had been successful.

Daniel emerged from the cellar and Yvette held up the hare in delight.

"Look! Tonight, we have fresh meat!"

Her happiness at the success seemed to make her natural beauty radiate even more enticingly than usual. Daniel had never seen her so happy before.

"Wow!" he said. "How did you manage to catch that?"

"Oh, we have a few snares around the place. Most often we don't get anything but today, we did."

"Well done! Do you need any help in getting it ready?" he asked.

"Can you skin and prepare a hare? I still have trouble picturing you as a farm boy."

Daniel put on a pose of affronted indignation.

"Give me that damn thing. I'll have it ready in five minutes!"

He took the hare and a knife and went outside.

Yvette called after him, "Be careful, that knife is very sharp. You're already damaged enough."

A loud *Hurrumph* came back through the door as he disappeared from view. Her laughter followed him as went to find a place to go to work on the carcass.

True to his word, he was back a short while later with the hare skinned, gutted and minus the extremities.

"I'm very impressed," said Yvette who was working at the kitchen bench preparing vegetables.

"But you were closer to fifteen minutes that five," she added with a smirk.

Daniel uttered another *Hurrumph* and went to sit down on the sofa to regain his breath. The process of preparing the hare had nearly exhausted him.

"How are you feeling?" asked Yvette. "You are certainly beginning to look better."

"I keep thinking that I'm doing OK, but any time I try anything even slightly strenuous, it just leaves me completely exhausted. It's the most stupid thing. I just don't feel sick, but I must be."

"You are sick, but you're doing well. Perhaps in a few more days, you'll be feeling stronger. If you push yourself too much now, you may go backwards. I know how boring it must be but please, keep on resting."

Daniel sat glumly. "All right nurse. If you insist."

"Since I am your nurse, I do insist!" laughed Yvette. She put down the knife she was holding and washed her hands in the sink. After drying them, she came around and sat beside him on the sofa.

The next moment just happened. It was beyond their control.

Daniel reached out and put his hand on the back of her head. Yvette leaned over to him and they kissed.

Yvette had lived in marriage with a kind and gentle man who she knew loved her, but Lucien's love was not physical, not romantic, not like this! This was something she had nearly given up dreaming about. Now it was real.

Daniel had been in love with her from the night at her grandparent's home. He knew it, but could dare not say so. Now for the two of them, it came rushing out in the overwhelming power and passion of this long suppressed moment.

They did not care what might happen next. Yvette stood up and took Daniel's hand. He got up also, and she led him into her bedroom.

Daniel had never been in there before, yet now he paid scant attention to the room itself. His mind was totally occupied by the beautiful woman in his arms. They both fumbled with the buttons, ties and clasps of each other's clothing.

Finally, freed of these things, they fell together into the bed.

After their lovemaking was over, Daniel lay back in the bed. He lay looking at the ceiling but not taking any of it in. Yvette lay nestled against him on her side with her arm across his chest and her hand against his face.

"You need to shave you know," she said.

Daniel smiled. "I guess it has been a couple of days…"

He held her closer.

Yvette asked, "When did you know? When did you first know?"

"At your grandparent's house. I knew then there was something. I've been fighting it so much since then. It was one of the hardest things I've ever had to do, going off on that trip to Oradour-Sur-Veyre. I just wanted to be here with you.'

Yvette just lay there and said nothing.

Daniel continued, "You know, I was actually glad I got sick. I haven't had to go anywhere. I could just be here with you. It's a funny thing. I've never been more unwell, but I've never felt more alive."

Yvette hugged him closer.

"I don't know what to say," she said, "I've never felt so free, but at the same time, I've never felt so trapped. Lucien is such a good man, but it's like I'm married to an older brother in so many ways. He cares for me. He loves me in his own way, and I love him too. He is such a kind man. You know that too! You've seen it! You like him also, I can tell. You can't deny it."

Daniel nodded silently.

Yvette continued, "But I don't love him. Not like I love you…"

"So you love me too then?" said Daniel.

"Completely," said Yvette, "I just don't know what to do next. How do I break the heart of the kindest man I shall ever know?"

Daniel lay there quietly next to her. The same thought was wracking his mind too. Yvette was right; he had come to like Lucien greatly in his time in this house.

As she had said, Lucien was a kind man, deeply damaged in a conflict that was not of his making. Now, there was another war and once again, he was a part of it. He was away from his home, helping fight this new war against that same enemy.

In the midst of that, Daniel was lying in Lucien's bed, making love to his wife.

He had never felt so conflicted.

"I thought love was supposed to be this beautiful thing. I didn't know it could come with such guilt."

Yvette held him closely. She was experiencing the same terrible flow of conflicting emotions. Perhaps for her, it was even worse.

"I know… I know…'

She began to cry. They held each other tightly as her tears flowed.

Chapter 6

2 June 1944: Chabanais, 50 km West of Limoges

The weather had taken a serious turn for the worse. The new day saw the arrival of heavy rain and strong winds. Atlantic storms were thrashing the coastline before blowing further inland.

Lucien's travels had brought him as far west as he intended to go. He had met with other Resistance cells over the last three days and told them all of the SS threat that lay to the south. The response was always the same.

C'est la guerre!

For his part, was coming to agree with them. It was war, and war is never without risk. In each town he visited, the local Resistance had greeted him warmly. They had shown him as much hospitality and generosity as the current austerity allowed.

Everywhere, the sense of anticipation concerning the impending invasion was palpable. Every evening, people would sit by their radios, listening to the BBC broadcasts from England, hoping for the key words that would signify that this night was THE night, and calling them to arms.

However, the weather had changed everything for the moment. There was no question of the invasion going ahead while the Channel storms were like this.

Lucien had chosen to stay in a small hotel this time, as he did not know anyone in this town. He had never visited the large crossroads town of Chabanais before. The local cell was one of the more active and it had taken him more than a day to make contact with them. It was the first town he had visited where he found himself treated with suspicion.

Throughout France, the Resistance movement had largely been born from Communism. The Maquis cell in Chabanais was one of the most ideologically Communist in the entire central Aquitaine region. They did not want to hear any calls for restraint from an outsider.

They took in the intelligence that Lucien had to offer but gave no hint that they would change any of their plans to accommodate such a possible threat. Lucien could only repeat his message that they plan well and be prepared.

Now, he sat in his hotel room and ate a small meal. The money that Daniel had given him certainly helped with his travels, but it was now almost gone. He had resolved that it was time to start heading home. He had done all that could have been expected of him.

He would try to find transport back to Limoges in the morning.

He could at least be content that every cell he had met now had the best information available as to the German presence in the region. That alone was worth the effort. What they did with that information was now up to them.

After he finished eating, he took off his clothes and changed into an old pair of pyjamas. He sat on the edge of his bed, deep in thought.

Despite Yvette's assurance that there was no cause for concern regarding having Daniel staying in their house, his imagination was beginning to run away with unbidden thoughts of the two of them together.

He knew she had agreed to marry him, more because it allowed her the chance to remain close to her grandparents rather than because she loved him. They were the only family she had ever really known. It was a very pragmatic decision on her part. She had since come to love him, but not in a deeply physical way; he knew that.

His mind dwelt on the reality that his constant anxiety, whenever they tried to be intimate, had resulted in her perpetual disappointment with him as a lover. That realisation just seemed to make things worse. The outcome of course, was that he had never been able to give her a child. He knew what a deep disappointment that had been to her. It just added further to his sense that he had been less of a husband than he might have been. Could he really blame her if another, younger man caught her eye?

He had always been conscious of their age difference but he had tried to brush it aside as being of no consequence. Now, it seemed as though it was becoming a wall between them. For the first time, he began to think of himself as an old man while she was still full of youth and life.

He began to dread what he might find when he got home. Eventually, he fell asleep but his dreams, when they came, were troubled.

He awoke early the next morning. He had no need of alarms to rouse him. He was a farmer, waking up early was deeply ingrained in his routine.

There was an omnibus service that would take him part of the way back to Limoges. It was slow and most likely, he would be asked to show his identification papers at one or more points along the journey, but that was expected.

The omnibus would take him to the next town, a larger village called St Junien. He had met the local Maquis in St Junien on his way out to Chabanais. He knew they were more hospitable and would be helpful in arranging discrete travel back to Limoges.

The weather made the trip to St Junien even slower than usual but at least it kept the Germans and the *Gendarmes* indoors. In the end, Lucien had not been asked to produce his papers once, except for when he bought his ticket.

Once in St Junien, he made his way to the *patisserie* where he knew that the baker was also a member of the Resistance. He hurried into the shop, water cascading from his outer coat, thanks to the still-heavy rain.

"Good morning to you, *Monsieur* Briand," he said as the baker emerged from the back room. "Wonderful weather you have laid on for me!"

Phillippe Briand was also a veteran of the previous war. The two had served together in the terrible fighting around the shattered citadel town of Verdun.

Phillippe was delighted to see his old comrade again. "This is the second time you have visited in three days, Lucien. Are you planning on settling down here?"

Lucien laughed. It was good to have his mind taken off his worries, even if only for a brief while.

"No, Phillippe! I am merely trying to find my way back to Limoges. The company in Chabanais was not as hospitable as I had hoped."

"Ah yes!" said Phillippe. "They are a law unto themselves around there. I often wonder what they will do to keep themselves busy after the war. They will no doubt, be looking for someone new to hold grudges against, once the Germans have been booted out."

Lucien finished taking off his wet overcoat and hung it up on a hook near the front door.

"Come on through, old friend," said Phillippe, holding open the door to the back room. "I was about to stop for lunch. Please join me. Guess what! I even have some real coffee!"

Lucien was amazed. "I haven't tasted coffee in over a year! How did you find it?"

"I have my sources," said Phillippe, tapping the side of his nose. "In my business, sometimes we have to be a little… shall we say, resourceful when it comes to finding ingredients. I've got to know a few people…"

"Fair enough," said Lucien, "I shall ask no more."

The two of them shared a companionable lunch. It was the best Lucien had eaten in months. Being a baker, Phillippe had fresh bread, still hot from the oven, as well as ham, dried sausage and several cheeses. Better still, the wonder of fresh coffee!

"My God!" said Lucien after they had finished. "If I was to eat like that every day, I'd be too fat to work the farm."

Phillippe smiled happily. "Your timing was perfect. I only got the coffee this morning. It might be the last I can get until after the war. Even the black market is struggling these days. So much of everything is being sent to Germany now."

"I know," replied Lucien, "the bastards have left me with so few animals; I may not be able to have a market season this year. I'll need to keep every new born to stock up the herds again."

Phillippe nodded sympathetically before changing the subject. "Anyway, you said you were on your way back to Limoges?"

"Yes," said Lucien, "I've done what I can around the cells. It's time I was going home."

"Well, I can't take you, but I know someone who can get you most of the way there. There is a delivery truck here in town right now. He is from a town north of here, called Oradour-Sur-Glane. He will be heading back up there shortly, I believe. From there, there is a tram service into Limoges. It might be too late to catch it by the time you get there today, but it will be an easy journey tomorrow."

"That will be fine," said Lucien. "Where can I find this man? How did you know about him?"

"Where do you think the coffee came from?" said Phillippe with a grin. "Come with me. I'll take you to him."

They both went back out into the shop. Lucien retrieved his overcoat from the hook whilst Phillippe put on his. Locking the door to his shop behind them, Phillippe then led Lucien off towards a bar a few hundred metres down the same road.

He knew the delivery driver would be in there having lunch of his own. Phillippe spotted him as soon as they walked through the door. Lucien went to the bar and ordered three glasses of *pastis* as Phillippe went over to ask the driver if he would take a passenger back with him to Oradour-Sur-Glane.

Lucien joined them a minute later with the alcohol. The driver accepted his glass with no apparent sign of gratitude.

He looked up at Lucien. "I am told you are wanting a free lift back to Oradour. I don't do free lifts, *Monsieur*."

Lucien was taken aback by his surliness. "I had no expectation that it would be free, *Monsieur*. I would be happy pay for the fuel if that's what you mean."

"Ten francs, *Monsieur*."

This was extortionate for such a short distance. It was also nearly a quarter of what money Lucien had left.

"That would leave me with too little to go home from Limoges, *Monsieur*. Would you accept five francs?"

The man thought about it for a few seconds and then took a large sip of wine. Suddenly, he broke into jovial smile and said, "Actually, I would have accepted two, but since you've offered…"

Lucien stood there, mouth open like a fish.

Both Phillippe and the man laughed.

"My name is Rene, *Monsieur*. I believe your name is Lucien?"

"It is. That was a clever trick, *Monsieur!*"

Rene was still chuckling. He leaned forward and said quietly, "Don't worry, Monsieur. The money will not be for me. It will be used wisely."

Lucien caught his drift. Rene was clearly Maquis also. Lucien felt better now but it still left him with a tight budget to get back to Flavignac.

Rene indicated for Lucien to sit down and join him. Phillippe then patted Lucien on the shoulder and said, "Well, I must get back and open the shop again. *Bonne chance* to you, my old friend. I hope we will see each other again soon, and under better circumstances. *Au revoir.*"

Lucien stood again and embraced his friend before Phillippe turned and left the bar. Lucien resumed his seat. Rene was nearly finished his meal and drank the last of the heavy aniseed liquor Lucien had bought him. Normally diluted with water, he drank his neat.

"Well now!" he exclaimed. "Phillippe didn't even touch his glass. I cannot stand to see such waste!" He took the glass for himself and took a large sip. Clearly, he was a man well accustomed to heavy drinking.

Lucien realised that he had not yet touched his own.

"I had best drink mine before you set your eyes upon it as well," he said with a grin.

"*A la votre!*"

Rene lifted his glass and swigged down the remainder.

The drive up to Oradour-Sur-Glane took nearly an hour. It was less than fifteen kilometres, but Rene's small lorry was old and slow. They were also several unexpected stops, waiting for unfenced cattle to amble off the road. This was a dairy region and there was nothing unusual in cattle being left to roam about unchecked. They knew where they lived and always found their way home in time for milking. Small-lot farmers in rural France could not always afford to effectively fence their fields.

They drove into the town from the south over a stone bridge, which crossed the Glane River, a small and pretty stream. The road took them past a large, ancient church on the left and then up the main street.

Lucien noted the tracks that the tram would use to take him into Limoges the following day.

He had never been to this town before and he was surprised at how prosperous it seemed. The town had a nice feel to it.

Rene dropped him off at a small, but neat looking hotel on the main street. Lucien looked up at the name of the establishment: Hotel Milord.

Rene had explained that he did not live in the town. He still had another eight kilometres to drive before he was home. He did make one important point though to Lucien before he left.

"There is no Maquis cell in this town, *Monsieur*. Best not to make enquiries if you understand me. Just find a room for the night and take the tram tomorrow."

"Thanks. I will keep that in mind. Thanks for the lift. *Au revoir!*"

Rene crunched the ancient vehicle into gear and set off up the street.

Lucien looked around for a minute and then headed into the hotel to see if they had a room that was not too expensive. They had a small room with no bath that he could have for seven francs. That would do.

Madame Helene Milord, whose family owned the hotel, ushered him upstairs. She showed him to his room and left him there to settle in.

Lucien had little luggage, just his backpack with some changes of clothes and his shaving kit.

It was now after four p.m.; too early to eat but perhaps enough time to have a wander around the town. The rain had abated for the moment, though the sky was still threatening. Lucien hated wearing the overcoat for long periods. Its bulk was too restricting for a man used to working around a farm.

He decided to take a chance and leave it behind to air in his room, while he went for a walk.

He nodded to Helene Milord as he went out into the street. She gave him a fleeting smile in return. She was a busy woman.

Lucien wandered first up the street to the tram terminus to buy a ticket to Limoges for tomorrow. He was advised the tram would leave at nine a.m. sharp. He did not need to come up to the terminus. It would stop for him outside his hotel.

The cafés were back in the direction he had come from. He wandered back down the street, noticing a prominent looking mechanics business, which also ran a Renault car sales concession as well. He would have loved to have a car of his own. Perhaps after the war…

He finally reached a café called *Le Chene Vert* (The Green Oak). It seemed as nice a place as any, so he went in and ordered a glass of red wine. He took his glass and sat himself at a table looking out the window as the world went by.

His thoughts returned to what he might find when he got home. *Would Daniel still be there? Would Yvette be with him?* It was hard to rid himself out of these thoughts. They nagged at him relentlessly.

The rain had started falling again, so he was tied to his seat in the café until it lifted enough to head back to the hotel. Several other locals were there also, but they seemed content to leave him alone rather than try to engage him in conversation. In wartime, it was often best to let strangers be.

Eventually, after nearly two hours, there came another break in the rain so Lucien took the chance to head back to the hotel. He went to lie down on his bed for a rest before going down to the restaurant to have a meal. He did not realise how tired he was. He did not wake for the meal and slept solidly until nearly six a.m. the following day.

***

Daniel awoke once more in Lucien and Yvette's bed. As always, he felt a pang of guilt, but then he looked at the beautiful young woman sleeping beside him. Once again, he pushed the guilt to one side and just lay there gazing at her. He knew that there would have to come a time of reckoning when Lucien returned.

That might be anytime now. Last night would be the end of it. They could no longer allow themselves the joy of sleeping together until the pathway to a future they could share had been decided.

As hard as it was, he must return to the Mouse Hole. Their all-consuming desire for each other notwithstanding, it was where he should have been. Their shared passion had made them careless to the risks of being caught with her, should anyone, especially German patrols, decide to visit.

The heavy rain and wind of the last several days had helped them feel secure from that possibility. The weather had sheltered them, with a blanket of isolation, from the rest of the world.

Yvette would still go out and feed the animals twice a day but any other work outside was not possible. It also meant that no one else was likely to visit. They had their world to themselves. They had spent their time in that world mostly naked in bed together. Their lovemaking was frequent; their passion was endless. Neither spoke of it, but they each knew it would soon have to end. Each time might be their last.

Daniel dragged has gaze away from Yvette and looked at the calendar hanging on the wall nearby. It was the 5th of June. The moon would be full for the next few nights. It was the optimum time for the invasion. The thought brought him back to reality.

He leaned over to Yvette and gently shook her. "Wake up, Sleepy Bones. The day is upon us."

Yvette mumbled back, "No… No… Make it go away!"

"I'm sorry, but there are pigs and goats to feed. You know they don't like to be kept waiting."

Yvette groaned again in resignation, but lay there for a few more moments to try to shake off the sleep. Then, with a sigh, she threw back the blankets and sat up, her legs draping over the side of the bed.

As always, Daniel gasped in wonder at how beautiful her body was. Lithe and slim from all the walking and exercise that farm life provided. He knew he had fallen deeply in love.

Yvette looked over her shoulder and saw Daniel gazing at her.

"Now, don't you look at me that way again! We shall never get anything done around here."

He smiled. "Yes, you're right." He was trying to sound determined and resolute. "It's past time to get up. Come on, my love, let's get moving."

"I like it when you call me 'my love' you know."

Daniel smiled. "I like saying it." Then a cloud came over his face.

Yvette saw the change in his expression and knew what it meant. She was feeling the same sensation. Terrible guilt.

"We need to get dressed and clean up this room," said Daniel, trying to sound resolute. "He might be back today. I need to go back down into the Mouse Hole."

Yvette thought she would cry. "How can I go back to what was? I cannot possibly give you up now. I love you so much!"

Daniel stood their looking at her. "That's the first time you've said that. I love you too. I want to be with you more than my life, but I just don't know what to do to make that happen. Not without being totally cruel to a man who's only ever shown me generosity and kindness."

This time Yvette did burst into tears.

***

Lucien had packed the few possessions he had brought with him and had eaten a simple breakfast in the hotel's restaurant. His long sleep had refreshed him. He now felt far more positive about going home than he had for days. Perhaps he was just letting his imagination run away with him. As soon as Daniel was well enough, he would be on his way again.

All would finally return to normal in his and Yvette's life together.

The rain was not as heavy today, but the wind was driving it hard. He was thankful he had arranged his ticket for the tram the day before. He simply waited in the hotel's restaurant for the tram to appear outside the door.

Sure enough, shortly after nine a.m., the little tram slowed and stopped outside. Lucien got up from his seat by the window and went to leave. He turned and said *au revoir* to Helene Milord as she stood at the reception counter of the little hotel. She smiled and waved back as Lucien went outside into the scudding rain.

It was only a few steps to cover before he clambered aboard the tram, but he still got well soaked, even from that. He showed his ticket to the Conductor who clipped it and handed it back. Lucien chose a seat on his own, put his bag on the brass, overhead carrier and sat down.

The little tram was quite new. The service had been running since well before the war. This was a new carriage however, and even though it was shaky, it was dry and the wooden seats were well shaped and comfortable.

Lucien was one of several passengers that had boarded from the hotel, but no one had tried to sit alongside him. He was grateful for the solitude. The tram was now moving slowly through the town as it headed back along the road that he had travelled when he entered Oradour-Sur-Glane.

Once outside the town, the tramway parted company with the road as the tracks began to veer towards the east, heading towards Limoges about thirty kilometres away.

Lucien looked at the weather and shook his head. There was no way the Allies would attempt the invasion in weather like this. There did not seem to be any end in sight to the storm system. They might lose the entire full moon period when a well-lit night and favourable tides would be so vital.

He felt his shoulders slump slightly as a sense of resignation came over him. At least another month with no action. He was beginning to understand why all of the Maquis groups he visited were so prepared to ignore the threat of the SS Division to the south. They were completely pent-up with barely contained nervous energy. They were like greyhounds in the starting cage.

They were desperate for the gates to be flung open and to be let loose!

Lucien lost himself in these thoughts as the tram slowly wound its way through the beautiful countryside of the central Limousin region. It stopped several times in small towns and villages. As some passengers got off, others got on.

It was nearing eleven a.m. when it finally reached the terminus in Limoges. The worst of the weather had noticeably abated, but it was still unpleasant. Checking that his overcoat was secure, he left the shelter of the tram and stepped out into it.

He stood under the large awning of the tram depot as he got his bearings. The tram depot was in a part of Limoges unfamiliar to him. His most sensible course was to get in touch with Angeline and see if she could use her contacts to help him arrange a passage back to Flavignac.

He studied a map of Limoges on the tram station wall and worked out where he had to go to find her clothing store. It was more than half a kilometre from the tram station, so walking in this weather was not an option. He did not want to have to pay for a taxi from the limited funds he had left, so waiting for a bus was his only option.

Buses did not run as often as they did before the war, so that meant another hour of waiting. One had just left while he was looking at the map, but that could not be helped. He knew he would have to be lucky to get a ride back to Flavignac today.

One more night away then.

It was well after one p.m. when he finally found Angeline's shop. He knew that she counted several Wehrmacht officers among her clientele, so he watched carefully from a discrete distance until he was content that it was safe to enter.

The front door activated a small bell as he opened it. This brought Angeline out from her sewing room where she had been busy working.

She seemed unsurprised to find Lucien there.

"I was thinking that I might be seeing you soon," she said with a smile. "I thought it might have been yesterday but as you can see, I missed it by a day. How are you, Lucien?"

"Wet and hungry!" said Lucien. "This weather has just been bloody terrible for days now. Even the damned ducks are drowning!"

Angeline laughed. "Come inside, you idiot! Give me your coat, I have a fire going through here. We'll get you dried out and fed."

Lucien kissed her on the cheek and followed her through into the large back room where two other women worked at sewing machines. They both looked up at him as he came amongst them. Their looks gave away no emotion.

"It's quite all right, girls," said Angeline. "This is Lucien. He is a very dear old friend. I've known him for a great many years."

"This is true," said Lucien, "and still she talks to me. It must be my charm!"

The two women visibly relaxed and looked at each other, grinning. They both turned and went back to their work.

Angeline took Lucien's arm and led him to a table at the back of the room.

"We had our lunch over an hour ago but there is still some soup and bread left. Would you care for some?"

"Would you mind?" replied Lucien.

"Not at all. I would be delighted. Please, sit down." She indicated a chair at the table, close to a wood-fuelled stove that was still burning slowly. Lucien began to feel himself warming up almost immediately.

Angeline placed a bowl of onion soup and a length of baguette in front of him. He gratefully started eating.

As he ate, Angeline leaned closely against him and said softly, "We can't talk here…"

Lucien understood.

After he finished, she took away the plates and said, "If you like, you are welcome to wait upstairs for a while. I still have plenty of work to do down here for the next few hours. I cannot really take a break. It wouldn't be fair to my girls now, would it?"

"I completely understand," said Lucien. "Would you mind if I was to lie down and perhaps have a short sleep?"

Angeline smiled happily. "Please be my guest. We have a few more hours of work to do, but after that, you can regale me with stories of your travels."

Angeline handed Lucien his overcoat back to take upstairs with him. She did not want to have a man's coat so conspicuously apparent, in case other clients might call in.

She showed Lucien to her bedroom and went back downstairs to continue working.

"And just who was that?" asked one of the women.

"A very old and dear friend. I do not often get to see him. He lives in Paris and his work has him travel around a lot. He sells industrial equipment. He's only here for the day." Angeline made up the story with practiced ease. She wanted neither of the girls to know the truth.

The two women finished their day's work at five p.m. As soon as they left, Angeline went upstairs to join Lucien.

"You took a risk coming here you know!" she said sharply. "I get German officers coming unannounced into the shop far too often these days."

"I waited a while before I came in. I took no chances."

Angeline exhaled and relaxed slightly. "It's more that I was concerned about my girls. One of them is currently seeing a German Lieutenant. I have no doubt she'll tell him that I've had a male visitor."

Lucien now looked concerned. "I'm so sorry; I would never have knowingly done anything to put you in any danger."

"It's OK. I'm sure we'll be fine. I told them you were an engineering equipment salesman. Down just for the day from Paris!"

"Dear God! Could you have thought of something that I know less about than engineering equipment? I wouldn't know a Flange Gasket from a Pressure Valve."

"What on earth are they?" asked Angeline, actually sounding impressed.

"I have absolutely no idea!" replied Lucien, "I've just heard the names before."

They both stared at each other for a few moments before each spontaneously burst into howls of laughter.

Out on the street, just under the bedroom window, the seamstress with the German boyfriend heard the laughter coming from above. She could tell it was genuine.

It's OK, she thought, *he's just here for a fuck.* She stepped away from the shelter of the building and headed off into the rain.

Angeline sat beside Lucien on the edge of the bed. "So tell me, how did you go convincing the other cells to show restraint against the Germans? Did they hang on your every word?"

Lucien smiled and shrugged. "How do you think I went? Exactly the same response as I got here. Even more so in some places. I think I am actually coming to agree with them now. The Germans will do whatever they want, no matter how much or how little we act."

Angeline nodded. "I could have told you that. In a way, I did, but I guess you had to learn it for yourself. It's like I said about you before, you're just a kind man at heart. You would love to see nobody get hurt when the Allies arrive, but it won't be like that. It can't be! People are going to get killed. It's inevitable."

Lucien let out a long sigh. "I know that. I always did. I just didn't want… God! I don't even know any more."

He let his upper body fall backwards onto the bed.

Angeline turned towards him and lay on her side. She put her hand on the side of his face and the two of them kissed.

In an instant, Lucien forgot all his angst about Daniel and Yvette. He forgot the inhibitions, which had plagued him years before with Angeline. The two of them pulled at each other's clothes and threw them carelessly onto the floor. Lucien buried his face in her breasts and kissed her with desperate passion. Angeline's yearning was equally desperate. She had not been with a man since her husband had died. She craved the physical contact of another. It had been too long.

Moreover, she had never forgotten Lucien.

Lucien lay back in Angeline's bed feeling a contentedness he had never known. He had made love to a woman with no nervousness or inhibition. Everything had worked! *Why had it never been like this before?*

Angeline lay snuggled tightly in against him, delighting in the contact of their skin.

"Can you please tell me why I could never get you to do that to me twenty years ago? You know I wanted you to."

Lucien was silent for nearly a minute.

"You know that I had been shot… in the war… in the lower part of my abdomen?"

"Yes, of course I do."

"Well, I had problems for a long time afterwards. I had problems not being able to control it when I pissed, and I had… other…"

"You mean you couldn't get it up?" said Angeline. "I can't say I noticed any problems just now. If anything, it was rather impressive!"

Lucien basked in those words. He hugged her closer.

"I really don't know w-why?" he stammered. "I-I've never been much good with Yvette. I always get so nervous."

"Ahh," said Angeline, "there's the problem. You let your worries ruin your life. Well, if you ever were injured down there" she pointed playfully, "then you certainly seem to have healed remarkably well."

"Amazing, isn't it?" said Lucien in wonder.

Lucien felt completely relaxed and calm. He needed the chance to talk more.

"You know, I have been dreading going back home. I've been feeling that I would get home to find Yvette with another man. We have been harbouring an operative sent over by the SOE."

"She's been with an Englishman? Surely not!" said Angeline with a wicked grin.

"No, he's French."

"Well! That's all right then," said Angeline. "Now, please go on."

Lucien looked at her grinning at him. He could not help but smile back.

"He was an army lieutenant who made it across to England in 1940, after France fell. You met him at Yvette's grandparent's farm. He had been visiting some Maquis cells to the west, but caught pneumonia on the way back to our farm. He's too sick to go anywhere else. Yvette is looking after him."

"So, you think he might be sleeping with her now? I seem to recall that he was very good looking."

Lucien winced at her blunt words.

"I have been allowing myself to imagine it happening. It certainly is possible, I guess. They are alone together in our house."

Angeline looked at him. "Was that why you came here? Were you looking to get some kind of revenge on them? For something that you don't even know is happening?"

Lucien lifted himself up on an elbow and replied earnestly, "No! Not in the slightest. I came here because I had nowhere else to go. I had hoped that you might know someone who could get me back to Flavignac. What happened now was... beyond my wildest dreams. It was the most extraordinary moment of my life. I've never known that it could be that good!"

Angeline suddenly laughed aloud.

"You do realise now that if they *haven't* been carrying on together, then you're the one with some serious explaining to have to do!"

Lucien flopped onto his back and joined Angeline in laughter again.

"And that is a totally new situation for me. Can you believe it?"

Angeline then looked at him deeply. "Well, if they have been, I shan't complain. Your world won't end."

She lay close against him again and both lay quietly, listening to the sounds of the storm outside.

Angeline had got dressed again and left the room. While she was out, Lucien had started to put on some clothes.

Angeline came back into the room more quickly than he expected. She was carrying a radio.

"I need to plug this in. It's nearly eight o'clock. The BBC will start broadcasting soon."

The radio warmed up and Angeline carefully tuned it to the BBC's broadcast band. As usual, the broadcast was simply short messages that made no sense to the casual listener. Angeline was listening out for the code word that signified her Resistance cell. After the code word, the message itself would follow, she would copy it down and then decrypt.

However, no code word came. There was no message for them tonight.

"That means no invasion tonight. Not at all surprising really. The weather is hopeless."

Lucien agreed. "I'm not surprised at all. It's just not possible with storms like this. They may lose the full moon altogether. Another month of waiting."

"We can't change the weather. Only God can do that," said Angeline. "We can only wait and see. Maybe tomorrow…"

She turned off the radio and unplugged it. She left the room again to return it to its hiding spot. She went downstairs and returned after a few minutes with some food.

"Here! We may as well have something to eat. Then we can go back to bed. You can explain to me again about the physical problems you claim to have when making love. I think I missed them last time."

Chapter 7

5 June 1944: Morin Farm, Outside Flavignac

Daniel awoke with a start. He was back down in the Mouse Hole. Yvette was not with him. He felt an immediate, sharp pang of loss. Then, as the fog of sleep lifted, he remembered their discussion the previous evening. Lucien could come home at any time. They were at the limit of the length of time he had suggested he might be away.

The rain was still falling but not as heavily. The wind had fallen away also.

Perhaps the weather might be turning for the better.

Daniel was far from being back to full health, but he knew he was on the right path. He was feeling stronger every day and small exertions were not getting the resultant coughing spasms and chest pains that they were a week earlier.

He wanted Yvette. She must be upstairs in her room. Lucien was clearly not coming home in this weather. Why were they apart?

Despite the near pitch-blackness that existed in the Mouse Hole, he leaned across the small space towards where he knew the table was. He always left a box of matches at the same spot on the table so that finding them in the dark would be simple.

He reached out his hand and found the matches straight away. He opened the box and took one out. Striking it against the rough side of the box, it ignited first time. With its light, he then found and lit the candle in its holder.

Its meagre light seemed amplified in the confines of the tiny room.

He lay back on the bed and gave himself a minute to finish waking up.

Once he was fully alert, he leaned across to the table again and picked up his wristwatch. The time was after seven thirty. At least he was not sleeping in until mid-morning any more. He wound up the watch and strapped it onto his wrist.

He sat up and swung his legs over the edge of the small bed. Leaning forward, he reached over to the inside of the panel that closed off the Mouse Hole. He gently pushed outwards and the panel fell free, allowing the limited light available in the cellar to flow into his tiny room.

Picking up his clothes, which lay piled on the small chair, he bent over and stepped out into the comparative spaciousness of the cellar. He listened carefully but heard no sound coming from upstairs. He replaced the panel and got dressed into his clothes.

Making his way up the stairs from the cellar, he opened the door that led into the main room of the house.

No one was about. He went over to the doorway into Yvette's bedroom and looked in. The bed was empty.

He made his way over to the front door, opened it and looked out. He could not see her, but after a few moments, he could hear her voice, talking to the pigs as she fed them.

Knowing now where she was, he relaxed, closed the door and found his way over to the sofa. Yvette had not yet started a fire and the room was chilly. Even though it was supposed to be the beginning of summer, the weather had been so bad that the unseasonal chill cut through him.

He went over to the fireplace and started to prepare the kindling. By the time Yvette had finished tending to the animals, the fire was well ablaze and the room was warming nicely.

She had seen the smoke from the chimney and guessed Daniel was up, before she returned to the house.

Her heart leapt when she came in and saw him there. He had also set the fire in the wood stove and was beginning to boil up some water in the kettle to make tea. She caught him in the middle of these homely activities.

"My goodness! What a wonderful housewife you will make for someone one day."

Daniel looked up from the stove and smiled at the sight of her.

She ran to him and they locked in a tender embrace that did little to erase their absence from each other's presence during the night.

"Last night was horrible!" she said. "Was it as bad for you as it was for me?"

"No!" said Daniel. "It was much worse."

They continued to cling to each other. Eventually, Daniel held her at arms-length. "I do trust Madame slept well in her boudoir of solitude." he said with a grin.

Yvette responded in kind, "Madame had a most atrocious night thank you. She was acutely aware of the absence of certain body parts!"

"My goodness! How unfortunate! Is there something that I may be able to provide you with now to help you recover from the disappointment of the evening?"

Yvette laughed and held him close. "Let me think on that. It may take a cup of tea first to help me remember."

"Don't take too long," said Daniel. "I'm a sick man!"

"You're a lying swine!" replied Yvette happily. "You're getting better every day. In fact, if I didn't know any better, I'd swear you were malingering. Are you trying to take advantage of my innocent nature?" she fluttered her eyes at him.

Daniel laughed. "So, you have worked out my evil little game!" he said in theatrical horror. "*C'est la vie*. I'll have to go back to begging on the streets."

They both laughed and fell into each other's arms again.

Yvette finally broke free from him and went over to the kettle. She spooned out some tealeaves into the teapot and poured in the now boiling water.

There was bread from yesterday's baking that was still fresh, and they ate that along with cups of the tea.

"I haven't been up to visit my grandparents for several days now, you know. I must go up this morning. Will you be all right on your own for a few hours?"

Daniel looked somewhat taken aback. "Do you have to? It doesn't look like Lucien will be back in the immediate future?"

Yvette felt a sudden, unaccustomed flare of annoyance. "I haven't been up to see them for over four days! I'll be able to blame the weather for it but you and I both know the real reason. I have no doubt that they will be missing me also! I don't want them to have to come down here in the rain just because they might be worried about me. You will just have to do without me for a few hours."

I'm sorry!" said Daniel, suddenly feeling contrite. "I was being selfish. I guess I've just got used to having you to myself. I don't suppose I can go up with you?"

The heat of Yvette's outburst quickly passed. "No, my love. That wouldn't be a very good idea. At least not now. I would like the chance to talk to them in private first. I can talk to them with complete honesty. I need their advice. I hope you understand."

Daniel nodded. "Of course, I do. I shall be fine. Is there anything that needs to be done here while you're away?"

"No, not really. Please try to stay out of sight if you can. I can't imagine we'll have any unexpected visitors with the weather like this but never let your guard down."

Daniel looked suitably chastened. "Don't worry, I'll be good."

The weather was becoming more settled as Yvette approached her grandparent's old home. Even fleeting patches of blue sky came and went, breaking up the unrelieved grey of the last few days. The ground though, was still muddy and sodden underfoot as she made her way up to the back door of the house and knocked. Her grandmother, Delphine had seen her coming and was opening the door before Yvette had finished knocking.

"Come in, my darling. We were beginning to wonder if you had forgotten we were here."

Delphine closed the door and led Yvette into the kitchen.

"I'm so sorry, *Mamie*, the weather has kept me very close to the house. And I've also had to keep an eye on our sick guest. He's definitely getting better now, so I can have a bit more freedom."

Delphine looked at her with a quizzical eye. She knew her granddaughter well enough to know when she was not telling the full story. However, she decided not to push too hard. Yvette would speak in her own time.

"Anyway, how are you coping? Is there anything you need? You haven't been to the market for a while. There must be things you are running short of?" she asked.

"You're right, *Mamie*. We've been all right but I do need to get a few things. I shall make a list when I get home. If you have any spare eggs and maybe some milk, that would be wonderful."

"Certainly. We have enough of both. Anyway, let me get some water boiling. We can have some nice tea. Now tell me what you've been up to in this weather. You must be enjoying the company of a young man, closer to your own age?"

She had chosen her words carefully.

She knows! thought Yvette.

Yvette tried to collect her thoughts for a moment, but a flood of emotion got the better of her and she simply dissolved into tears.

"Oh *Mamie*! What have I done? How did this happen?"

Delphine crossed over to her and hugged her closely, just letting her cry and release the pent-up emotion.

She was still sobbing deeply when Bernard came inside a minute later. He had been outside in the garden.

Delphine looked at him and nodded gently. Bernard got the message. He said nothing. He simply came over and spread his arms around the two women.

Presently, Yvette began to regain her composure. Delphine led her to an armchair and let her sit.

"I shall just go and finish making the tea. Bernard, will you come and help me please?"

Bernard followed her back into the kitchen.

"It is as we thought," said Delphine quietly, "she has fallen in love with the Lieutenant."

Bernard did not look surprised. He and Delphine had noticed a change in Yvette since the young soldier had come into their lives. They both cared deeply for Lucien, but they each knew that his and Yvette's marriage was not a passionate one. Something like this was always a real possibility. Now, it had become a reality.

"Well then," said Bernard, "what happens now? It will break Lucien's heart."

Delphine looked closely at her husband. Their own marriage had been long and happy. They had married for love over sixty five years earlier and had never fallen out of it. It had always troubled them that their beloved granddaughter lacked that same joy in her own marriage.

Delphine finished preparing the tea. She put the pot and some cups onto a platter and carried them out into the lounge room where Yvette was still sitting. Bernard followed her, carrying some milk in an old porcelain jug along with some sugar cubes and a plate of homemade biscuits.

"My goodness, real sugar!" said Yvette, trying hard to sound cheerful despite the redness remaining around her eyes.

"We still manage to have a small amount that we keep aside for special occasions," said Bernard, "there haven't been too many special occasions in recent years, so it's lasted quite well."

Yvette smiled. Her grandfather could always find a way to bring a little bit of humour into most conversations. It helped put her more at ease.

Bernard picked up the teapot and poured the steaming hot drink into three cups. He put a little milk into Yvette and Delphine's. His own he left black. He put a cube of sugar into each of the cups and handed them to the women.

Delphine and Bernard both sat down next to each other on the lounge, facing Yvette. For a moment, all three sat quietly stirring the tea.

"Now, my Darling, do you feel up to talking to us about this?" asked Delphine.

Yvette took a deep breath and slowly exhaled. "I think I need to," she said.

5 June 1944: Limoges 9.42 A.M.

"I know I have no right to ask you. It's a long way out of your way. It will mean one more night away from home. I just don't like the idea of Martine doing all that driving on her own. It's not safe for a single woman. Are you sure you don't mind?" Angeline was feeling terrible for asking, but Lucien seemed surprisingly content after agreeing to her tentative request.

She needed someone to deliver several uniforms she had made. The customers were two German officers, just posted to a garrison in the smaller, regional city of Tulle, about one hundred km south of Limoges. They had received orders suddenly, and she had not had enough time to finish the uniforms before they left. They had paid her well, to have them delivered as soon as they were finished.

It meant a chance to get into a regional Wehrmacht base on legitimate business. It was a rare opportunity to pick up some fresh intelligence, all under the guise of delivering uniforms to the newly arrived officers.

It was too good an opportunity to pass up.

For his part, Lucien was keen to go. The car they would take could drop him back in Flavignac, or even back at Yvette's grandparent's house as it made its way back to Limoges.

He was more than happy to have an extra day to try sorting out his feelings, before seeing Yvette again.

He was discovering emotions he had long sought to suppress. He had no idea how she did it, but Angeline had a way of putting him at such ease, that he could forget all the inhibitions that consumed him when he was with Yvette. He felt as though he was reading a new book, written in a style that was so much easier to understand. That, however, did not ease the conflict that now troubled him.

A little bit more time might be a good thing, especially with an important task to distract him. It would be good to fill his mind with other things for a while.

"I assure you, I'm quite happy to do this. I know the local Maquis well. They were the ones I went with last month, when we checked out the SS operating to the south. I'm the best person to go."

Angeline looked at him pensively. Things had happened between them very quickly and she knew he was still a married man. However, her long dormant feelings for him had rekindled fast. She wanted him somewhere safe, not in the lion's den.

"It's all right!" said Lucien, trying to sound soothing. "It's a simple chore. I won't have to do anything that will look suspicious; I'll just keep my eyes open and take in as much as I can. Then we'll be on our way. No problems at all."

"Will you have somewhere safe to stay? It'll be too late to come back this afternoon."

"Of course," said Lucien, "that is the least of our problems. If we need to, the Maquis there can get me back home tomorrow. Just in case your girl wants to come straight back to Limoges today and not do the detour to drive me home."

Angeline was going to have Martine, the young seamstress with the German boyfriend, do the driving. She was a good driver and knew several of the German soldiers stationed around Limoges. Her presence in the car would help if they encountered any unexpected stops for inspection. They also carried official passes, all duly signed by the local occupation Authorities in Limoges. They were after all, delivering German uniforms, properly ordered and paid for, to their rightful owners.

Angeline and Lucien left her upstairs apartment and went down the stairs into the workshop. She had told Martine about the job and the girl was delighted to have the chance to go on such an adventure.

As far as she knew, it was a very simple delivery drive and Lucien was going along merely as a companion. A young girl driving alone, might prove too much of an enticement for an opportunistic scoundrel!

The money the German officers had paid Angeline for the delivery was ample to allow her little Renault to be filled with petrol. The return trip was less than two hundred and fifty km. One tank of petrol should be enough but Angeline gave Martine a few extra francs, in case it were needed.

The new uniforms had been well pressed and neatly wrapped. Angeline placed them carefully on the back seat of the little car. It was parked in a narrow lane-way at the rear of Angeline's shop.

She went back inside and returned with a road map and the passes given to her by the Germans. She handed them to Martine who reached inside and placed them in the glove compartment of the car.

Solemnly, Angeline handed Martine the keys to her Renault.

"I love my little car. Please take good care of it for me."

Martine giggled. "You know I am a good driver. I'll look after it for you."

Angeline smiled. "I certainly know you are a better driver than he is!" She gestured towards Lucien. "Don't let him anywhere near the keys or you'll wind up in a ditch somewhere!"

Lucien could not help himself. All three of them laughed. Angeline could make him laugh at himself in a way that made him feel more comfortable with the person that he was.

As much as he loved Yvette, that was something she had never been able to do.

He had a lot to think about over the next day.

Martine settled in behind the wheel and Lucien climbed into the passenger's seat alongside. She turned the ignition key and pulled out the starter knob, the motor singing into life. With a wave to Angeline, they set off on their way.

The drive down to Tulle took over two hours and they had to show their papers three times. Sure enough, the documents were all correct and they had no trouble with the local Vichy *Gendarmes*.

Lucien remained quiet throughout most of the drive and Martine soon gave up trying to engage him in conversation. She could not understand what Angeline saw in him. He was not bad looking for an older man, but he seemed sullen and withdrawn.

Oh well, he was not her problem. The weather was improving and the rest of the drive was easy, albeit largely spent in silence.

Tulle was a large enough town to get lost in without difficulty. They had to stop to confirm the directions to the German barracks. Once they arrived, they presented their passes and were promptly shown through to the Officer's quarters to hand over the uniforms.

Lucien was surprised. He had expected there to be a larger force garrisoned here. It was only about two companies in strength. There were no tanks, only a number of lorries and half-tracks, although there may be some that were out on manoeuvres. He mentally tucked the information away.

After they left the barracks, they found their way to a *patisserie* in the centre of the town to stop and have a late lunch.

Lucien looked at Martine, "Are you keen to get home? I am quite able to find my way back to Flavignac from here, if you would like to go."

Martine looked unsure. "*Madame* Angeline was very insistent that I get you to Flavignac safely. It is too large a detour to do that and get back to Limoges today. Shouldn't we wait until tomorrow?"

Lucien smiled and said, "It's quite all right. I know some people in this town. Any one of them will be happy to put me up for the night and see me on my way tomorrow. There is no need to worry about me, I will be fine. Just tell Angeline that I pulled rank!"

"Are you absolutely sure? I don't mind staying overnight, really."

Lucien gave her his most ingratiating smile. "I will be absolutely fine. Besides, I would like to see some friends and we may have a drink or two. I'm sure you will be far happier knowing you were on your way back to your home and your boy-friend."

At the mention of her boyfriend, Martine picked up. Angeline would not be expecting her to be back until late tomorrow morning! Perhaps Lucien's offer might turn out to an opportunity for her to have an unexpected romantic evening. In addition, she would not have to get up too early the next morning. Finally, the thought of having to sit next to this silent, enigmatic man for several more hours of driving did not appeal to her at all.

"Well, if you really don't mind. I would like to get home tonight if possible."

"Excellent, then!" said Lucien, "I shall see you back to the car and you can make your way back home. I'm sure I shall get to see Angeline again soon, so please tell her not to worry. Tell her I insisted. She will be fine."

After Martine had left on the return drive, Lucien set off across town to a hotel where he knew the patron was a member of the local Maquis. They had become friends when he had accompanied Lucien on their intelligence-gathering trip the previous month.

He entered and went over to the Bar where he ordered a small beer and took a seat. Presently, the man he was looking for came in from a back room.

Lucien called out, "*Bonjour,* Paul!"

Paul Launay looked around in surprise. "My God, Lucien! What are you doing here?"

"Just missing your company, Paul. I was hoping you may have a spare room for the night and perhaps a glass or two of Pastis."

Paul laughed in delight.

"Well, this is a rather unexpected pleasure. As it turns out, I do have a bottle of Pastis behind the Bar here. I do hope you don't have plans of trying to drink me into bankruptcy?"

Lucien laughed. "Not at all, just mild penury."

Paul brought over two glasses of the aperitif and joined Lucien at the table. The Hotel Bar was mostly empty now that the lunch crowd had left. The two men felt comfortable enough to talk quietly without having to go into another room.

"Now tell me, Lucien, what really brings you here?"

"As it turns out, simple circumstance. I was in Limoges and I needed to get home. This was the best I could do at short notice. Is there any chance there might be someone going in the direction of Flavignac tomorrow that I could perhaps cadge a lift with?"

"I don't know. I can put out a couple of quick enquiries for you. If there isn't, I'm sure we can make some kind of arrangement to get you there."

"Many thanks, Paul. I appreciate it. I have just got back from a visit to the Wehrmacht barracks here in town. I thought they would be here if greater force. There's not much more than a company of them."

"What the hell were you doing going there for? Did they call you in?"

"No, not at all!" laughed Lucien, "if you must know, I was delivering German officer's uniforms. How is that for an excuse?"

"I'm sure there's a fascinating story behind that, but did you see anything of interest?"

"Only that it is a much smaller unit than I would have expected. Perhaps they are relying on the larger Division to the south if they need back up?"

"Perhaps," said Paul thoughtfully, "the Wehrmacht don't usually like being too reliant on the SS. We knew that the local presence was not large. We've kept this area nice and quiet as per the orders from London. The German's have obviously thinned out their numbers here in the last few days. A week ago, they were much stronger. They obviously feel they can move troops away from here."

"Perhaps they're starting to send troops up north, in case of invasion."

"Almost certainly," said Paul, "it must be soon. The weather is starting to show signs of improving. Maybe, in the next few nights…"

"I certainly hope so," said Lucien. The waiting is driving me mad. This fucking weather must be behind the delays. I'm sure they would have been here by now if the weather was good."

Paul leaned forward. "Tell me honestly, where do you think they'll land?"

Lucien thought hard. "I think it might be in Normandy."

Paul looked surprised. "Normandy? Not in the Pas-De-Calais?"

"That's where the Boche expect them to land. It will be far too heavily defended. It would be suicide. No, it has to be Normandy."

"Well," said Paul, "with any luck, we might just find out soon."

Paul showed his guest into a spare room. He invited Lucien to have dinner with him and his wife that evening. Lucien gratefully accepted.

Thanks to the tender ministrations of Angeline, Lucien had not had much sleep over the last two nights. Exhaustion was catching up with him now. Paul told him that they would eat at about eight p.m. so Lucien took the opportunity to catch a couple of hours of sleep.

5 June 1944 Morin Farm, Outside Flavignac, 3.15 P.M.

Daniel was resting on his bed down in the Mouse Hole. He was keeping a keen ear out for the sound of any movement coming from the room above. By now, he was completely familiar with the sound of Yvette's footfall. He lay there, listening in anticipation of her return.

Eventually, there came the sound of the front door opening. His attention focussed in anticipation. *Would it be Yvette's tread or something more manly? Would it be Lucien coming home?*

The sound was of a softer tread, it was Yvette. He waited a few moments longer to see if there might be a second set of steps accompanying them. There was not. She was alone.

He heard her voice call out to him. "Daniel?"

"Coming!" he called out. Clambering out of the confines of the Mouse Hole, he made his way up the stairs from the cellar.

As soon as Yvette saw him, she ran to him and embraced him with a desperation that took him by surprise.

"Are you all right? What has happened?"

Yvette managed to compose herself. "Nothing bad has happened. I have been with my grandparents most of the day. We have had a long talk together."

"Was my name mentioned?" asked Daniel pensively.

"Many times as a matter of fact," replied Yvette, "never in anger, so please don't worry. My grandfather doesn't want to come down here and put a pitch-fork through your chest or anything like that."

"Well, that is certainly a thought to cheer me up. I can stop updating my Will then."

Yvette smiled. "Believe it or not, they are very supportive. They love Lucien, as do I, but they know that he was never the right man for me. They don't know you at all really, but they trust me and my judgement. All we have been talking about is how this will affect Lucien. There is no way out of this without someone being hurt badly. The question is, who will be that person?"

Daniel looked pensive again. "Either Lucien, or the two of us."

"That's right," said Yvette, "I've never felt such happiness, and I've never felt such guilt and sorrow. I just don't know what to do."

Daniel crossed the room and opened the front door. He took a few steps outside and looked up the pathway and in the direction of the road. There was no sign of anyone. He went back inside and closed the door behind him.

"Who knows what the near future will hold for us. But right now, we need to be together."

Yvette ran to him and hugged him as tight as she could. They fumbled with each other's clothes as they made their way into Yvette's bedroom. For the moment, they did not care who might catch them. They just needed the reassurance of each other's love.

5 June 1944: Tulle, 7:36 P.M.

Lucien made his way downstairs into the Bar. Paul was serving behind it, and he smiled when he saw Lucien enter the room.

Lucien came over to the Bar and took a seat.

"Can I get you a drink, *Monsieur*?" asked Paul.

"A glass of red wine would be appreciated, *Monsieur*," he replied.

Paul poured out two glasses and passed one to Lucien. "My wife, Marie will have dinner prepared shortly. We can eat in our kitchen, away from the prying eyes of the customers."

Paul indicated to his serving staff that he was leaving. They would be running the bar and restaurant from here on, for the evening.

Paul led Lucien out of the public Bar, through the hotel's main kitchen and into a smaller, more private, family kitchen beyond.

Lucien had never met Paul's wife Marie before.

"*Enchantee,* Marie," he said as he kissed her on both cheeks.

"*Enchantee,* Lucien," she replied with a smile.

Marie left the two men to talk as she went back to her cooking.

"Dinner will be in about another fifteen minutes. Not too long now," she called out.

Paul went to the kitchen door and locked it. He did not want anyone coming in while he was tending to the next part of his evening ritual. That involved setting up the radio and listening to the BBC's eight p.m. service to the occupied countries.

He turned on the radio and waited while the valves warmed up. There were still several minutes to go until the hour ticked over.

Marie already had the table set as Paul and Lucien took their seats. She had the meal preparations all in hand.

They began to eat just the broadcast was beginning. As usual, there were notices going out to many different groups. More than usual in fact. Paul was beginning to relax. He had not heard the code word for his own group and he was thinking that there would be nothing for him tonight.

Then the word *"Pamplemousse"* (Grapefruit) crackled through the speaker.

It was his group's code word. The following message was for them.

He hurriedly grabbed the pad and pencil he kept close by, and wrote down the words as they came.

Lucien and Marie had both stopped eating. Their eyes were fixed intently on Paul, in anticipation.

He got up from the table and went over to a kitchen drawer. He pulled it out completely and reached into the cavity that it left behind. After a few seconds, he pulled his arm out, holding a small book. It was one of the codebooks that Daniel had brought with him from England.

Paul returned to the table and began thumbing through the pages eagerly.

As he found the words corresponding to the ones in the message he had just received, he wrote down their decoded meanings.

Soon he finished. He looked breathless. He held up the decoded page to show Lucien.

The invasion was tonight… and it was Normandy!

The Invasion

6 June 1944: Normandy

The history books tell us that the 6th of June, 1944 was the day that the Allied armies began to land on five selected beaches in the Normandy region of western France, to begin the task of the liberation of Europe.

However, the invasion actually began late in the evening of the 5th of June. The first paratroopers began to land before midnight on that evening.

The first Allied casualty actually died on the 5th, shortly before midnight.

He was part of a British paratroop assault on one of two strategic bridges over the Caen canal, behind Sword Beach, the most easterly of the five designated invasion beaches.

His unit (the British 6th Airborne) had an image of the winged horse Pegasus as their emblem. The bridge they captured and held has, henceforth been known as "Pegasus Bridge."

He was but a part of the vanguard in the largest assault in human history.

Paratroopers from the US, Great Britain, its Commonwealth, France and many other countries began to descend upon Normandy.

It was their task to try to capture strategic points inland from the beaches.

Meanwhile offshore, a staggering armada of ships was gathering, about to send tens of thousands of troops and their equipment ashore.

They were beginning the liberation of a Europe held in shackles for the last four years by Nazi Germany.

Whilst the weather had relented somewhat from the storms of the preceding days, it was still bad enough that the airborne troopers were dropping, all too frequently, far from their intended drop sites.

The German defenders had taken advantage of the winds and heavy rain by deliberately flooding many fields throughout the region as an invasion precaution. Other fields and farm lots had flooded naturally, as small rivers and streams broke their banks. All too often, allied paratroopers found themselves descending into shallow lakes instead of the fields and pasturelands indicated on their maps.

As a result, a number of men drowned where they landed, unable to free themselves from their equipment, the weight of which held them underwater in the flooded fields that should have welcomed them.

Most of their comrades survived though, and were able to form into fighting units and commence the great task for which they had trained so long.

As the incoming waves of troops advanced from the beaches, they started to meet up with these airborne units. The roadways and bridges these advanced troops had captured, often with heavy casualties, would now allow the incoming waves of troops to move further inland from the beaches, securing the initial bridgehead.

Some invasion beaches, however, proved more costly to secure than others.

The American troops landing at the beach code-named 'Omaha' suffered horrendous losses due to well-positioned, stoically manned German defences. The defenders had the great advantages of height and a commanding field of fire.

The Americans finally broke through but forever after, they called the beach "Bloody Omaha".

The Allies had been so successful at deceiving the Germans as to the intended invasion site that it would take several days before properly coordinated, well organised opposition could be brought to bear against them.

The overall Commander of the German forces manning the western defences, the famed Field Marshal Erwin Rommel, was back in Germany on the invasion night, attending his wife's birthday party.

As for Adolf Hitler himself, he lay soundly asleep in his bed in Berlin.

No one was prepared to suffer his wrath by awakening him from his slumbers. They decided to let him awake of his own accord before advising him that the Allied invasion had begun.

When he finally did awaken, his immediate response was to push the point that these landings were only a diversion. The real invasion was surely to happen at the *Pas-De-Calais,* where the English Channel was at its narrowest.

By the time this error in the German's thinking had been rendered obvious, the Allies had secured their bridgehead and the invasion was gaining an unstoppable momentum.

The Allies needed ports in order to land supplies, equipment and reinforcements in bulk.

Allied planning anticipated that no natural ports could be captured without enormous loss of life, so they made their own artificial ports and brought them with them.

These engineering marvels were known by the code-name 'Mulberry'. Despite their enormous size, their design and construction was carried out under the greatest secrecy.

After the initial bridgehead was secured, these 'Mulberry Harbours' were then floated across the Channel, to be sunk into place off their designated beaches and pressed into immediate service.

Thus, within days, the bridgehead had its support infrastructure in place. Short days after the initial landings, supplies and reinforcements were thus pouring into Normandy as the push to free a subjugated Europe finally began in earnest.

However, the German Resistance was just beginning to get itself properly organised...

Chapter 8

6 June 1944: Valence d'Agen

News of the invasion started coming through before dawn. Initial thoughts were that it was a ruse by the Allies to disguise their real intent. They had not received any orders yet, but the men of '*Das Reich*' were alert and preparing. If this was a ruse, then the real invasion must be close.

Lammerding called an immediate meeting of all senior officers as soon as news he had confirmation of the events in Normandy.

The officers gathered in the house he had requisitioned as his personal Head Quarters.

"Good morning, gentlemen. It appears that the waiting is over. I can confirm that the Allies have been landing in force up in Normandy. It appears that airborne troops began landing during the night and seaborne troops and vehicles at first light this morning."

"At this stage I have received no orders to mobilise but we should proceed in the expectation that they will come at any time. Perhaps Group are still waiting to see if this just a diversion in force before they commit us. Whatever, my orders to you now are to make all preparations for our immediate mobilisation. Now go to it, make haste, gentlemen."

The assembled officers began to file out of the room. Lammerding caught the eye of Lt Colonel Stadtler, and motioned him to remain.

After the others had left, Lammerding took Stadtler aside. "I want you to be at the head of the line when the order to move comes. Your Regiment has the most veterans, particularly Diekmann's Battalion. Have them move out first. I have no doubt we will be encountering vigorous Maquis activity from here. They will take gloves off now. We must be ready to hit them hard, whenever they appear."

Stadtler nodded in agreement. "This could be the chance we've been waiting for to get at them. Diekmann is the perfect choice. He won't give them an inch."

Lammerding looked at him steadily for a moment before he spoke again.

"These Communist bastards are likely to try and hit hard and then disappear as fast as they can. They dare not stand and fight. They will melt back into their villages like the dogs they are. I am advising you now to exercise your judgement as to how you respond."

Stadtler considered those words carefully. Such instructions were commonplace during their time in the Ukraine. There, he had not been 'Ordered', merely 'Advised'. That advice always allowed for a great deal of latitude.

"Am I to take it then that we are authorised to undertake retaliatory action against civilians if necessary?"

"If you deem it appropriate, yes!" replied Lammerding.

"To what extent?" asked Stadtler.

"That is where you must use your judgement. If you choose to act, then make it a real statement! Let them know that any action against us will rebound against them in deadly force. If need be, make it hurt!"

"Very well then, sir," said Stadtler, "I shall use my discretion. It is about time some of these French learn what being at war really means. They sleep snugly at night while our families in Germany suffer. If we hear so much as a peep out them, they will soon regret it."

"Excellent!" said Lammerding in satisfaction, "brief your officers well. Now go and attend to the arrangements. Heil Hitler!"

"Heil Hitler!" replied Stadtler, snapping to attention and saluting.

He spun around and left the room immediately.

Stadtler found Major Diekmann, deep in discussion with Captain Kahn and Lieutenant Barth.

"Ah Gentlemen. It is good that I find you all together. As soon as we get the order to move out, Otto, your battalion is to take the lead position. Have your wits about you. We are likely to be encountering resistance activity from here on. General Lammerding wants his best men on hand to receive them."

Diekmann smiled a wolf's smile. "Excellent news! The men are restless and spoiling for a fight. Any idea when we move, sir?"

"Not yet. The order could come at any moment. I believe we are only waiting for Army Group HQ to decide if this is the real invasion or simply a diversion. It certainly looks like the real thing to me. The Allies are landing in their thousands."

"Indeed, sir!" replied Diekmann, "that's what we were just discussing ourselves. Our preparations to move are all but done. There is little left, still to be packed and stowed. We can move as soon as the order is given."

"Once again, you exceed my expectations, Otto. Good work. Now I must attend to the other battalion commanders. I hope for their sakes they are as organised as you! Heil Hitler!"

"Heil Hitler!" came the response from all three officers.

Stadtler turned and headed off.

Diekmann turned back to Kahn and Barth. "Once the last of the preparations are made, have the men stand down and get some food. It could be a long day."

"Yes sir!" they both replied.

***

Yet, still the order to mobilise did not come.

The Brigade stood at readiness for the remainder of the day. As evening began to descend, it was clear that no order to move out would come until the following day at least.

Tents previously stowed, were unpacked and put up again for the night. Men remained in a state of heightened tension, desperate for the call to action to relieve the stress of the continued waiting.

Cooks prepared evening meals for the hundreds of men of the battalion as they settled in for a night of tense, sleepless anticipation.

The order to move would surely come soon. What was keeping it?

Chapter 9

6 June 1944: Tulle, South of Limoges

The day dawned; still, overcast and threatening, but no one was considering the weather. The word had spread along the fine tendrils of the Maquis network like a wildfire.

All across France, Resistance groups were gathering. Hidden caches of weapons were unearthed and made ready for use. Their plans were simple: attack and harass any German units they encountered making their way to Normandy.

Paul Launay had managed to get a few hours of sleep, but roused himself before four a.m. to begin preparations for the day. He knew it would not be long before there came the first surreptitious knocks at the back door from his Maquis comrades.

Shortly after Paul came down stairs and into the kitchen, he was joined, shortly afterwards, by Lucien.

"Well," said Lucien, "it looks like I'm going to have trouble finding a ride back to Flavignac today. I might as well stay here and join in the fun."

"Wonderful!" said Paul, "we will need every able-bodied man today. We should be able to muster nearly sixty from around here. Others will join us but they need to come from further away. It'll take them time to get here."

"What are we doing? I presume you've had this day planned for some time?"

"We have indeed," said Paul, "the local Wehrmacht garrison will likely mobilise immediately. We need to hit them as soon as they are clear of their barracks."

"While they are still in the town?" queried Lucien. "Wouldn't it be better to wait until they are out in the countryside itself? Less chance of civilian casualties that way."

"Yes, that is true, but it is also what they would be expecting us to do. Inside the town, they are more likely to be off guard. If we set ourselves up well, we can catch them all the way along their line. They have no idea how well armed we are here. We can hurt them hard and fast. Don't forget, Lucien, we are technically civilians too. We must all be prepared to accept our share of the risk. France is not going to be liberated without blood being shed."

Marie came into the kitchen to join them just as Paul was making this point. Lucien had no chance to reply.

No sooner had she walked into the room than the first gentle knocks sounded at the back door. The Maquis cell was gathering.

Over the next hour, the numbers had swelled to over fifty. Men and women, all ages, all ready at last to take the fight to the Germans out in the open.

Paul outlined his plans once all had settled.

The German garrison was towards the southern end of town and the most likely route they would take, if they were to head north, would be straight up the main road that lead towards Limoges. There was no logical reason for them to go any other way.

The Tulle Maquis had long since scouted out the best positions from which to ambush a column as it moved along this stretch of road. They were organised into six sub-groups. These had trained together and had their own leadership structure.

They were as well prepared as they could possibly be.

Paul looked around the room and made eye contact with the five other leaders of these groups. Three of them were men and two were women. Their genders did not matter. Their leadership qualities did.

Each group was responsible for the secure storing of their own weapons. Only a select few in each group knew where these stores were. The never shared this information with fellow Maquis from outside their own sub-groups. That way, if any one person were to be captured and interrogated, they could not give away enough to cause the entire cell any irreparable damage.

Paul raised his arm to draw everyone's attention. "It's time to get out the weapons. Everyone must have a Sten gun, a pistol and plenty of rounds of ammunition. Also grenades! Carry as many as you can manage. Now divide into your groups and let us get about it! We need to be in our positions within the next half hour. The Germans could be moving at any time."

The room began to clear quickly and with remarkable silence, given the number of people gathered.

Once the others had all gone, Lucien turned to Paul.

"Where do you want me? Shall I join in with your group?"

"That would be best, I think. How are you at handling a Sten gun?"

"I've never fired one. Good with a pistol though… or a Maxim!"

Paul laughed. "We don't have too many Maxim machine guns around here I'm afraid. I haven't even seen one since 1919."

Marie had begun to make some coffee. Today was special. Today she would use the last she had saved.

Paul looked at Lucien. "The Sten is a very simple gun. The British just about make them from scrap metal. They are not much to look at but they are effective. Just remember that they can jam easily, so only fire very short bursts. Two seconds at the most. And they ride up with the recoil so you have to learn fast to pull down as you fire or else everything will go over their heads."

"No time to practice so I'll have to learn on the job. No doubt I'll get the hang of it quickly enough," replied Lucien.

He paused. "Is that actual coffee I smell?"

Marie could only manage a half smile. "I have been keeping some aside for just this day. I don't know how good it is."

"It smells superb!" said Lucien.

The three of them sat in silence as they drank their coffee. Each deep in their own thoughts as the true magnitude of what they were about to do finally began to dawn upon them. It had all been words and romantic bravado up until now.

Before this, they had done little more than blow up railway tracks and cut telephone lines. Nuisance activities.

Now, it was about to get real. Today it would become war.

6 June 1944: Morin Farm, Outside Flavignac

Daniel had finished feeding the animals and was taking his turn going around the snares to see if they held any more rabbits or hares. Yvette had left nearly an hour earlier to go and visit her grandparents. Daniel's health had improved to the extent that he could now provide active assistance in tending to the running of the farm.

Movement in the distance caught his eye. Yvette was running down the path from her parent's house. Waving her arms frantically as she ran, she was making directly towards him.

Soon, she was close enough for him to hear her words. "The invasion! It's begun!"

Daniel felt as though a bolt of electricity had gone through him.

Yvette was breathless as she reached him. They fell into each other's arms and kissed.

Yvette started talking quickly, her excitement now boiling over. "It's in Normandy! It began in the night. That's all I know right now."

"Your grandparents heard it on the radio?" asked Daniel.

"Yes. They were about to come down and tell us, but I got there first."

"Well!" said Daniel, "I can't stay here, out of the fight. I should be well enough now to get up to Limoges and contact the Maquis leadership. I'm sure they can find a use for me."

Yvette suddenly looked distressed. "You mean you want to go? You want to leave me?"

Daniel tried to soften the blow.

"You know I don't want to, but I have to. I am a soldier. It's why I'm here. The last thing I want to do is leave you, but I have no choice. You must realise that!"

Yvette burst into tears and clung to him. "Oh, Dear God! I have been dreading this. I've prayed so hard that this day would never come."

"We both knew that something was bound to happen," said Daniel. "Either Lucien would return and we would have to face him, or else something like this. It had to be."

"I just didn't want it to be so soon. I just wanted things to stay as they were," said Yvette through her sobs.

After a minute, Daniel stepped back and held her shoulders at arm's length.

"My darling, I swear to you, I will come back. I know you will worry about me; I will certainly worry about you, but I promise you, I will come back to you. Now come on, let's start getting things ready. I don't have too much to have to pack."

Yvette had become calmer, but the dark thoughts remained. They started to walk back to the house.

"I wonder where Lucien is?" said Yvette, exchanging one difficult subject for another. "I had expected him to be back before now. Just one of the several things I've been dreading..." She gave a wry smile at the thought.

"I've been thinking the same thing actually," said Daniel. "I didn't think he was going to take this long. It may be that he's become caught up with a Maquis cell wherever he is. He might not be able to get here for a while now. When I get up to Limoges, I'll ask some questions. See if I can find out."

"How will you be able to let me know?" asked Yvette. "If Lucien can't get word to me, how do you expect to be able to?"

"I'm not sure yet. Your grandparents are part of the network. We'll talk about it with them. They are likely to have some contacts. They may have some ideas."

Daniel left her for a minute as he went down into the cellar to retrieve his overcoat, valise and back pack from the Mouse Hole. He made sure all the timber panelling was carefully back in place before he returned upstairs. The clandestine little room was once again invisible to all but the most thorough examination.

Yvette had not moved from where she stood when Daniel went into the cellar. Her head was so full of conflicting emotions, she was scarcely able to think.

"Are you all right?" asked Daniel tenderly. "I can't bear to see you looking so miserable."

Yvette suddenly shook her head, clearing her thoughts. "I'll be fine!" she said in a determined voice. "Come! We have to go up to see *Mamie* and *Papie*. They will know what to do to get you on your way. They even have a car though I don't know how much petrol it has left."

Daniel smiled to see her regaining control. "That's good. I also have more equipment stored up there in that old cellar under the tumbled down barn. I have a Sten gun and extra ammunition up there. I suspect I might need all that!"

He handed the leather valise he had brought with him over to Yvette.

"There's nothing in it now that could incriminate you. If you just store it somewhere, it'll just look like you own it. Hopefully, I can come back for it soon." He smiled at her and she hugged him.

She put the valise into her bedroom and together they left the house and began the walk up to her grandparent's house.

6 June 1944: Tulle. Late morning

Everyone was now in their designated place. They had planned for this moment for years. There were over forty Maquis, all arranged in their respective small groups. Each of these units had taken up their selected ambush sites in the upper floors of buildings lining the main road.

Altogether, the length of the ambush ran for well over a hundred metres. Two and three story buildings on both sides, lined the street for almost its entire length. Once the German column was fully committed on the street, it would have nowhere to go to escape the ambush.

Now they just had to wait. The German garrison would surely mobilise and be on its way to the invasion grounds soon. Surely soon.

Lucien was with Paul and two others on the upstairs floor of a private residence overlooking the road. The owners of the home were not given a choice. They had locked themselves in a cellar at the rear, desperate to remain out of harm's way.

The house Paul had selected was the second last in the long string of sites. The second furthest away from the garrison. When the column reached the furthest, the Maquis there would open fire. That would be the signal for all the units stretched out along the road to commence their attacks. Their positioning should bring the entire German column under fire.

The waiting continued.

Paul checked his watch for the umpteenth time, it was nearing midday. He looked over at Lucien who had been particularly quiet for most of the morning.

"Are you all right, Lucien?" he asked.

"I'm OK. I'm just thinking; Yvette would have no idea where I am. I have no way of getting a message to her. Can I ask a favour of you, please? If something… happens to me, can you get a message to her and let her know?"

Paul nodded slowly. "Of course, my friend. It would be my honour."

Lucien paused for a moment. He clearly had not finished.

"And another thing also if I may… can you please let Angeline Blanchard up in Limoges know as well? She and I have become… well… rather close," said Lucien sheepishly.

Paul stared at him for a moment and then burst into laughter. "You crafty old bastard! You, of all people! I can hardly believe it! Now I'm going to make sure you survive. I've just got to see how you explain your way out of this!"

Paul leaned back against the wall near the window. He was still chuckling happily.

He glanced out the window once again, as he had been doing for the last few hours. This time though, there was a hand waving from a window across the street. They were indicating down the road, in the direction of the German barracks.

Paul carefully peeked around the edge of the window and looked down the street. There was obvious movement underway. Very soon after, the clattering sounds of heavy, moving metal on cobbles began to filter up the street. The first German half-track vehicles were beginning to move. These were armoured troop transport vehicles. They would take the lead positions in the convoy. The regular lorries would be following them with perhaps, some smaller cars for the officers.

Paul looked back up the street towards where the first unit were in position. He saw a hand wave from a window up there. They were alert to the growing activity as well.

Lucien had moved in beside Paul at the same window. They exchanged glances, each sensing the apprehension in the other. Paul looked towards the other two Maquis in the room with them. They held positions at the other windows, weapons at the ready.

Paul peeked out of the window and down the street again. The column's first vehicles had now left the barracks and were moving down the road towards them. Before long, they would be passing the first of the ambush units. Everyone knew his or her roles. It was vital that those units closest to the barracks hold their fire until the lead vehicle of the column had come under attack at the far end of the road.

The column continued uninterrupted. The plan was working. The sound of the half-tracks was near deafening now as the column drew closer. The noise as they crunched along the ancient cobbled street echoing and amplifying off the buildings as they passed.

The half-tracks had armoured sides, but were open at the top. That made them vulnerable to attack from the buildings above. Paul, Lucien and the others each reached for grenades. It should be easy to drop them into the half-tracks as they passed. The effects should be devastating.

The sound grew in intensity as the half-tracks drew closer still. The column was now fully formed and underway. Paul had another quick further look and confirmed that there were no more than a dozen vehicles in total. No tanks. Excellent.

Everyone moved away from the windows as the first vehicles drew past them. The Germans would be keeping a close watch on any open windows as they passed. The ambush could backfire quickly if the Germans saw anyone in the windows above.

The lead vehicles now passed below Paul and Lucien's room. They pulled the safety pins on their grenades, whilst keeping a firm grip on the priming levers. Only a few more seconds now.

Any moment now, the vehicles would be abreast of the first Maquis unit. Lucien waited for the first rattle of gunfire, scarcely able to breathe.

Then came the sound of four grenades exploding almost simultaneously.

Paul spun around and looked out of the window; the three others were only a fraction of a second behind. The first half-track had flames billowing from its open passenger compartment. The third vehicle in the column was directly below their window. They each released the primers on their grenades and dropped them down into the vehicle below. The Germans were still too stunned from the explosion in the lead vehicle, only moments before, to react quickly enough. The four grenades blew up in their vehicle as well, causing carnage.

Paul quickly snatched up his Sten and opened fire onto the half-track caught in between of the two disabled vehicles. One of the other Maquis in the room joined in immediately. The first unit also opened fire on the same vehicle, creating a cross fire between the two positions that was murderous to the troops trapped in the open vehicles below.

All the way down the road, the other Maquis units had opened their attacks on whichever vehicle was nearest. The Germans were caught in the open, completely unprepared to be under fire so soon after leaving their barracks.

These were well-trained, professional soldiers, however. They quickly took stock of the situation and started to fight back. They were far more heavily armed than their Maquis opponents, and quickly pinpointed the windows from where the firing was coming.

Shocked and stunned troops were spilling out from the lorries and half-tracks. They took cover in doorways, behind the now stationary vehicles and anywhere that was immediately effective. Within seconds, the Maquis were taking return fire. These experienced and determined Wehrmacht troops quickly steadied. They were now hell-bent on exacting retribution for this outrage.

Gunfire was now echoing up and down the street as the Maquis continued to use the advantage of their elevated positions to good effect. The Germans continued to recover from the mind-numbing shock of the initial attack. Professional soldiers, they were now responding with a focused fury. Their heavier calibre machine guns were now into the action, clearing the windows above of all but the most foolhardy of Resistance fighters.

In bare seconds, the momentum of the battle switched.

The weight and ferocity of the German response was quickly threatening to overwhelm the Maquis. Each separate unit was finding itself increasingly isolated, and fighting for its life.

In the first three half-tracks, the uninjured survivors from the grenade attacks had managed to get out and find cover behind the armoured sides of their crippled vehicles. They knew their attackers were immediately above them. The Maquis had used grenades on them; now they responded in the same way.

Two troops pulled the pins on their stick type grenades and hurled them towards to windows of the first ambush group. One missed its target and fell back onto the road, exploding harmlessly in the open, but the other one found its mark.

The grenade's explosion in the confines of the room was tremendous. Of the four Maquis, one was killed outright and the other three were injured and concussed. The Germans threw a second grenade into the room and immediately after it exploded, rushed the doorway and charged up the stairs.

Bursting into the room, they fired their machine guns at anything that looked human. Within seconds, all the Maquis were dead. Their bodies torn to shreds from the effects of the grenades and the torrent of machine gun fire.

The Germans quickly called out to their comrades in the street that the room was now secure.

They then turned their attention to the other room in the building across the street, from where Paul, Lucien and the others were still firing.

Paul immediately grasped the gravity of their situation.

"OK! Time to get going. Everyone out NOW!"

The other two Maquis did not need to be told twice. They both bolted for the door and raced down the stairs to disappear out the rear of the building.

Paul turned to Lucien. "Come on, get moving."

Lucien did not budge. "You go. I'll fire for a few more seconds to cover you. Then I'll follow."

Paul did not have time to argue. He turned and raced after the first two.

Lucien turned back to the window and open fire with the Sten. He had the satisfaction of seeing a German soldier drop to the ground as he fired at him.

The noise from his own gun prevented him from hearing the sound of a German grenade as it flew through another window and thumped onto the floor, only a few metres away.

The explosion, an instant later, blew him across the room and slammed him into the wall. He collapsed to the floor, injured and stunned. Moments later, German troops burst into the room firing wildly. One of the bullets hit Lucien in the left shoulder and he slumped further, groaning in agony.

A German soldier approached him, drawing his pistol. He started to take aim at Lucien's head but his Corporal called out, ordering him to stop.

"Take him alive. Hand him over for interrogation."

The Germans removed any weapons he had and carried him downstairs, dumping him unceremoniously in the street, under guard.

After a few minutes, Lucien slowly began to regain consciousness. He was aware of an agonising throbbing in his shoulder and a dazzling brightness. He turned his head to the side so that he was no longer looking straight into the sun.

One of the German guards noticed he was conscious. He came close and looked into Lucien's eyes. The German hawked up a mouthful of phlegm and spat it all straight into his face. Then he stood up and kicked

Lucien hard on his bullet-wounded shoulder. Lucien's mind screamed in agony and he passed out again.

6 June 1944: Briand Farm, near Flavignac. Mid-Afternoon

Daniel was deeply uncertain as to the reception he would get when he and Yvette arrived at her grandparent's house.

He had no reason to believe it would be welcoming. As it turned out, he was wrong.

"Welcome, my dear boy!" said Delphine as she embraced Daniel. Bernard's embrace was no less warm.

Yvette could see Daniel begin to relax almost immediately. She herself was also uncertain how their meeting might go. She began to feel more at ease as quickly as did Daniel.

"Hello *Mamie*," said Yvette kissing her grandmother on the cheek. "*Papie*, have you heard any more news?"

"There's been a lot. I have not bothered putting the radio away now. I suspect the German's will have more important things on their minds than inspecting the home of an ancient couple like us," said Bernard with a chuckle.

He took Yvette by the shoulder and led her and Daniel through into the lounge room.

Delphine remained in the kitchen, starting to get some food prepared. She had guessed that neither Yvette nor Daniel would have eaten much this day.

Bernard looked closely at Daniel. His chest was still heaving after the exertion of the walk. "You still seem very short of breath after your walk up here. It's only two kilometres. Do you honestly believe you are fit to go into action? Because I don't!"

Daniel was somewhat taken aback by Bernard's directness. "I have no choice! It's what I was sent over here to do. It's what I volunteered to do!"

"Be that as it may, I've seen people with pneumonia before. It takes months to recover fully. You have barely had three weeks. If you push yourself too hard now, it will almost certainly come back, probably worse than before."

Daniel sat down in an armchair. "I can't sit back and do nothing. I've come all this way and taken virtually no part in anything. How can I look my compatriots in the eye if I don't seek to do my share? I'm not an invalid!"

Bernard sat down on the sofa, not taking his eyes off Daniel. Yvette sat on the wide arm of the chair, alongside Daniel.

"I'm sorry to break the news to you, but you are an invalid," said Bernard. "Do you think that there has never been another soldier who was unable to fight due to sickness? It is common. It is nothing to be ashamed of."

Daniel looked crestfallen. "This is maddening. It is so frustrating!"

Yvette looked at her grandfather and then at Daniel. "*Papie* is right you know. You have had a serious illness and you are only just starting to recover. You're not ready yet."

"Is this why you wanted to bring me up here, so you can all gang up on me?"

Bernard laughed. "Not at all. I actually wanted to see you anyway. We know what you mean to Yvette and I believe you feel just as strongly about her, but that is not the issue right now. Your health is! Surely even you can see how much that short walk has left you gasping. You're clearly not ready."

Daniel slumped back into the chair. The truly maddening part for him was that he knew they were right.

"Then there must be other things I can do to help?"

Bernard shrugged. "There are bound to be. Not today though. It is too late now to arrange anything for today. You can both stay here tonight. Hopefully we will be contacted shortly by our local Maquis cell and they can let us know how you can help."

"Are you sure they're coming?" asked Daniel.

"Of course, they will! Don't forget, we have a small arsenal stored here. They will need to retrieve those weapons very soon. In fact, I was actually expecting someone to have been in touch before now. Just be patient."

Daniel looked at Bernard and saw him in a different light. For his age, he was still a robust man and clearly not to be underestimated. Daniel could not help but imagine what a figure of authority he must have been in his youth.

Yvette sensed it was time to change the subject. "Have you heard any word of Lucien, *Papie*?"

"Nothing yet. The last word that I heard was that he was in Limoges, but that was two days ago. I'm very surprised he isn't back here by now…"

His sentence tailed off. They all knew what Lucien returning home would mean. All three of them went silent as they contemplated the reality of seeing him again.

The mood soon lightened as Delphine brought a tray of food into the lounge room and placed it on a low table.

"Now! Come on! You must all be hungry."

She turned and went back out into the kitchen to fetch another tray, this one with the teapot and cups.

"Now come on, start eating! I won't tell you again!" she said.

Daniel and Yvette both remained pensive, but only for a few moments longer. Despite her concerns, Yvette made a conscious effort to appear more cheery and lift the mood.

"Yes *Mamie*, you're right!" She looked at the man she loved. "Daniel, have some cheese, please. We need to be happy now. This is a great day! France is being set free again!"

6 June 1944: German barracks, Tulle. Late Afternoon

Lucien lay on a stretcher. They had carried him under close guard to a small room in the German barracks. A German physician had bandaged his bullet wound, and the larger of the numerous lacerations he had received from the grenade blast. They had, however, given him no analgesia to ease the pain. They wanted him conscious.

An army Major entered the room and brought a chair over to where Lucien's stretcher lay. He sat himself down on it and stared thoughtfully at Lucien for several long seconds before he spoke in fluent French.

"Well, my friend. You and your comrades caught us well and truly by surprise this morning. I must congratulate you. We had not credited you with being quite so audacious as to attack within the town itself. I can assure you, it's a mistake that we will never make again."

"Now there are a few questions I would like to ask you, as one soldier to another, and I strongly suggest that you think carefully about answering me truthfully. As you no doubt realise, we are regular army. *Wehrmacht*. We prefer to go about our business with as much honour as circumstances allow. To the south of us, there is a large Waffen-SS Regiment preparing to move north and join us. I have no doubt, their methods of questioning prisoners will be quite different to mine."

The Major waited for Lucien to respond. Lucien lay there without speaking.

"So, what's it to be then?" asked the Major with indulgent patience.

Lucien turned his head away.

The Major continued on, regardless. "I would like you to tell me a few names if you would be so kind. I am sure that in a rural centre such as this, you would all know each other well. You would be well aware of the names of the other members of your cell."

At this, Lucien could not help himself. He let out a short laugh.

"I don't come from here. I just happened to be in town. I offered to help. I don't know any names here."

"Really! Is that so?" replied the Major. "In that case you will be of no use to us at all. I might as well just shoot you now."

Lucien winced at the thought. "I thought you said you were honourable?"

"*Touché, Monsieur!* You have called my bluff!" said the Major. "But on the other hand," he continued, "if that is true that you are not from here, then you are clearly involved with another Maquis group somewhere else. I'm sure there is much that you can tell us about that one. Don't you think?"

"But first of all, it appears I have forgotten my manners. Please allow me to introduce myself. My name is Major Krebbs. I was a part of the column you attacked this morning. One of my close friends is now dead as a result of that attack. Several others I know well are badly wounded, one has lost an arm. You might be able to guess then, right at this moment, I am not feeling particularly well disposed towards you and your comrades."

"My own conscience won't allow me to do to you what I really want, but I am more than happy to hand you over to the SS when they arrive tomorrow. They will have no such qualms. Now please my friend. Let us start with something simple. What is your name?"

Lucien did not acknowledge the question.

"Please *Monsieur*, as any captured soldier knows. He is permitted to tell his name, rank and serial number. There is no shame in your telling me that. The Geneva Convention stipulates that you are allowed to pass on such basics. Now, once again, what is your name please?"

This time, Lucien spoke before he had a chance to think clearly.

"Lucien."

"Ahh!" said Major Krebbs, "you do have a voice and your name is Lucien. That is an excellent start. Now, your last name please?"

Lucien's mind was foggy with pain and now that he had given out his first name, he did not see what harm his last name could do.

"Morin," he replied.

"Lucien Morin!" said Major Krebbs scribbling down the name. "What an excellent start. And where might you be from then, Lucien Morin, if you don't come from here?"

Suddenly, despite the pain, Lucien realised the danger. If he said anything even close to the truth, he would be placing Yvette and her family in the gravest of peril. He had to think of a town far enough away from Flavignac to keep them safe, but not so far as to make his presence in Tulle seem too unlikely.

Where had he been recently that could deflect the Major away from Yvette in Flavignac or Angeline in Limoges?

One name leapt into his head.

"Oradour," he said.

Krebbs wrote the name down immediately. "See. That was not too hard now, was it? Now you must excuse me. I have to go and consult a map. Do not worry, *Monsieur*, I shall be back soon to continue our little conversation. *A bientot*."

6 June 1941: Tulles. Late Afternoon

The Maquis survivors from the day's ambush had initially dispersed to the safety of the countryside beyond the city. Yet they were far from finished. They began to regroup and commence spontaneous attacks against any German soldiers they encountered.

There were short and vicious firefights going on throughout the suburbs and the nearby countryside for the remainder of the day.

German casualties began to grow. The Maquis knew their town and from where best to attack. They also knew where best to hide afterwards.

Paul Launay returned to his hotel as discretely as possible, once the streets had cleared following the initial ambush. He had been unable to do anything more than look on from a hidden position, as Lucien was captured and taken away. It was clear though, that he had been badly wounded.

One of Paul's first actions was to take Giles, one of his young employees, aside and give him the instructions that would take him to Flavignac and then, on to Limoges.

He knew Giles had a good bicycle and that he was an enthusiastic rider. Giles lived with his parents, just outside of the town. Paul realised that if Giles could get home safely, he would be past the worst of the German threat and could be on his way in relative safety.

After Giles had left, Paul turned his attention to finding his wife Marie. She was safe, hidden in the cellar.

Apart from a few overnight guests, there were no customers in the hotel that day. The fighting had kept everyone not actively involved, huddled securely behind their own doors. Paul and Marie went around the hotel and ensured all the external doors were securely locked and bolted from inside.

Paul was torn. As a Resistance leader, he knew he should be out there fighting. However, he had become separated from his cell as they had dispersed following the ambush. The fighting was now so fluid that he had no idea where to go to link up again with the others. To go out on the chance of a random meeting with other Maquis would be to invite capture by the Germans.

As much as he hated the feeling of isolation, staying put was by far the most sensible approach. The darkness of the coming night would give him the chance to go out again, looking for the others.

6 June 1944: Valence d'Agen. Late Evening

Lammerding called another meeting of his senior officers.

"Well, gentlemen, I have finally received our orders to move. Due to the hour, we shall get underway in the morning, before first light. We are to travel north until we get to a city called Tulle. It appears there has been an incident involving the local Communist Resistance and a *Wehrmacht* Regiment based there. Group HQ would like us to… err… lend our expertise to the task of teaching the local townsfolk a lesson they are unlikely to forget."

"The distance is about two hundred kilometres so we must be underway early and stop for nothing. If you encounter anything that looks even slightly suspicious, then use absolute force to deal with it. I want at least a vanguard battalion in Tulle by tomorrow evening."

Diekmann stepped forward. "Do you still wish us to take the forward position, sir?"

"Actually, Major, given the changing nature of our task, I think it's preferable to have Major Kampfe take his Reconnaissance Battalion out first. You follow close behind. This is no longer a simple re-deployment. Do you all agree?"

The assembled officers all spoke their agreement in unison.

"Very well then!" said Lammerding. "You have your orders, gentlemen. Have a pleasant evening. Dismissed!"

Major Helmut Kampfe went over to Diekmann as the two of them left the meeting.

"I do hope I'm not stealing your thunder at the front of the column, Otto?" he said with a laugh.

Diekmann smiled tolerantly at his friend. The two of them had served together for years now, and had become regular drinking buddies.

"If it can't be me at the Head of March, then it might as well be you, Helmut. I do see the sense, though. If we are to move into an active viper's nest of these Maquis bastards, then a Recon Unit is best to have up front. For my part, I hope we do run into them. We've been patient for far too long."

"I couldn't agree more, Otto." said Kampfe, "Let's get about them, and then we can go and say hello to the Americans!"

"If that isn't something to drink to, I don't know what is!" replied Diekmann.

The two of them set off towards Diekmann's tent where a supply of good, confiscated Cognac awaited them.

Chapter 10

7 June 1944: Briand Farm, near Flavignac, Mid-Morning

The radio news from the BBC was sounding very positive. After initial strong resistance in the American sector, the Allies were now beginning to move inland in force. In some areas, the worst obstacles were in the form of flooded pastures and muddy roads. The German resistance was still to get itself properly organised. At this early stage, it was all looking very promising.

There was still no news of Lucien and it was with mixed feelings that everyone under the roof of the Briand farm was growing more anxious.

Despite everything, Daniel had liked Lucien; the others all loved him in their way. They were all worried.

Yvette had gone back down to their farm to tend to the animals. The many duties of a farmer could not simply be ignored. There were hungry livestock demanding to be fed and let out to pasture.

She had not yet returned when a teenage boy on a bicycle, rode in from the south. He steered his machine into the farm and rode determinedly towards the house.

Arriving outside the front of the house, he got off the bicycle and called out loudly.

"Is there anybody home?"

Delphine and Bernard had been watching him as he came up the road.

Delphine went outside to greet him and ask what he wanted. Bernard watched from inside the house as Delphine and the boy talked. He heard mention of the city of Tulle, to the south.

His heart skipped a beat as he saw Delphine put her hand to her mouth in shock. He hurried to the door and called them both inside.

Delphine was too shocked to speak. The boy took off his hat and came inside after her.

"*Bonjour Monsieur*. My name is Giles. I am looking for Monsieur Bernard Briand. I have some news from Tulle that concerns him."

"*Bonjour* Giles. I am Bernard. Have you ridden all the way here from Tulle? It's nearly ninety kilometres! You must be exhausted! What have you to tell us that so important?"

"Yes *Monsieur*, I have been riding since early this morning. The leader of the Maquis in Tulle has asked me to ride and tell you. We attacked a German column in Tulle yesterday. We hurt them badly but we had a couple of casualties ourselves. I have to let you know that *Monsieur* Morin has been badly wounded and captured by the Germans."

Bernard could almost feel himself age several years in that moment.

"Morin? Lucien Morin? Are you certain it was Lucien? What was he even doing in Tulle? He was up north in Limoges the last we heard!"

"I don't know the answers to those questions *Monsieur*, all I know is what I have been told to tell you. I am told that he has been badly wounded and captured by the Germans after the Maquis ambushed their column yesterday. Several people saw him being carried off by them after the attack finished."

They all just stood in silence.

Daniel had been standing in the kitchen, staying out of sight. However, he had heard everything.

He came into the lounge room to join the others. He held out his hand to the boy, who reached out and shook it.

"*Bonjour* Giles. I am Lieutenant Martin. I could not help but hear what you said. You say Lucien was part of this attack? How did it go?"

Giles could only shrug. "It seemed to go well at first. Then the Germans began to fight back. We had to break off and escape into the woods behind the town."

"How many did you lose?"

"I'm not sure *Monsieur*, several at least."

"Dear God! This could to end very badly. Who can guess what the Germans are going to do now?" asked Daniel, speaking as much to himself as to Giles.

Delphine had sat down and was weeping quietly, trying to remain stoic, but unequal to the task. The emotion was too great.

Daniel motioned to the boy to come out into the kitchen. "Please let me get you a drink, you must be parched after that ride."

"Thank you, *Monsieur*. I do need a drink, but I also have to be on my way. I have to ride up to Limoges next. There is someone I have to notify there also."

"Notify who?" said Yvette, walking in through the back door, having just returned from her farm.

Daniel immediately reached for her and hugged her tightly.

She sensed something was very wrong.

"What is going on here? Who are you?" she said, her eyes fixed on Giles.

Bernard heard her voice and came into the kitchen as well.

"This lad's name is Giles. He has ridden all the way from Tulle with news of Lucien," he said.

Yvette freed herself from Daniel's embrace and came over to her grandfather.

"What news?" she asked in a tremulous voice.

Daniel and Bernard looked at each other and then at Yvette.

"It seems he has been wounded in a Maquis attack on a German column," said Daniel, "the Germans have captured him."

Yvette's legs gave way and crumpled underneath her. She sat on the floor and burst into uncontrollable tears.

Daniel reached out to try to comfort her but she pushed him away. At this moment, his touch only added to the profound wave of guilt that was suddenly consuming her.

Daniel understood. He stood up and led Giles out of the kitchen, back into the lounge room. Bernard remained in the kitchen with Yvette.

In the lounge room, Delphine was still crying. Wishing to leave her to the privacy of her despair, Daniel indicated to Giles to follow him through the front door and go outside.

"I'm sorry, Giles. I didn't get you your drink of water."

The young lad smiled sympathetically. "That is all right, *Monsieur*. I saw a pump as I rode into the yard. I will get a drink there. I must be on my way. I'm so sorry that my news is not better."

Daniel put his hand on Giles shoulder. "It is only the beginning I'm afraid. It is going to get a lot worse than this. Are you sure you'll be all right to ride all the way into Limoges? It's a fair distance."

Giles looked affronted. "*Monsieur*, I am very fit, and I have an important task!"

Daniel could not help but smile. "Be safe then, young Giles. Godspeed to you."

"*Merci, Monsieur. Au revoir!*" He started to ride off. His next task was to find a woman in Limoges by the name of Angeline.

"*Au revoir!*" called out Daniel in reply. He turned and went back into the house.

7 June 1944: German Barracks, Tulle. Mid-Morning

Major Krebbs looked in on Lucien again. Lucien had been drifting in and out of consciousness since the previous afternoon. He had eaten nothing and managed barely a sip or two of water since being taken into custody.

Krebbs had hoped to keep him awake so he could continue questioning him, but Lucien's condition was worse than it had initially appeared.

Krebbs was *Wehrmacht*, not SS. He was not a member of the Nazi Party. He was a career soldier who viewed his enemy very differently to his compatriots in the Waffen-SS. There were lines of behaviour he would not cross. In the hours that had passed since the ambush the previous day, his anger had settled and he now viewed his captive through calmer eyes.

He knew the Maquis were not regular army. He knew that many were Communists. He knew that it was the fate any captured Maquis, to be shot as terrorists. He accepted that, but he did not want to be a part of any instance of torture. That was behaviour unworthy of a civilised people. In spite of all that he had seen in the war thus far, he still tried to retain his civility and humanity.

He stood over Lucien as he lay there on the stretcher that had been his bed since he was brought in the previous day. Lucien had lost a great deal of blood and was murmuring quietly as he lay in a shallow, troubled sleep.

His face was glistening with sweat and his skin colour was considerably paler than when Krebbs had first seen him the previous day.

Krebbs had orders to withhold morphia from captured Maquis. He knew the Gestapo would want any captives to be lucid when they arrived to start their own interrogation.

Nevertheless, despite himself, he could not help but have an admiration for these people.

He could hear occasional bursts of gunfire out in the more distant streets as the Maquis continued to mount attacks against any Germans they encountered.

They were only defending their country against an invader after all. In their circumstances, would he be any different?

He tried to push those thoughts from his mind, yet he remained troubled. He knew what would happen to Lucien once the Gestapo or the SS arrived. He knew the SS were coming up in force from the south and were likely to be arriving before the end of the day.

Somewhere in his soul, he found himself wishing that Lucien would succumb to his wounds before they arrived.

He was aware that Lucien had stayed behind to cover his friends whilst they retreated. As a soldier, Major Krebbs could respect that.

Suddenly, Lucien opened his eyes and Krebbs knelt down beside him.

Lucien spoke weakly, "May I have some water, please?"

Major Krebbs reached for a tin cup of water that had been left beside Lucien's stretcher.

He gently held the cup to Lucien's lips and poured a tiny sip into his mouth. He did this several times as Lucien struggled to swallow each sip.

Eventually, Lucien put his hand on Krebbs' arm and said, "Thank you... thank you..."

Krebbs put his hand on Lucien's good shoulder in a reflexive, kind gesture.

Lucien managed a weak smile. "A fine example of the master race you are, my friend."

Krebbs could not help but smile back.

"And a fine example of a Communist bastard you are too, Comrade."

The two remained in silence for a while.

"I suspect this isn't going to end very well for me, is it?" murmured Lucien.

"It's not looking too good," replied Major Krebbs after a moment's consideration.

"Oh well," said Lucien, "you weren't able to get me in the last war. I'm very impressed by all the trouble you've gone to... to get me in this one."

Krebbs chuckled softly, but with genuine humour. "Well, you must realise, we Germans hate to leave a task unfinished. So, you served in the last war?"

Lucien made eye contact with Krebbs for a moment, and then looked away.

"Yes. I was at Verdun. You even managed to hit me! Bullets and gas! I must say though, the bullets you're using today seem to hurt a lot more."

"That's because they are Nazi bullets. They hate Communists, too!"

Lucien managed another weak smile. "*C'est la guerre.*"

Krebbs looked thoughtful. "*C'est la guerre.*"

He stood up and looked down at Lucien. "There will be a large SS Battalion arriving in a few hours. No doubt, they will wish a few moments of your time. There will be little that I can do. I'm sorry…" He looked genuinely sad.

Lucien looked up at him. "*Auf weidersehn* then, *Herr* Major… and thank you for the water."

Krebbs nodded, turned and left the room.

Alone in the room again, Lucien stared up at ceiling. His mind, dulled from the pain, thirst and loss of blood was not able to process very many thoughts, but chief amongst those few, was utter dread at what the coming hours might bring.

***

The rumble of vehicles arriving from the south grew louder. The clock had gone four o'clock in the afternoon as the first armoured half-tracks from Major Kampfe's advanced Reconnaissance Battalion began to arrive in Tulle. The remainder of his battalion and that of Major Diekmann would all be arriving over the course of the next few hours.

Kampfe immediately reported to the Barracks and demanded to see the Commanding Officer. He was still out in the field, so Kampfe demanded the presence of Major Krebbs instead.

Kampfe and Krebbs saluted and shook hands.

"Would you be so kind as to tell me what has been happening here, *Herr* Major?" said Kampfe.

Krebbs offered him a seat and went into detail about the events of the last day and a half.

"Are you holding captives that are available for interrogation?" asked Kampfe.

Krebbs nodded. "We have one. He is badly wounded and may not last long if the interrogation is too… intensive."

"I see," said Major Kampfe. "Have you spoken to him yourself? Have you been able to get anything worthwhile out of him?"

"A little," replied Krebbs, "it appears he is not from here. He just happened to be in town when the news of the invasion came through. He threw in his lot with the first Maquis group he came across."

"Do you believe him?"

"I have no obvious reason not to. I did manage to persuade him to tell me the name of the town he is from though."

"And that is…?"

"He says it is called Oradour."

"Well, that is a start. He may well have contacts there. Have you checked where this town is?" asked Kampfe.

"Of course!" replied Krebbs. He hesitated over the next admission. "There seems to be some small confusion though. We looked over the maps and there seem to be two towns with similar names. One is called Oradour-Sur-Veyres and the other is Oradour-Sur-Glane."

Kampfe looked surprised. "Two towns? I wonder if our little friend might be trying a clever game with us. Have you pressed him further to find out which of the two?"

"Not yet," replied Krebbs, "he has been largely unconscious since then. I haven't felt compelled to press him too hard in his moments of lucidity."

Kampfe leapt to his feet in an instant rage. "You haven't felt compelled to press him too hard? What kind of pathetic nonsense is this? You *Wehrmacht* are an embarrassment! Take me to him immediately!"

Major Krebbs stiffened immediately. He was a proud officer and refused to be spoken to like that.

"How dare you! You will apologise and address me with respect *Herr Major*! I strongly suspect my service far outweighs yours."

"Really?" said Kampfe. "And just how long have you been in the service of the Fatherland?"

"Since before the Fuhrer became Chancellor. I joined the army in 1931."

"And how much of that time have you spent on the Russian Front, *Herr Major*?" asked Kampfe with a smirk.

Krebbs stood frozen. "I served in Greece, Crete and North Africa, *Herr Major*. I have not served on the Russian Front," he replied, knowing full well the rebuke this answer might bring.

"Then allow me to put in a good word for you, *Herr* Major. It really is an experience you must not miss," said Kampfe with savage satisfaction. "Now, please take me to the prisoner."

Krebbs felt crestfallen and humiliated. He had served with distinction under Rommel in the *Afrika Korps* for nearly two years. However, that adventure had ultimately ended in defeat and evacuation. He knew the SS considered any connection with that campaign to be an embarrassment for Germany.

He had no choice but to comply with Kampfe's demand.

Major Krebbs led Kampfe to the room where Lucien was being held. Despite his condition, an armed guard remained at the door.

Lucien's condition had deteriorated even further since the last time Krebbs had seen him. Still unconscious, he was continuing to lose blood and looked deathly pallid.

Kampfe looked down at him in ill-disguised disappointment. "He is in worse condition than I expected. I doubt I'll be able to get much out of him like this."

Krebbs felt a moment of inner satisfaction at this admission from Kampfe. It was what he had been trying to say earlier when Kampfe had turned on him.

Kampfe reached out his right foot and used it to push Lucien's good shoulder. Lucien was rocked back and forth but did not respond at all.

"It seems he is completely unconscious. He is no value to me whatsoever." He turned to the guard still standing beside the door.

"If he shows the slightest sign of regaining consciousness, send for me immediately."

"Yes, sir!" said the guard smartly.

Kampfe then turned back to Krebbs. "Well then, *Herr* Major. Since he is unable to help us now, please show me on the map where we might find these two Oradours. I may wish to take some of my men and check them out myself."

7 June 1944: Briand Farm. Early Afternoon

Yvette sat next to Daniel on the old lounge. She had regained her composure some time ago, but still could not bring herself to show him any outward affection. She felt guilty and miserable.

Bernard and Delphine sat in the single armchairs.

"We have to go there!" said Daniel, "somehow, we have to find out where he is and what condition he's in."

"Out of the question!" replied Bernard sharply. "Tulle will be swarming with Germans now. Anyone coming into the town will be stopped. If they find someone like you, they will arrest you immediately. God alone knows what they would do to you."

"There must be some way to get in," said Daniel "we can't just sit here, not knowing…"

Yvette spoke up for the first time in a while. "There is a way, but it can't involve either Daniel or you, *Papie*. If *Mamie* and I can take your little van, we could get one of my remaining sows and take it into Tulle. We would simply look like local farmers wives, trying to get to market to sell a pig. We can act as though we have no idea there is anything going on. It could very well work."

Bernard and Daniel looked at each other. The idea had real merit.

Delphine spoke up. "I think it's a good idea. I am completely prepared to go. They are not likely to suspect an old woman and a pregnant farm wife."

"I'm not pregnant!" said Yvette in surprise.

"Perhaps not, but you will certainly look it when I get through with you!" said Delphine with a sly smile. "Come! We need to start getting you ready."

"Whoa! Aren't we rushing things a bit?" said Daniel, suddenly anxious at the speed with which the decision had been reached.

"Not at all," replied Delphine. "If we wait too long, we might start to find reasons to change our minds. Come Yvette, I have some old cushions we can work with to pad you out." The two women left the lounge room and went into Delphine's sewing room.

Bernard stood up wearily and turned to Daniel. "Come with me please, Lieutenant. I will need your help to get the van started up."

Daniel stood up and joined him as he went out into the yard.

Bernard had bought his Peugeot 4CV van a year before the war broke out. Despite his age, he had loved driving and the little van was perfect for the two of them, and for use around the farm. Even though it had hardly been driven in the last several months, it still started easily.

Bernard had a large drum of petrol, still nearly a third full, in the barn close by where the little Peugeot sat parked. Using an old pump and hose, he and Daniel filled the tank up to full.

Next task was the short, two-kilometre drive to Lucien and Yvette's farm to catch one of the sows and get her into the back of the Peugeot.

The Germans had only left them with a pig and two sows when they commandeered much of their stock earlier in the year. To lose one more would seriously compromise their ability to rebuild the herd later.

There was no time though, to consider any another option. A sow had to go!

Bernard backed the van up to the gate of their small paddock and Daniel set about trying to round up one of the reluctant sows. Bernard set up the ramp into the back of the van as Daniel tried to chivvy a sow towards it.

The sow was neither keen nor cooperative, but eventually Daniel managed to manhandle her into the back of the vehicle. By this stage, he was covered in mud and manure. His weakened lungs were protesting as he puffed in exhaustion.

Bernard could not help himself. He had to laugh at the sight that Daniel presented.

"I do hope you cut a more military figure when you are on parade, Lieutenant."

Daniel looked down at himself and smiled ruefully back.

"Oh well! You had best drive back on your own. I'll go inside, change into clean clothes and sit down for a few minutes. I can't go back with you in the van if I'm looking like this. I'll leave the seats filthy for Delphine and Yvette. I have no doubt they won't appreciate it."

"OK," replied Bernard as he got back into the van. "If you insist. I shall see you back up there."

Bernard put the car into gear and slowly started to head back up the laneway to his own farm.

Daniel locked the gate to the paddock and went back into the farmhouse. It felt very different this time, with neither Lucien nor Yvette there. He had been left on his own inside the house many times before, but now it felt markedly strange. He could almost sense the forces, changing his destiny, at work.

The thought left him feeling powerless, and somehow, lonely.

Yvette, Delphine, Bernard and Lucien were all playing their parts. Yet he, the one actual military officer amongst them, remained, obscure on the sidelines.

The war was not going to end overnight, and he knew his chance for action would come, but right at the moment, he felt humiliated by the circumstances that affected him.

He went around to the laundry at the rear of the house. He changed out of his filthy clothes and then cleaned himself up with water and a cloth. He left his dirty clothes in a bucket in the laundry, and then went back into the house to put on his one remaining set of clean clothes.

Lastly, he checked to make sure that the house was secure before beginning the tiring walk back up to the Briand Farm.

He pushed himself too hard at first, and very soon began to gasp for air. He had to rest for a minute before he could continue at a more sedate pace. He had no choice but to concede that his rehabilitation from the bout of pneumonia was, indeed, far from complete.

By the time he reached the farmhouse, Delphine and Yvette were already gone.

Daniel felt devastated.

Bernard led him inside and told him what had happened.

"When Yvette saw that it was only me in the car, she told Delphine to hurry up, so they could be on their way. She did not wish to see you before she left. I'm sorry, Daniel. It's not because she doesn't care for you, though. I can promise you that she does, but this trip is for Lucien. She has to know what has happened to him. Seeing you again just now would have been too hard for her. Please try and understand."

Daniel nodded glumly. He felt too wretched to reply.

Bernard led him back inside the house and set about pouring them both generous glasses of Armagnac. All they could do now was wait.

7 June 1944: Tulle German Barracks. Early Afternoon

News had just to come through from the town of St Junien, to the west of Limoges. The Maquis had risen up there as well. The local Resistance had blown up a railway bridge to try to hamper the Germans moving troops and equipment to the Front. They had killed two German troops during this attack. The French Resistance was clearly rising up everywhere. The Germans could not allow it to get out of hand.

General Lammerding was *en route* to Tulle, moving with the main body of the Division, still some distance to the south of the city.

Kept appraised of the events at St Junien by radio, he promptly issued orders for an immediate reconnaissance in force to be despatched to the area.

The logical officer to assign to the task was Major Kampfe. His own preparations for an investigation into that very region were already well advanced.

For Kampfe, the fastest route meant travel into Limoges and then turn due west from there. It meant having slightly further to travel, but the roads were much better. He wanted to be in St Junien that night.

Kampfe's Battalion was a specialist Reconnaissance unit. Smaller than most and equipped for speed and information gathering, rather than with heavier assault vehicles. Almost all of its larger vehicles were half-tracks and lorries.

They made their preparations quickly and were on the road before three p.m. Kampfe himself rode in a Kubelwagen, an open car with sides made from a heavy, corrugated metal.

Kampfe rode in the back seat and was carefully examining a map, familiarising himself with the area they were to investigate.

The name of a town only a short distance from St Junien leapt out at him.

Oradour-Sur-Glane!

This, Kampfe realised, must be the place to which the captured Maquis terrorist was referring. He sat back in his seat, deep in thought.

He would have to get a message back to General Lammerding at the first opportunity. He was now certain he knew the town from which the Maquis cell was operating.

Chapter 11

7 June 1944: Tulle, Late Afternoon

The drive from Flavignac to Tulle was uneventful. There was virtually no traffic on the slow, back roads and the little Peugeot settled into a nice rhythm. With Yvette driving, it took about two hours.

Sure enough, as soon as they joined the main road near the outskirts of the town, the German presence was everywhere. They were stopped several times by German patrols who demanded to see inside the van compartment. The sight of a large and far-from-happy sow had them all closing the door quickly and waving them through, after a quick check of their identity papers.

Yvette's plan was good. They certainly looked innocent enough in what they claimed to be doing.

As they neared the centre of the city though, the Germans troops they were now encountering wore different uniforms. No longer simple Wehrmacht, these were SS troops. The streets themselves showed signs of recent violence. Shattered windows and bullet holes marked many cars and buildings. The Germans looked edgy and alert.

They would need to be very careful from here.

No sooner had they realised this, than they were stopped once more, this time by the SS. They were brusquely ordered out of the car as several soldiers began to give the vehicle a thorough inspection.

Bernard had never used the van for smuggling contraband and both Delphine and Yvette were confident there was nothing incriminating there to be found.

The Germans, however, were most interested in the sow. It was clear that they had every intention of confiscating it.

Delphine stepped forward as they took it from the van and tied a rope around its neck to lead it away.

"But we need to sell it! Can't you see my granddaughter is pregnant! We need money to buy her supplies for when the baby comes!" she shouted at them with complete disregard as to how they might react.

They had fully expected this to happen and this was Delphine's chance to shine.

"You are nothing more than thieves! Brigands! You will leave us with nothing," she shouted at them as they led the sow away.

The Germans simply laughed at her and motioned for her to be on her way.

She stood there with her hands on her hips for a full minute after they left. She had worked herself up into a total fury and it was not abating quickly.

Yvette came over to her as she stood in the middle of the road and spoke to her quietly.

"Come now, *Mamie*. We must not make any more of this. We don't want them coming back. Let us go now."

Delphine's shoulders slumped and she slowly turned and began to make her way back to the van.

She had not paid any attention to the small crowd that had gathered to see what the commotion was all about.

Out of the crowd, a German officer came forward and approached them. His uniform was not SS. He was *Wehrmacht*.

"Please forgive the behaviour of my compatriots, *Mesdames*. Not everyone from Germany thinks like they do," he said to them in a quiet voice. They were both surprised at the quality of his French.

"We appreciate your apology, *Monsieur*," said Yvette, "but we are still without the pig we came here to sell. We have been left with nothing," she looked as though she was about to break into tears.

"How much do you believe she would have fetched at market?" asked the German Officer.

"We had hoped to get at least a hundred francs, *Monsieur*. She was an excellent sow," said Delphine, chiming into the conversation.

"Well, I don't have that much money on me, but may I offer you twenty? If that will help?"

Yvette and Delphine were speechless. This was the last thing they had expected.

Delphine regained her composure first. "That is extremely kind of you, *Monsieur*, I did not expect such consideration. Thank you very much."

The officer took out his wallet and removed all the notes he had. They indeed totalled twenty francs. He passed them over to Delphine.

Delphine stood there for a few moments, collecting her thoughts.

"I am not used to be shown such consideration by a German officer, *Monsieur*. I did not know that such honour existed in your army. May I ask your name, please?"

The Major offered an ironic smile at the backhanded compliment. "My name is Major Egon Krebbs, *Madame*."

"Well, it has been an unexpected pleasure to meet you, Major Krebbs. Please accept my thanks for your kindness."

The two women got back into the van and Major Krebbs leaned in towards the driver's side window.

"May I also offer you a word of warning, *Mesdames*? Please take great care around here over the next day or so. After what happened here yesterday and today, I fear that tomorrow will bring some unfortunate responses from my SS colleagues. If you are not planning to leave immediately, then I suggest that you stay indoors."

Yvette and Delphine looked at each other and then back at Major Krebbs.

"Might you not get in trouble for telling us such news Major?" asked Delphine.

Krebbs smiled. "Then I shall have to trust in your discretion, *Madame*."

He began to stand back from the car, then paused and leaned back in again. It seemed there was something he was desperate to tell them.

"Please understand *Madame*, not all German soldiers are SS. Not all Germans are Nazis. I can only wish… I wish…"

He could not finish the sentence.

He stood up and looked at both women with an unfathomable look in his eyes. He turned and walked back into the small crowd, which was still watching on curiously.

Yvette put the car into gear and started driving again. Apart from Delphine giving directions, they spent the next few minutes in thoughtful silence.

Bernard had given Delphine directions to the hotel owned by Paul and Marie Launay. He did not need to write them down; Delphine had an excellent memory.

They pulled up in front of the hotel. Apart from a number of people on bicycles, there was no other traffic on the street. Delphine got out and started knocking on the door as loudly as she could. Her knocking sounded like cannon fire in the largely deserted street.

After a minute, a woman came to the door. The two of them looked at each other through the glass panes.

"Can I help you, *Madame*?" asked the woman from the inside.

"I was hoping to see *Monsieur* Launay, *Madame*," replied Delphine.

"May I know who you are, please?"

Delphine put her head closer to the door and spoke quietly. "My name is Delphine Briand, *Madame*. We have come from Flavignac. This woman with me is Yvette. She is the wife of Lucien Morin."

The eyes of the woman inside the door flew wide open. She opened the door as quickly as she could after fumbling with the lock for a few moments.

"My name is Marie. I am Paul's wife. Please, come in quickly."

"What about the van?" asked Yvette.

"I will get one of our employees to drive it around the back. Please come in."

The two women grabbed the small leather bag with their changes of clothes and went inside.

Marie relocked the door and showed the two women through to the family kitchen where they had sat with Lucien, just two nights earlier, when the news of the invasion came through.

"Please, have a seat. Can I offer you a drink, or perhaps something to eat?"

Neither Yvette nor Delphine had eaten anything since breakfast. They were both hungry.

"If it's not too much to ask, a little food would be wonderful. Thank you very much," said Delphine.

Marie set about preparing the two women some food. She was trying to avoid making conversation for the moment. She knew of the situation with Lucien and she did not want to be the one to break the news to his wife.

She paused from her efforts in the kitchen for a moment. "May I have the keys to your car, please? I shall have one of my lads bring it around the back."

She left the room for a while and returned with a forced smile. Clearly, she was not yet comfortable with the presence of Delphine and Yvette in her home.

"It is being brought around now. I'm sure Paul will return shortly. He has gone out to check in on some of our... friends. Just to make sure they are safe. He's been gone most of the afternoon. I'm sure he won't be long." Yvette noticed she was repeating herself. She was clearly nervous.

Marie poured each of the women a glass of red wine and then returned to her food preparation.

To her undisguised relief, a few minutes later, Paul returned home through the back door.

"Ahh! My darling!" she exclaimed, "I have been so worried."

Paul could not help but notice Yvette and Delphine sitting at the table.

"*Bonsoir, Mesdames,*" he said, "I don't believe we have been introduced."

Marie had recovered her composure now that her husband was home.

"Paul, this is *Madame* Delphine Briand and her grand-daughter, *Madame* Yvette Morin."

Paul could not have been more shocked. "Good heavens! You must have travelled fast. I only sent Giles off last night. I presume you're here because he found you?"

"Yes, *Monsieur*," said Delphine. Yvette was too apprehensive to speak. "As soon as we heard the news about Lucien, we had to come. Can you tell us anything more?"

"Very little concerning how he is at the moment, *Madame*. But I can tell you both what happened."

Paul poured himself a glass of wine also, and sat down at the table with Yvette and Delphine.

Marie had finished preparing a platter with dried sausage and ham, cheeses, pickled onions and cornichons. She placed it in the middle of the table and gave everyone plates and cutlery.

They all began to help themselves to the food.

Paul began to tell the women everything that had happened since Lucien had arrived at the hotel two days earlier. He explained that, for

Lucien, it had merely been a very roundabout way of getting back to Flavignac, whilst helping a friend in Limoges. He had simply become caught up in events, after they had news of the invasion.

He told them how Lucien had stayed behind to provide covering fire as the others had fled. He was clearly moved by Lucien's bravery. He also told them of the state Lucien was in when the Germans carried him from the building, before they took him off into custody.

The women sat in silence as Paul told his story.

Yvette was the first to speak afterwards, "Thank you, *Monsieur*. Thank you for telling me everything."

Paul felt a small twinge inside. He had left out one important detail concerning a certain woman in Limoges, but he realised that no good could possibly come from passing on that particular piece of news.

"It is my honour, *Madame*. I wish I had some more information about how he is at the moment, but I do have to let you know though; a large SS Battalion has been arriving in town over the course of this afternoon."

"If they are to start interrogating him, with their methods... well... I fear for him."

Yvette's head fell forward into her hands and she began to sob.

7 June 1944: Tulle. Situation at Early Evening

The fighting around Tulle had not ended after the first street ambush. After fleeing the scene of the initial attacks, the various Maquis units had quickly found their way outside the city and immediately started to search out further opportunities to re-join the fight.

The savagery of their first attack had forced the Germans to retreat to their barracks. This emboldened the Resistance. Over the course of the remainder of the 6th of June, other Resistance units in the area quickly mobilised to join them. Very soon, their numbers were in the hundreds.

Organising themselves quickly, they moved back into town and commenced opportunistic assaults on any German troops they encountered in and around the city itself.

Surprising the Germans with the speed, ferocity and organisation of their attacks, the French Resistance fighters gained and held the early initiative in fighting on that first day.

Throughout the town and the surrounding countryside, many German units unexpectedly found themselves to be under fierce and sustained

Maquis attack. These assaults continued into the next day with the Germans taking heavy casualties, both in numbers killed and wounded, in addition to many troops being captured.

Their seized weapons were added promptly to the Maquis' stockpile of arms.

However, late on the 7th, the SS Units moving up from the south, began arriving in force and with their firepower, the momentum quickly swung back in favour of the Germans.

The SS descended on the city from three different directions. The Maquis quickly realised that these were very different types of soldiers now facing them. Forced to break off their attacks in the face of these remorseless troops, the Maquis went back into hiding.

Quickly enough, Tulle was secured once again and the Germans began to take stock.

The Maquis had hurt them. The SS were outraged that a rabble force of untrained Communist terrorists could dare to mount such attacks against them.

Attacks such as these could never be allowed to go unpunished. The time for retribution had arrived.

8 June 1944: Tulle. Early Morning

General Heinz Lammerding had now arrived in Tulle and after selecting a suitable building as his Head Quarters, immediately called a meeting of all available senior officers.

He was furious.

"By God! These bastards are going to pay! They are going to pay! If they want the gloves to come off, then so be it!"

The officers gathered around him stood silently. No one wanted to speak first.

Lammerding exhaled deeply. He allowed the emotion to pass. He replaced it with cold determination.

"All right then, gentlemen. They have had their moment of fun. Now it is our turn."

The others stiffened in their posture. They knew what was coming. All they needed to know was the magnitude of the response.

"We are going to round up every man in the town. Every man between sixteen and sixty! We are going to hang ten men for every one of ours they have killed! They are going to learn just what it is to take on the German army with acts of terrorism."

No one blinked. They had participated in mass hangings in the past. On the Eastern front, there had been instances when they had hung a thousand civilians. *Why should this large town in central France be any different?*

Lammerding looked around at the Officers assembled.

"Major Kowatsch, I am placing you in charge of the task. Organise your men. I want every man in Tulle rounded up and held. We will select from them who is to be punished."

Major Aurel Kowatsch came to rigid attention and nodded his assent.

"Yes sir. As you order!"

"You have my authority to conscript as many men as you require. Be thorough. Check every building if you have to, but be prompt. Do not waste a minute. I want these bastards on the end of a rope within twenty four hours."

"Yes, sir!" came the immediate reply.

"I am certain that you will need a large number of men. Conscript as much additional manpower as you require from any battalion that is available." He looked around the other commanders present. "Do you all understand this, gentlemen?"

Lammerding turned and looked at all the assembled officers.

No one dared speak out against him.

"Excellent! So then Major, as I said, gather all the manpower you need. Now then, go to it!"

Still at attention, Kowatsch extended his arm and saluted.

"Yes sir! Heil Hitler!"

He spun on his left heel and marched towards the door.

"Be thorough, Major!" exclaimed General Lammerding as he was leaving, "Don't let one of the bastards escape you!"

As he reached the door, Kowatsch turned and gave a rigid half bow towards the general.

"As you wish, General. Heil Hitler."

He left the room and closed the door behind him.

Once he was safely outside, he breathed in deeply and let out a long, slow exhalation. This was not the Eastern Front; these were not Russian peasants; this was France!

What had he just been ordered to do?

Lammerding turned to the other officers remaining in the room.

"Well, gentlemen, I have been receiving updates from Major Kampfe to the north-west of here. He is in the vicinity of a town called St Junien where there has been recent terrorist activity. He believes he has located a town near there where a terrorist cell is based. It is called…" he consulted a piece of paper, "Oradour-Sur-Glane."

He paused for a moment to collect his thoughts.

"I should like to have a demonstration made in this town. Make it quick. Make it hurt. Then we must get back to our main purpose. Our task is to get up to Normandy! We are needed at the front!"

"I want to be able to teach these damned terrorists a lesson they won't forget, but we need to do it quickly! We need to put this behind us and take our place fighting the Americans and the British."

Lammerding then turned directly to Diekmann.

"Major, I want you to prepare your battalion and be on your way as soon as possible. I want you to be in position to take directions from Major Kampfe. By now, he will have a good knowledge of the ground. I want you to teach that town a lesson it will never forget. Use whatever force you consider necessary. But get up there fast so you can be on hand to act!"

Diekmann promptly saluted and responded with "Heil Hitler".

He too, spun on his heel and left the room.

After he had gone, Lammerding spoke to the remaining officers.

"Well, gentlemen, I would like you to have your men at readiness to move at short notice. If Major Kampfe is correct, then we will be making another demonstration within the next two days. Major Diekmann will see to that. After that, however, we must be ready to start moving towards Normandy. Please prepare your battalions!"

Everyone stood to attention and saluted. A chorus of 'Heil Hitler' filled the room.

Major Diekmann searched out Captain Kahn and his other junior officers.

"Well, gentlemen, it appears we are being given a whole village to settle with. We are to move as soon as possible towards the north. We will form the battalion and move towards Limoges, then turn left and find a suitable place to wait until Major Kampfe completes his reconnaissance. It appears that he has uncovered which town is home to a nest of these Maquis vipers. Our task will be to clean out that nest"

Kahn, Barth and the other looked at each other in anticipation.

"Which town is it, Herr Major?" asked Lt Barth.

"Oradour… something," replied Diekmann, "I'll be given full details from the General shortly. Just remember what our tactics were back in the Ukraine, gentlemen. Why should these French be any different?"

The men looked around at each other. They had been waiting for a chance to take on the Maquis like this.

Diekmann added, "Ensure we are well stocked with demolition charges, incendiaries and grenades. As many as we can carry. It may turn out that we need to use them all."

They set to preparing their vehicles and their equipment. They would be moving out shortly.

***

Major Kowatsch followed through on his orders. It was an enormous task. Tulle was a large town, a major regional centre. A search of every building, to arrest every man between sixteen and sixty was not a task to be undertaken lightly. However, he had no option but to get underway.

He found a map of the city and sent word to have all his subordinate officers gather immediately.

Within a few minutes, these junior officers were present.

"All right, gentlemen, I have been ordered to undertake a mass round up of all male civilians in the city of Tulle. Everyone between the ages of sixteen and sixty! This is a large town. You have the general's permission to conscript any additional personnel you require from any outfit nearby."

"Now please, gather around the map. We will need to divide the town into sectors. Each of you will have the responsibility to completely comb your designated sector, and bring in every male in that age range."

There was initial silence in the room as everyone took in the enormity of the task.

"Where shall we bring them after they've been arrested, *Herr* Major?" asked someone.

The question caught Major Kowatsch short.

"I guess that is the first question we need to decide on. Does anyone have any suggestions?" he replied.

After a minute, one of the junior officers spoke up.

"There is a large open area in front of the Munitions Factory, near the river docks at Rigny. That would be perfect."

"I'm not familiar with the township," replied Kowatsch. "Can anyone else endorse this place?"

One or two other voices spoke up.

"I am familiar with the place, *Herr* Major," said a captain, "I think it's an excellent suggestion. It is all very securely fenced, so no one can escape easily, and there is lots of space to hold a large number of men. I think it would be an excellent choice."

"Very well then! It's decided," replied Kowatsch. "Now then, let's get to working out which sectors of the city we each cover, and how many men we will need. Come on now, gentlemen, General Lammerding is demanding action."

Once it was underway, the round up took on an inexorable life of its own.

No house, no workplace, no habitation of any sort was spared. No warnings were given, no doors were politely knocked on.

The Germans simply let themselves in or broke doors down. Extra troops patrolled back lanes to capture anyone trying to slip away from the rear of buildings.

As the roundup of men proceeded, the women and children left behind were told that it was a simple identity check. There was no need to worry. Nothing needed to be packed or prepared. Their men-folk were to be returned to them presently.

Eventually, the net brought in nearly five thousand men and older boys.

The next problem immediately presented itself. *How to go about selecting those for execution?*

Chapter 12

9 June 1944: Tulle, Morning

The Mayor of Tulle and other officials had been desperately negotiating with the Germans all night.

It soon came to light that, at the height of the fighting, a number of residents of Tulle had rushed to the aid of wounded German soldiers. Their quick intervention had thus saved many helpless soldiers from summary execution by the Maquis.

The Mayor and the town Prefect had used this news to extract certain concessions from the Germans.

The SS allowed them to go through the thousands of detained men and point out those who they were certain had not been involved in the attacks. Men who were vital to the continued running of the town's services.

This ultimately led to the release of nearly thirty-five hundred of the prisoners. A remarkable achievement, but one that still left over fifteen hundred men held in custody.

In a further development, the Germans had softened on the numbers of men who to be executed. Instead of ten citizens for every German casualty, they had brought the number down to three.

The Mayor, however, had not only pointed out the innocent; he had also surreptitiously indicated to the Germans those who he believed *had* been involved in the uprising.

These men were promptly removed for further interrogation. Several dozen men in total were thus given over. Their fates were sealed.

The Mayor and the other officials were then escorted away to see to the safe release of those whose freedom they had secured. This left the Germans alone, in charge of the next round of selections.

To choose those who were to die.

***

The second round of selections began immediately after the local Tulle officials had departed.

The remaining men could only look on helplessly as several German officials made their way around the assemble captives, and decided who was to be chosen. Their decisions were arbitrary.

There was little or no real evidence available to lay against any one of the captives. The choice came down to the caprice of the chooser.

In the end, the Germans selected a total of one hundred and twenty men whose fate it was to be hung. A further one hundred and fifty or so were chosen for deportation to Germany.

There were concentration camps waiting to receive the likes of them.

9 June 1944: Tulle. 2:00 P.M.
Morning had passed into afternoon and the SS had been busy.

Scores of troops had been pressed into preparing impromptu gallows, starting in the town square and then fanning out along the roads radiating outwards from there.

Any location capable of conversion into makeshift gallows was utilised.

Nooses were set in trees, from lampposts, in tall doorways. Anywhere strong enough to carry the weight of a man and high enough to be visible to the townsfolk.

Ladders had been set at the base of each gallows. Two German soldiers were stationed at each one.

Back at the Munitions Factory, the condemned were selected into groups of ten.

Arms tied behind their backs; the first group marched away from the Munitions Factory under heavy guard. As they drew closer the Town Square and saw what awaited them, the group spontaneously stopped walking, mouths agape at the sudden realisation of their fates.

Their SS captors started to lay into them with their rifle butts. No show of resistance, no matter how slight, would be tolerated. They had done this to thousands of others on the Eastern Front. They had mastered the techniques of mass control through violence.

The victims were led, sometimes dragged, to their own appointed gallows and forced to climb the ladders.

The nooses were placed around their necks, and tightened. Then the ladders were kicked out from underneath them.

The next group of ten followed shortly after the first. Seeing the sight that greeted them, their immediate reaction was more desperate than the first. The response of the SS guards though, was no less brutal and the outcome, no less certain.

On and on it went.

One group of ten after another.

A few, a very fortunate few, had their necks break in the initial fall. For them, the passing was quick. Most though, were not so lucky. They dangled, choking and kicking in agony, at the end of the ropes.

For some, a German guard might have the compassion to grab them by the legs and wrench them downwards, breaking their neck and completing the process. Others though, were ignored, left alone to strangle slowly. Others still, suffered capricious, callous abuses; being kicked, punched and spat on as they swung.

A tenth group had been assembled. As they were made ready to begin their march to the gallows, someone stepped forward.

A local priest, Father Jean Espinasse had been keeping count of the men as they filed past him on their march to the gallows.

A quick count of the tenth group showed that it held thirteen men, not the agreed number of ten.

Father Espinasse confronted the officer in charge of preparing the groups.

"This is too many! You agreed that there would be no more than ten in any one group. You must let me remove several of these men."

Immediately, Father Espinasse stepped forward and took four men from the rear of the group, reducing its number to only nine.

The Germans, watching on, were too bemused by his actions to respond.

Retaining his place in the remaining nine, was Paul Launay.

The Germans had arrested him as they made their rounds of homes and businesses the previous day. His wife Marie had been frantic with terror as they took him away at gunpoint.

Yvette and Delphine had been up in a room that Paul had offered them for the night.

The sounds of Marie's distress had brought them both downstairs, just as Paul was being led away.

He had given his wife the most positive smile he could manage, as he was marshalled out of his home in front of the three women. He knew then that he was unlikely to ever see it, or them, again.

Somehow though, the Mayor had not selected him as being a member of the Maquis, even though he knew the Mayor must have had strong suspicions. He had begun to hope his luck might hold.

It didn't. He became one of those randomly selected, as the Germans made their own choices as to who should face the gallows.

Paul, along with the other eight, had his hands tied behind his back. They and their German guards walked the same path trod by the groups that preceded them. Paul looked about constantly, taking in for the last time, the sights of the beautiful medieval town that had been home for his entire life.

He had accurately guessed, as had the others, what now awaited them. They had heard no sounds of gunfire, so they knew it was not to be a firing squad.

That left hanging.

That also explained the small groups. Easier for the guards to manage.

There were no gallows left in the town square. Paul's group was led to a line of trees along an avenue he had always loved. Ropes had been strung from them, with a ladder and guards awaiting each man.

Several of his comrades fought back and tried to escape, only to be viciously beaten with the butts of the rifles held by their captors.

He was no less terrified than any of his friends, but Paul was determined to face this as bravely as he could. He was a Resistance leader. He would resist up to the end.

He climbed the ladder at his appointed gallows and stood still as one of the guards climbed up behind him. The guard reached over Paul's shoulder to take the noose and place it around his neck. The German tightened the noose but left the large knot directly at the back of Paul's neck.

Paul knew what this would mean. His neck would not break. His windpipe would be crushed and he would slowly strangle to death in agony.

He weakened.

He turned his head towards the German guard and whispered to him.

"Please, *mein freund*. Please move the knot to the side."

The guard looked into Paul's eyes and somehow found the compassion to do so.

As the guard retreated down the ladder, Paul began to take the final steps up to the very top.

He was still mid-stride on the last rung when the ladder was kicked out from underneath him.

His awkward fall only exacerbated the action of the now, well-placed knot.

His neck broke instantly as the rope arrested his fall. His death was as quick and as clean as he could have dared wish.

***

After the intervention of Father Espinasse, no further groups were led away to be hung. Thus, in an entirely arbitrary act, the number of those executed was left to stand at ninety-nine.

For the twenty-one men spared the gallows, however, it was merely punishment delayed, not salvation.

They were included with the other group, whose fate was to be a transfer to Germany, and on to eventual incarceration at the Dachau Concentration Camp.

Most would never get to see their homes again.

9 June 1944: Tulle. Earlier in the Day

Lucien was still lying on the same stretcher he had been left on for over two days. It was now caked in the blood that had been seeping from his wounds the entire time.

Flies hovered noisily around him, as he lay in a state of near complete unconsciousness.

So close was he to death that even his guard no longer bothered to remain nearby, simply coming to check on him on an irregular basis.

His skin was starkly pallid and the smell of putrefying blood was everywhere in his small cell.

Major Krebbs had looked in on him earlier in the morning but could see that there was nothing further that could be done for him.

Somehow though, Lucien's eyes opened once more as a moment of consciousness returned to him.

He lay there, thinking with a clarity that had eluded him since the grenade had exploded so close by.

His thoughts now were simple; they were of Yvette and Angeline.

How he wished he could see them both again. Just to thank each of them.

He wanted to thank Yvette for being such a good wife to him, when had been able to offer her so little as a husband.

Especially, to Angeline for reawakening in him so much that he had thought was lost forever. The thought crossed his mind that despite everything, he had been a far luckier man that he had ever realised.

He had known the love of not one, but two extraordinary women.

Presently, he found himself wishing that Yvette had indeed found a new love in Daniel. The thought of her discovering the complete happiness that he been unable to provide, suddenly became the only thing that mattered to him in that moment.

Eventually, he allowed himself to believe that she had indeed found that love. He was sure of it. The reassuring thought stayed with him… and then drifted away.

His guard came in shortly afterwards to check on him.

He could see immediately that Lucien had died. It was strange though, his eyes were open and he appeared to be smiling.

9 June 1944: Paul and Marie Launay's Hotel. Late Afternoon
Marie Launay was inconsolable.

She had just heard the news that Paul was among the executed in the town centre.

Delphine and Yvette both held her, as she wept uncontrollably in the middle of the kitchen. They could offer no words of comfort that did not sound trite. All they could provide was the simple warmth of their physical presence.

After several minutes, they were able to lead her to a chair at the table where she sat with her face buried in her hands.

Yvette found a clean tea towel and offered it to her.

Meanwhile, Delphine began searching the cupboards until she found what she was looking for. A bottle of Cognac.

She poured a generous serve into a glass and gave it to Marie.

"Here, my dear. Drink this. It will help."

Delphine then poured smaller serves for herself and Yvette. The alcohol might help them as well.

Their own concerns continued to haunt them. Neither had any idea concerning the situation with Lucien. Not many people in Tulle knew him. If he was one of the hanging victims, there was no one likely to recognise him. Even if they did, nobody knew that Delphine and Yvette were in town and waiting for any news of his fate.

There was no alternative. They would have to go out into the town centre and confront the sight of the executed men. They had to see for themselves.

The thought made both women recoil in horror.

Yvette looked at Delphine. Her grandmother was now in her 80s, and yet she still possessed such strength of both character and constitution. *Would that be enough to help her face this?*

Yvette looked inwards and wondered whether she could get through it herself. Especially if one of the bodies was indeed that of Lucien.

She steeled herself and looked at her grandmother. They owed it to Lucien. They had to know what had become of him.

After what seemed an age, there was a gentle knocking at the back door of the hotel. It was a small group of women, friends of Marie. They had heard the terrible news and had come around to be with her. They all thanked Delphine and Yvette for their kindness and then took over the task of offering such solace as they could, to their deeply grieving friend.

Delphine and Yvette caught each other's eye. "We have to go and look *Mamie*. Don't we?" asked Yvette.

Delphine could only nod.

They had already packed the few clothes they had brought with them in a small valise.

They went over to where Marie sat, and each kissed her on the head as she continued to weep.

The both smiled weakly at the group of women, and left the room through the back door.

Bernard's little Peugeot van was parked nearby. Yvette took her place behind the wheel as Delphine slipped in beside her.

They both looked at each other again, and Yvette started the engine.

They approached the town centre down a tree-lined avenue, only to be greeted by the confronting sight of the first dangling corpses.

Both of them involuntarily gasped and put their hands over their mouths as they recognised Paul. His body hanging limp, his head at a grotesque angle.

Yvette had to stop the car. She could not drive any further. The scene was shocking, a cruelty beyond their understanding.

She and Delphine got out of the car and, supporting each other, began to make their way along the line of hanged men.

The Germans had made sure that the spectacle would be as profoundly distressing as possible.

Slowly, the two women made their way past every single one of the ninety nine corpses arranged around the city centre.

None of them was Lucien. *Was this good news? Where could he be?*

Each lost in their thoughts; they found their way back to the car. This time they avoided looking at the bodies as they passed them. None was Lucien. No matter how distressing the sight, that thought at least, was a comfort.

Once they were back in the Peugeot, Yvette looked at her grandmother and said, "We have to go to the German Head Quarters. They will surely know."

Delphine looked at her as if she had gone mad.

"You can't be serious! They would probably arrest us as being accomplices. Even if they didn't, they would not tell us anything."

"I don't see any other choice, *Mamie*. Otherwise, we may never know. You can stay in the car if you choose. I'll leave the key with you. But I have to go in and ask."

Yvette had a steeliness about her, to which Delphine had to concede. She had made up her mind.

The German barracks were only a few minutes' drive away.

There was a heavy presence of large vehicles and well-armed guards around the building. They had no choice but to park some distance away, and walk back.

Delphine had accepted that she needed to go in with Yvette. Waiting alone in the car would have been intolerable for her.

The two women got out of the car and composed themselves. Linking their arms, they set off, making their way towards the large building that garrisoned the regular German *Wehrmacht* forces in Tulle.

They were surprised at how easily they gained admission to the building. Two armed guards stood either side of the main door, but neither challenged them. Once inside, there was a desk where a corporal sat. It was clear that this was the reception area.

Taking a deep breath, Yvette started towards the desk. She had travelled no more than a couple of paces though, when a voice called out to her.

"Good evening, *Mesdames*. I was upstairs and saw you both coming."

It was the German Major from the day before.

"Good evening, Major…" began Yvette.

"Krebbs, *Madame*."

"Yes, of course. Thank you. Good evening, Major Krebbs."

Delphine quickly joined them. "Good evening, Major."

Krebbs smiled at them both. "And how may I be of assistance ladies? It is not often we get visitors here. Not through choice anyway," he added wryly.

Faced with actually having to ask the question, Yvette nearly lost her voice. Delphine stepped in and spoke.

"We are hoping that you might be able to give us some information about someone who we believe was captured by your comrades during the fighting a few days ago."

Major Krebbs raised his eyebrow in surprise. Seldom were people quite so blunt in asking questions such as this.

"I was involved in that fighting myself. I lost a few friends. You have taken quite a risk coming here and asking such questions, Madame. What is this person to you?"

"He is the husband of my granddaughter!" Delphine looked at Yvette who still had the false pregnancy bulge under her dress.

Major Krebbs looked at Yvette again and slowly nodded.

"When was the last time you saw him, please?"

"Actually, we haven't seen him for weeks. He disappeared some time ago," said Delphine.

Krebbs looked at Yvette. "Is this true, *Madame*?"

"Yes Major. We had no idea where he was. Then a friend got word to us that he had come to Tulle and was caught up in the fighting."

"I see. How do you know he was captured, *Madame*? Perhaps he has just vanished into the night along with the other Maquis. Perhaps he is among those who was hung today?"

"He wasn't, *Monsieur*! We have been and checked. He isn't one of the dead," said Yvette.

"Are you certain he was captured, *Madame*? How can you be so sure?"

Yvette looked at Delphine. She would have to tell Major Krebbs more than she wished. She was beginning to realise what a terrible mistake coming here may have been.

"We had heard that he had been wounded and brought here, *Monsieur*!" Yvette blurted out.

"Really?" asked Major Krebbs. "Would you be so kind as to tell me his name?"

Yvette swallowed hard. "His name is Lucien Morin."

Krebbs looked at both women in amazement.

"Would you please both come with me, *Mesdames*? I would like to talk with you in a more private setting."

Krebbs led the two women up a flight of stairs to his office on the first floor. It looked out over the front entrance of the building.

Yvette realised he must have been in here when he saw them approaching.

Krebbs offered seats to both women as soon as he had closed the door behind him.

He then went behind his desk and sat down in his leather chair.

He looked intently at both women for several seconds before speaking.

"Do you realise the enormous risk you have taken in coming here and asking such questions? It should be my duty now to arrest you both. You have just admitted to being very close associates of a known Maquis terrorist!"

Yvette broke out in a cold sweat. What had she got Delphine and herself into?

Krebbs sat back in his seat for a moment before leaning forward again.

He looked at Yvette. "I wasn't lying when I said that I had lost friends in the attack that you husband was a part of, Madame. The Maquis ambushed us, right here in town!"

Krebbs took a deep breath and let out a long sigh.

"For better or worse, the SS have exacted a terrible revenge upon this town today. I have seen quite enough death for one lifetime, I can assure you."

He looked steadily at both women and then made up his mind.

"I am afraid that I have to tell you some sad news. Lucien passed way this morning, here in this building."

Both women gasped in shock. Yvette slumped in her chair.

"I had spent some time with him after he was brought in. I had tried to interrogate him, but he was too badly wounded to tell me much. I assure you, I merely asked him questions, no more."

Delphine asked in a weak voice, "Would it be possible to see him?"

The Major shook his head. "That would be most inadvisable, *Madame*. Too many people here would see you, and you would most certainly then be detained. As it is, I am very much in two minds as to what to do now. It is certainly my duty to have you both arrested immediately."

He paused and smiled.

"I have no desire to do that. There has been quite enough suffering in Tulle for one day."

"I do have one question for you both though; Lucien told me that he came from a place called 'Oradour'. Would you please be so kind as to enlighten me as to which one?"

Yvette and Delphine looked blankly at each other and then at the Major.

"We don't live in any 'Oradour' *Monsieur*," said Delphine, "we live on a farm outside Flavignac. Perhaps he was just trying to protect us."

"That would seem most likely, *Madame*," said Krebbs, "it does rather solve the riddle. I do have to say though, that I am glad neither of you will be involved. Any town with the name 'Oradour' in it is probably a good place to avoid over the next few days."

He did not elaborate any further. They had the feeling that he had spoken an unguarded thought. The two women looked at each other. Perhaps the Major might also have been offering them a hint of... something?

He broke the moment and brought them back to the current situation immediately.

"Now *Mesdames*, I beg of you, please don't make me regret what I am about to do next. I am going to give you a pass that will get you out of the city of Tulle. It will be under my signature. I trust you will use it to go directly to your home and remain there. Please say 'yes' before I change my mind."

Delphine nodded vigorously. "Of course, Major. We will go straight home."

"Good! I trust that your vehicle contains nothing that will cause either of us any difficulties?"

"No, *Monsieur*. Nothing I swear!" replied Delphine.

"Very well then."

Krebbs took out a large pad of printed forms and tore the topmost off. He spent a minute filling it out and signing it. Then he took a rubber stamp and embossed the document.

He looked at it for a moment before handing it over to Delphine.

Yvette was still sitting silently in her chair, trying to process the news about Lucien's death.

She looked up. "Did he suffer, *Monsieur*? Lucien?"

Krebbs answered as honestly as he could. "He would have been in considerable pain, *Madame*. I have no doubt. I am sorry. I wish I could say otherwise."

Yvette nodded. "Lucien chose his own path, *Monsieur*. I thank you for your compassion. You are a rare man, Major. I'm glad it was you who was with him. You might not have been a friend, but somehow, I struggle to see you as an enemy."

For a moment, Major Krebbs could not speak. He was a soldier certainly, but he had always tried to be a decent man as well. Not an easy task with the world as it was.

"Thank you, *Madame*. Now it is best that you both be on your way. It is late in the day and you have some driving ahead of you. *Bonne chance*!"

All three stood up and Major Krebbs came around from behind his desk. Yvette went up to him and kissed him on the cheek.

"Honestly, *Madame*! Now I won't be able to sleep tonight!" said Krebbs with a warm smile.

Delphine reached out and shook Major Krebbs' hand.

"Please accept my best wishes, Major. I sincerely hope you are able to return to your own home one day. After the war, Germany will need such men as you. Heaven knows, the whole world will."

Major Krebbs led the women out of his office and down the stairs to the foyer. He watched them as they made their way back towards their van. Then he returned to his office and sat for a while, lost in his thoughts. He realised that he had let slip more than he should when he told the women about Lucien's mention of a town called Oradour.

It occurred to him now that since Lucien's use of that name was simply a ruse to divert attention away from where his family really lived, he should pass that on immediately.

He was well aware of the methods of the SS.

If they believed that there was appropriate cause, they could exact a retribution upon a whole town that would be cataclysmic.

He rang down to the switchboard and asked to speak to Major Kampfe.

"I am sorry, *Herr* Major," came the reply, "Major Kampfe cannot be contacted at the moment. He has left with his battalion on a manoeuvre to the north."

"Can you tell me who his superior officer is? asked Krebbs.

"I believe it is a Colonel Stadtler, *Herr* Major." came the reply.

"Can you please put me in touch with him?"

"Yes sir."

Krebbs waited whilst the call was connected. After a minute came the response.

"Stadtler here."

"Good evening, *Herr* Colonel. Please forgive the intrusion. My name is Major Krebbs. I am an officer at the garrison in Tulle."

"Please go on," replied Stadtler tersely.

"Well Colonel, I have been working with Major Kampfe of your Regiment. He believes we may have had a lead as to the location of a Maquis cell to the north-west of here. I believe he may be on a reconnaissance sortie to investigate that lead."

"Yes, that is indeed what is happening. How can I help with regard to this?" asked Stadtler.

"Well sir, I now believe that it is likely be a false lead. I think the name of the town may have been given to us as a deliberate red herring."

"And what is it that makes you think this, Herr Major?"

"Well sir, I believe the man, when being questioned, told us the name of a town well away from where he really lived. In order to protect his family from retribution."

"That is an interesting possibility, *Herr* Major, but one that is no longer relevant. We now have men in force in the area near that town. I can let you know that there has been serious Maquis activity there as recently as today. They have just blown up a bridge and killed at least two German troops."

Krebbs inhaled reflexively in surprise.

Stadtler continued, "So you see, *Herr* Major. Even if it was not his intention, the name of the town he gave us has proven to be very much the centre of an active terrorist cell. I thank you for contacting me but I can assure you, we have a response plan to this attack and it shall be implemented very shortly. Good night, *Herr* Major."

"Thank you, *Herr* Colonel. Heil Hitler," replied Krebbs.

"Heil Hitler," came the abrupt reply.

Krebbs put down the phone and sat back in his chair.

That was most unexpected news. He could not believe that Lucien would sell out another cell, even if his family were the motivation. He did not seem the type.

It must simply to be one of the strange coincidences of timing that can occur in a war. There were Maquis cells all over France. They were all starting to become active since the invasion.

Just a simple coincidence.

***

Yvette and Delphine had got into the Peugeot and, without a word, started the motor, turned the vehicle around, and left Tulle behind them.

Major Krebbs' official pass saw them through two checkpoints and safely on their way home.

Both remained silent for the greater part of the journey. They were each so lost in their thoughts that neither of them felt much like conversation.

Night had fallen before they were even half way. They encountered no other traffic on this rural road. The Germans were using the main road to Limoges, further to the east.

The occasional badger or deer was all that they saw, as the road brought them closer to home.

By the time they arrived back at the farm, it was nearly ten p.m.

Neither Bernard nor Daniel had gone to bed. Both men had spent the last days worrying. They were deeply relieved at the sound of the approaching Peugeot.

Bernard went to the passenger's side and embraced his wife as she got out of the car.

Daniel waited with some trepidation as Yvette slowly emerged from behind the wheel.

She stood and looked at him for a few seconds before she completely dissolved into tears and fell into his arms.

She had fought hard to suppress the torrent of emotions that had been eating away at her as the events of the last few days had unfolded.

Now it had all become too much.

Daniel had to carry her inside. She had become too emotionally exhausted to walk.

Bernard supported Delphine as they entered the house together.

Daniel placed Yvette down on the lounge so he could sit beside her.

Delphine sat in one of the armchairs as she tried to compose herself. It would be up to her to tell the men of the horrific events that they had witnessed in Tulle.

Bernard produced a bottle of Armagnac and poured out four generous serves.

Yvette had now stopped crying and was slowly regathering her composure. Now she just lay still on the lounge with her head resting on Daniel's lap.

Delphine took a sip of the spirit and looked at Bernard and then at Daniel.

She began to tell them of what they had seen.

The men sat, listening in horror as the tale unfolded. Neither had believed that so-called civilised men could be capable of such despicable, inhuman behaviour.

This was not war.

It was not even murder.

Perhaps there was not even a word for it.

Yvette just lay there, staring blankly ahead as Delphine continued.

Finally, as her grandmother told the story of what had happened to Lucien, she closed her eyes, and began to weep quietly again.

Eventually, Delphine had exhausted herself of all detail. She fell back into the chair, closed her eyes and began to rub her temples. She was far too exhausted to think any more.

The last twenty-four hours had shown her horrors that she could never have imagined.

Bernard sat thoughtfully before he spoke.

"I can't understand what has happened to Germany. To the German people. They were not like this in the last war. Lucien would have vouched for that. They were the enemy, yes, but they fought honourably. What is so different now, to make a people become like this? Do the ordinary people in Germany know that their soldiers are doing things like this? I just don't understand…"

Finally, Bernard stood up and went over to Delphine. "Come, my darling. You need to sleep. We can talk more in the morning."

Daniel looked down at Yvette. She had fallen asleep where she lay. The mind-numbing events of the last few days had finally taken their toll.

Bernard and Daniel exchanged tired smiles, as he led Delphine away to their bedroom. Bernard reappeared shortly after and asked Daniel what he wanted to do.

Daniel responded, "I think we'll just stay right here if you don't mind. She's finally asleep. I can't bring myself to wake her again. Would you be so kind as to turn off the light?"

Bernard did so, and retired to his bedroom. Daniel arranged a cushion behind his head and hoped that sleep would soon come to him as well, even though his mind struggled with the horror of the events Delphine had recounted. Eventually, somehow, sleep managed to find him.

It was now slightly after midnight. The clock had ticked over to the 10th of June.

.

Chapter 13

9 June 1944: St Junien – The Situation at the End of the Day

The first units of Major Diekmann's Battalion had begun arriving in St Junien late the previous day.

Alongside elements of Major Kampfe's Reconnaissance Battalion, they began to set up a bivouac in the surrounding fields. The officers though, promptly helped themselves to any accommodation to which they took a liking, within the town itself.

As men and vehicles continued to arrive, they quickly stretched the limits of the town and the fields beyond.

Soon, there was no choice but to send the overflow of incoming troops to another town, Rochechouart, a further ten kilometres to the south-west.

The SS troops, as they wandered around St Junien made little attempt to hide their contempt for the local residents.

Several incidents occurred throughout the day. Spontaneous, unprovoked attacks by SS troops, against anyone who had the simple misfortune to encounter them, were commonplace.

In Rochechouart, the situation was even worse.

German troops started firing on farmers working in the fields. One elderly woman was shot and killed as she made her way home from shopping at the local market.

SS officers did little to reign in the behaviour of their men.

On the morning of the 9th, Major Diekmann sought out Kampfe's temporary Command Post. He was keen to catch up with his friend, and get an up-to-date briefing on what Kampfe had been able to learn thus far.

He approached a sergeant who appeared to be the most senior soldier present.

"I am sorry, *Herr* Major, but Major Kampfe is not here. He has gone out scouting to the north of Oradour-Sur-Glane," said the sergeant.

"He left early this morning. I believe by now he will be north of the town. I don't know how long he is intending to be."

Diekmann looked concerned. "Did he go on his own? Did he not take additional troops with him?"

"He went in the *Kubelwagen, Herr* Major. Just himself and a driver. I believe he wanted to be able to move quickly and not raise too much attention," said the sergeant.

This news left Diekmann feeling deeply unsettled. A senior German officer, moving alone in this area would be taking a tremendous risk. Still, Kampfe was very experienced. He would have been aware of the risk and had obviously dismissed it. Diekmann had no option but to trust in his friend's judgement and wait for his return.

He left the Command Post and returned to his own bivouac on the edge of the town. With much to ponder, he was still undecided as to what extent and form their action against the town of Oradour-Sur-Glane would take.

Then, late in the day, two visitors arrived at the German Command Post. They brought with them news which changed everything.

They were pro-Nazi, French informers; members of a group called the Milice.

Their news had the Command Post scurrying to summon Major Diekmann urgently.

The Milice were an underground organisation, loyal to the French Vichy government. Pro-fascist, they had proven themselves instrumental many times in helping infiltrate and break down Maquis cells. Clearly, they had their agents at work here as well.

Diekmann arrived soon after, demanding to know what was so important that his evening drinks with his junior officers had been disturbed.

A corporal saluted and said, "I believe you will wish to hear this, *Herr* Major!"

The two Milice informants were immediately brought before Diekmann.

"Who are you? What have you to tell me?"

"Good evening, sir," said one, "I have some news concerning Major Kampfe. I have to report that he has been captured, and is being held by local terrorist Maquis to the north of here."

Diekmann inhaled sharply! "The hell with them! The bastards! Where are they holding him?"

"We don't know for certain, sir. It's possible that he is being held not far from here, possibly somewhere between here and Oradour-Sur-Glane."

That town again! thought Diekmann.

"Another thing, sir," said the informer, "there are rumours that the Maquis intend to set fire to him and burn him alive tomorrow, as a demonstration to the SS."

Diekmann stood there, unmoving, for several seconds, processing this ghastly news.

Kampfe was a good friend. Diekmann felt a wave of horror wash over him. An uncontrollable fury immediately set a fire within him. It burned as never before.

The Maquis had pushed too hard, they had just made it personal.

Diekmann now knew what form the retribution would take the following day.

Tersely, he thanked and dismissed the Milice informers and went back to meet with his officers. He wanted to sit with Heinz Barth and the others, and get drunk.

He needed to drink, to simmer in his fury… and to plan.

***

10 June 1944: Near Flavignac, Morin Farm. 6:15 A.M.

Yvette woke from her sleep with a start. She still lay on the couch with her head on Daniel's lap. He was snoring, uncomfortably propped up, using a cushion as a pillow.

It took several moments for her to process her surroundings. She sat up and looked at Daniel. Her movement had awakened him also.

He rubbed his neck as he awakened, squinting in discomfort from his awkward sleeping position.

For the first time in days, Yvette smiled. A wan smile, but a smile none the less.

"How are you, Yvette?" asked Daniel with some hesitancy.

She leant her head against his shoulder. "I'm OK. I am with you. I will be all right."

Daniel smiled also, a wave of relief finally unburdening the emotional baggage he had carried for the last two days. He was worried that he had lost her.

"You didn't speak at all last night. I've never felt so concerned for anyone in my life."

"I know," replied Yvette softly, "I still don't think I can speak about it. Maybe someday. Not now."

Daniel nodded. He wanted to speak but could not find any words. He just held her. To his immense relief, she responded and hugged him back. More tightly than she had in a while.

The pathway back to finding her inner peace might be long, but he had resolved to be there, to help guide her along it.

They both understood that the way forward was clear for them now, but it was not the time to talk about it. Lucien deserved at least that much respect.

Eventually, Yvette released him and stood up.

"It's not the most romantic thing I will ever say, but it's been a long time since I've been to the lavatory. You must excuse me!"

Her sense of humour was returning. Daniel chuckled in relief as she left the room.

Shortly after, Delphine appeared from the bedroom, still tying the cord on her dressing gown.

"I've just had a thought, something that the German Major said. It seemed like he let it slip by accident. Now, I'm not so sure."

Daniel looked at her attentively. "What was it he said?"

"He said something about any town called Oradour would be a good place to stay away from over the next few days."

Yvette returned from the lavatory as she was speaking.

"That's right. That had slipped my mind. What do you suppose he meant?" she asked.

Bernard emerged from the bedroom and wandered through, into the kitchen. He filled the kettle and lit the gas burner.

He called out from the kitchen, "If no-one is prepared to start making the tea, then it looks like it will have to be me!"

Delphine chuckled. "You poor old man! You make it better than I do!"

Kettle on the hob, Bernard joined them in the lounge room. "Now what was that you were talking about a moment ago?"

Delphine looked at him. "The Major mentioned something quite disturbing about a place called Oradour. It sounded like something bad going to happen there very soon."

"How would he know that? I thought you said he seemed like a very decent man, for a German!"

Delphine smiled. "He is a decent man! He said that Lucien had told them that he came from a place called Oradour. Most likely trying to protect us by giving the name of a different town to where he really lived."

Daniel spoke up, "I have been to a place called Oradour; Oradour-Sur-Veyres. I walked back here from there, in fact. In the rain! It's how I got sick. Do you think that's the place they're looking for?"

Bernard pondered the thought. "I doubt it. That town is to the west from here. The Germans will be wanting to move more to the north. That way, they'll be in the right direction to keep on going up to Normandy. There is another town of that name up there." He thought for a moment. "Oradour-Sur-Glane! That's the name, that must be the place."

Yvette suddenly felt a chill run through her entire body. "What could they be planning? Surely, what they did in Tulle is enough, isn't it? Surely, they can't plan to do anything more!"

Daniel had a sinking feeling. "If the SS think there is a major Maquis cell based in Oradour-Sur-Glane, and they can easily go through it as they head north…" He left the sentence hanging.

The mood had suddenly become very bleak again.

"What can we do?" asked Delphine. "Can someone go up there and warn them?"

"It might already be too late," said Bernard, "I shall turn on the radio. Perhaps there might be some news."

Bernard waited while the radio's valves warmed up. He then began to scan the radio stations he could receive. The most likely broadcast came from Limoges, but the Vichy government controlled its content and censored it heavily.

He tried the BBC, which was now constantly broadcasting to occupied Europe. However, it did not even mention the massacre at Tulle. Between the Germans and Vichy, news of that horror had been effectively suppressed thus far. All that came through from England was news of how the invasion was progressing.

Bernard left the radio on, but turned the volume down.

"So what do we do then?" he asked, "Do we continue to just sit here?"

Daniel had already decided. "If you would be so kind as to lend me your car, I will go. I have to!"

Yvette screamed in protest. "No! Not you! I forbid it! Not you too!"

She hurled herself at him and held him as if he might simply disappear. She had already suffered as much loss as she could cope with. She could not lose Daniel as well.

Bernard and Delphine stood there in shock. They had never before seen their granddaughter react like this.

Daniel took her by the shoulders, "I have said it in the past. I am a serving soldier! It is my duty to go. I swear to you, I will be careful." He looked into her eyes. "Besides, I have too much to live for now, to take unnecessary risks."

"Why can't we just find a telephone and ring someone there?" said Yvette. "Surely that would be the easiest thing."

Daniel shook his head. "That was my first thought. The call would have to go through the switchboard in Limoges. Since the invasion, the Germans will be monitoring all calls, even more closely than before. It's more than likely a phone call would just alert any SS units near Oradour-Sur-Glane to act immediately. Even worse though, it would also tip them off to Bernard and Delphine. They would undoubtedly send a patrol here to arrest them… and you! I'd rather try to get there by car. It's the safest choice!"

Yvette suddenly regained her composure. Her posture, as she sat, became erect.

"In that case, I shall go with you," she said simply.

Daniel, Bernard and Delphine, all stood there with their mouths agape.

Despite the tension, Yvette suddenly laughed at the sight. "You look like a school of goldfish! There is no debate to be had here," she continued, looking serious again. "I will go with you. I can be useful. I still have my pass from Major Krebbs. It is valid for twenty four hours and dated from yesterday evening. It is still fine to use."

Daniel wanted to say no, but he wanted, still more, to be with her. He nodded his head in agreement.

"Well, if you are both to go, then you shall need to get moving. I shall get you both something to eat on the way," said Delphine.

"Aren't you going to try and stop her?" asked Daniel.

Delphine replied, "No, not at all. In fact, I agree with her. She needs to be with you. I know how useful she can be. Also, her presence may stop you from doing something rash!"

Daniel shrugged. "Then it's decided. Let's start getting ready."

"I shall go and fill up the car," said Bernard. He took the keys out to the Peugeot, drove it into the barn and set about filling it again from his supply of petrol, also topping up the radiator.

Once he had finished, he parked it again in front of the house.

Meanwhile, Delphine had prepared a small picnic hamper in case they got hungry. Yvette and Daniel had readied themselves quickly.

Whilst Yvette and Delphine had been in Tulle, Daniel had brought up some of his supplies from the other farm. He had also been into the armaments cache, concealed in the old derelict shed at the back of the Briand farm.

He knew he could not carry much, in case they were stopped and searched. He slipped a magazine fed pistol up behind the dashboard of the Peugeot, loosely held in place by the car's instrumentation wires. It would rattle as they drove and might even damage a wire or two, but it would make no noise if the car were stationary at a checkpoint.

Most importantly though, it would be easy for him to reach in an emergency. Next, he put several spare magazines in a paper bag and stuffed them up into the springing under the passenger's seat.

Hopefully, the sight of an attractive young woman, combined with a valid pass would be enough to get them past any German checkpoint without being searched too thoroughly.

Bernard appeared from inside the house carrying a road map of the Limousin.

"Here," he said, "you might need this."

Yvette and Daniel embraced Bernard and Delphine. It was time to go.

Daniel was driving this time. He felt a little self-conscious taking over the driving, but the sight of a woman driving a man would draw more attention.

They left the farm and turned towards Flavignac. From there, they could pick up the road to Limoges easily, or go more directly via St. Junien, using smaller and more uncertain back roads.

After they had settled into the drive, Daniel voiced the question that had been troubling him. "You know, assuming we can get into Oradour, and we get there and find nothing has happened yet, what the hell do we do then? Who do we talk to? How do we make them believe us?"

Yvette did not know the answers; she could only sit in silence. It was a question for once they got there.

Chapter 14

10 June 1944: St Junien, 9:30 A.M.

Diekmann stabbed at the map with his finger. His officers had gathered around him at a large table in the dining room of the Station Hotel. He had requisitioned the building the previous day to serve as his own battalion command post.

"Gentlemen, today we are going to see blood flow! We are going to remove this pathetic little collection of hovels from the map. We will teach France a lesson today it will never forget. Are you with me?"

The coterie of officers around him snapped to attention immediately, raised their arms in salute and responded as one, "Yes sir! Heil Hitler!"

Diekmann had to pause a few moments to allow his self-control to resettle. He had been simmering with pent up rage since the previous evening's news about the capture and possible fate of Major Kampfe.

He did not know where the Maquis were holding him. That did not matter. He was convinced he knew where the Maquis cell was based, and that town was now squarely in his sights.

That town was Oradour-Sur-Glane.

It lay little more than 10 kilometres from where they all now stood. It was time to prepare.

He called out the names of the two lieutenants in the room. "Barth, Kleiss! You are each to prepare your companies. Captain Kahn, you are to make sure that everyone has all the grenades and demolition charges that they can carry. I want incendiary charges also. Make sure there are plenty of those!"

"Kleiss, you are to take your company around the town and to approach from the north. You are to seal off that exit. Spread your vehicles and men in a wide arc, so that you can cover both the roads and the open fields on either side, in case someone tries to escape that way. If you encounter anyone on the way in, arrest them also. Bring them with you to the town as well."

Lieutenant Kleiss snapped his heels together and said, "Sir!"

"Barth, you are to take your company and approach from the south. Go into the centre of the town and start the process of rounding everyone up.

You, Kahn! You will follow behind Barth and seal off the southern route, out of the town. You will deploy your men similarly to Kleiss. Fan them out to cover the countryside as well as the roads. Make sure your men at the extreme flanks are in touch with Kleiss'. I want the town surrounded!"

"As with Kleiss, arrest anyone you encounter along the way and bring them in with you. You are to let no one escape. No word of our presence is to be allowed out!"

All eyes remained locked on him.

"The plan is the same we have used in the past on the Eastern Front. We will tell the villagers that it is nothing more than a simple identity check. Insist that everyone has their ID papers. Nobody is to be excluded. Babies, elderly, bed-ridden; I want them all!"

"What time are we to go, sir?" asked Kleiss.

"I'm going to send in a couple of half-tracks shortly. They will do nothing. Just be there to help the locals get used to the sight of us. They will be under orders to be friendly."

He then looked straight at Lieutenant Kleiss, "You will have the furthest to travel, Lieutenant. I want you on the road no later than eleven a.m. Take a wide path. Don't make your destination obvious. I do not want anybody in the town to suspect anything. I want you to move into the town at precisely two p.m. Three hours should be enough of time for you to get in position.

Kleiss nodded and spoke, "Indeed, Sir. That should be ample. We will time it so that we enter the town from the north, at the same moment that you approach from the south."

"Very good, Kleiss. Now, gentlemen. Do you have any questions?"

There was silence.

"Excellent then!" said Diekmann.

"Let us start preparing. Remember, plenty of demolition charges and incendiaries. I want nothing left of this town."

He looked around the assembled officers one last time.

"All right then, let's get moving, gentlemen."

10 June 1944: The Road North-West of Flavignac. 9:50 A.M.

Daniel and Yvette had decided that they would try going directly. Once they had passed Flavignac, then there was a left hand turn that would put them onto a road leading in the direction of St Junien.

It was a narrow road, mostly used by farmers, and not well maintained.

The driving was slow. Yvette knew there was a much better road to the north, but that was likely to be heavy with German vehicles. Best to avoid that one if they could.

The odometer in the Peugeot told them how far they had travelled. Once they felt sure they were most of the way to St Junien, Daniel pulled over at a turn off onto a muddy farm road. He wanted to check the map again. His guesswork was good. They were no more than a few kilometres from St Junien now.

Oradour-Sur-Glane was only ten kilometres or so from there.

The question that concerned them both centred on the whereabouts of the SS. They must be somewhere around here. Could they be further north? Could they have already left? Perhaps they were worrying over nothing.

For her part, Yvette was hoping that Major Krebbs had passed on the information that Lucien's use of the name 'Oradour' had been a red herring. Is so, then any German units in the area might have been advised of that by now and withdrawn.

There may well be nothing to worry about after all. She hoped that might prove to be the case. Still, she had seen for herself just what the SS were capable of doing.

She had to be sure the town was safe.

If it was not and she had not tried, how could she ever look at herself again?

Daniel had finished with the map and passed it over to Yvette. He was content that St Junien was very close now. If there was a large German presence in the town, then they should expect to encounter checkpoints soon.

His senses started to prickle as he felt his alert levels rising.

Yvette was sitting close to him in the narrow confines of the cabin. She was now looking intently at the map. Daniel looked across at her, taking in her beauty and the alertness of her mind. He was surprised at how deeply in love with her he had fallen.

He put his hand around the back of her head and drew her close.

It was the first real kiss they had had since she heard the news of Lucien's capture, three days earlier.

After they drew apart, Yvette smiled at him and said, "I'm so sorry to have put you through this. I had to know about Lucien… what had happened to him. I loved him also, you know. Not like you, not like this, but he was such a kind man. He looked after me so well."

"It's all right," replied Daniel, "I truly do understand. While you were gone, Bernard told me a great deal. He and Delphine both cared for him also. They admired him. I did too, even though I didn't know him as well as you did. It's just such a shame what the last war did to him."

Yvette nodded. "He did a very heroic thing, you know… at the end. He stayed behind to cover some others as they escaped from a building. Whatever he may have lacked, it certainly was not bravery. He will never know it, but that act was most important gift he ever gave me. I will now always think of him as a hero. I will always be proud of him. That is something I will treasure."

Daniel nodded quietly and turned his head to look at his watch again. It was now after ten a.m.

He put the car into gear once more and turned back onto the road.

Barely a minute later, his suspicions about the proximity of German troops proved frighteningly correct.

The road was twisty, the verges heavily overgrown with trees and dense foliage. Scarcely a kilometre past where they had stopped, the little Peugeot rounded a blind corner to be confronted by a German roadblock, less than one hundred metres ahead.

Daniel braked hard as soon as he saw it. The little van came to an immediate halt.

This put the four Germans standing at the roadblock on instant alert. Three were carrying machine guns, which they promptly levelled at the Peugeot. The fourth was now hurrying towards a motorcycle, which was propped on its side-stand, several metres behind the roadblock.

Seeing this, Daniel slammed the van into reverse and started to take it back around the corner from which they had just emerged.

The Germans sentries yelled out at him to stop, but that was no longer an option. His behaviour guaranteed the Germans would demand to inspect the car thoroughly. With the concealed gun and ammunition, that inspection would be their death warrant. Daniel accelerated harder.

The Germans started firing.

Their machine guns were not accurate weapons at this distance, but with the hail of bullets they spewed out, a number of them hit the Peugeot.

Yvette let out a cry of pain as the car rounded the corner and briefly found cover for a moment. Daniel braked hard, crunched the gearbox into first and spun the steering wheel, desperate to take them back the way they had come.

The little car was agonisingly slow to accelerate but it gradually began to put distance between them and the roadblock.

"Are you all right?" he demanded of Yvette, his voice edgy with concern.

"I think I'm OK. I've been hit in my arm. I don't think it's too bad. I can still move it. I think the bullet went right through."

Daniel nodded. It was not good, but it did not sound life threatening.

He looked back in the mirror. To his horror, the motorcycle was in pursuit and closing the gap very quickly. Once it caught them, they were gone.

Daniel acted immediately, out of instinct and training.

Rounding another blind corner, he saw a chance. Grabbing the handbrake, he spun the van to a stop in the middle of the road, driver's side facing back in the direction from which they had just come.

Reaching under the dash, he grabbed the pistol he had hidden there and flicked off the safety catch. Next, he flung open the car door and levelled the pistol at the corner. A bare second later, the motorcycle emerged from around that corner, heading straight towards the parked van now blocking the road. The rider lifted his head in shock at the sight directly in front of him.

Daniel began firing immediately. The motorcycle was now less than thirty metres away.

Two bullets hit the German rider in quick succession, both of them close to the centre of his chest.

The rider was trying to swerve at the same moment the bullets hit him.

He came off the bike and continued to slide along the road, carried along by his own momentum. He came to an abrupt stop when he hit the Peugeot.

His bike, freed from its rider, kicked, bucked and careered past the front of the van, disappearing off the road to come to a halt in the heavy hedgerow just back from the roads edge.

Daniel looked down at the German soldier lying on the road beside the car. Although fatally wounded, he was still alive and desperately gasping for air in his final moments.

Daniel had no time for compassion. He slammed the door shut, put the car into gear again and headed back down the road in the direction of Flavignac.

They were never going to make it through to Oradour on this road. It was time to get away before more soldiers appeared.

The most important thing now was to get Yvette back home for medical attention.

She was clutching at her left upper arm and examining the wound. Blood was beginning to weep from in between her fingers.

"Is that the only one?" asked Daniel.

"I'm fairly sure it is. Nowhere else hurts!" she replied.

"Good." Daniel exhaled slowly. He was starting to come down from the adrenalin rush.

"That's going to make an incredible story to tell our grandchildren!" he said.

He kept a constant check on the rear-view mirror. There was no sign of further pursuit. Soon, he was able to settle down to a safer speed as they continued back to Bernard and Delphine's farm.

They would be able to look after Yvette there. There were plenty of good medical supplies stored along with the arms cache in the derelict shed.

After Yvette was secure, he would head out again afterwards to try to get to Oradour-Sur-Glane on his own.

Yvette would not like it, but he was going.

10 June 1944: St Junien. 1:20 P.M.

There was an initial rumble and a burst of blue exhaust smoke as the first half-track started its engine. Moments later, another joined it, and then others as the air quickly filled with the cacophony and smells of the many large diesel engines coming to life.

Diekmann had completed his preparations, everyone had their orders and all knew what their roles were to be.

After waiting for a few minutes to allow the engines to warm up to operating temperature, Diekmann picked up the microphone from his vehicle's radio set.

"Lieutenant Barth, you may move out."

Barth nodded to the driver of his half-track. The large vehicle crunched into gear and the convoy began to move.

Oradour-Sur-Glane was only ten kilometres away.

It would not take very long to get there.

10 June 1944: Oradour-Sur-Glane. The Morning

The past few days had been grey and overcast. This morning was not much different. A little rain scudding through, every now and then.

Every so often in recent days, a tiny bit of blue sky had occasionally appeared. Not much, but enough to offer a tantalising glimpse into the summer that lay just around the corner.

Not this morning though. The lowering sky and the light rain were back.

Robert Hebras had just returned home from helping a neighbour work on his car.

Just the day before, he had been laid off from his job as an apprentice mechanic in Limoges.

His former employer had had an altercation with a German officer who then threatened to have all of his younger workers conscripted into a forced labour program that would see them shipped off to Germany. Robert's employer had immediately laid all the young apprentices off, trying to save them from this fate.

The forced labour program was intended to keep able-bodied young men away from the lure of joining the ranks of the Maquis, as much it was about providing labour in a manpower-stripped Germany.

Whatever the reason, Robert, who was eighteen years old, was now home with his family. All except for his father, who was out of town helping a friend prepare some cattle to be taken away by the Germans. The friend had been told just the day before they were being requisitioned and he needed the help of Robert's father with the task.

Two German half-tracks had arrived in town an hour earlier. They had parked outside the town's grocery store.

They did nothing. The men inside just watched on as the town went about its business, even though their presence was making some of the townsfolk nervous.

The sight of German troop vehicles was not common in Oradour-Sur-Glane.

Shortly after, Robert met up with his friend, Martial Brissaud. Both typical eighteen-year-old boys, their conversation was largely about football and girls. Both were expecting to take part in a local football match the following day.

Elsewhere in town, The Green Oak Café, simply known as The Oak by all the locals, was enjoying its usual busy Saturday lunchtime crowd.

Oradour had quite a few cafés for a town of its size.

The pretty town was a popular weekend destination in the area. Since the tram to Limoges had been installed after the last war, 'townies' as the locals liked to call them, would regularly make the journey to enjoy Oradour-Sur-Glane's hospitality on a Sunday.

Today though, was Saturday and all the guests were locals.

As mid-day slid lazily into the early afternoon, the weather started to improve. The sun began to shine through, and the early afternoon warmth was making the streets, damp from the earlier rain, start to steam.

Monsieur Compain, who ran a small *patisserie,* was just readying another batch of pastries to go in the oven, preparing for the afternoon trade.

Other businesses around town were getting ready to close for the week, or had closed their doors already, as they enjoyed their lunch breaks.

Monsieur Desourteaux who ran the town's garage was preparing to close the business for the day. As well as running the most prominent business in Oradour, he was also the mayor.

As the sun continued to warm the day, many women took their washing down to the river Glane, near the bridge that formed the southern gateway into the town. Washing clothes in the small river's clear water had been the habit of generations.

Upstream, some men, their weeks work now behind them, fished for gudgeon in the river. A popular recreation.

2:00 P.M. It begins…

Some townsfolk who lived on the northern side of the village noticed with surprise, a column of German half-tracks and lorries pull up, just at the town's edge. They proceeded no further. They just waited there.

What was clear, however, was that they had intentionally blocked off the road.

Only minutes later, another column of half-tracks and lorries began to approach from the south.

This column did not stop at the town's edge. It crossed over the bridge and began to move slowly up the main street towards the centre of the village. There it stopped, close by the town's grassy central reserve, popularly known as the Fairground. Some of the half-tracks turned onto this flat, open parkland and drove to its farthest end. There, they stopped.

Robert Hebras' friend Martial was immediately gripped with fear. He had not had any real contact with Germans soldiers so far. Their sudden presence in town had him deeply scared. His mother had told him many times, "If you see the Germans, run!"

Thus far, Oradour-Sur-Glane had managed to avoid unexpected visits by the occupying army.

In fact, in a very real sense, the war had almost passed the town by. With only a few minor inconveniences, life had carried on there, much as it had before.

All of that was over now. Even though the residents did not yet realise it, the war and its horrors had finally come to Oradour-Sur-Glane.

For his part, Robert was quite used to being in the company of Germans. He saw them all the time at his job in Limoges. His reassurances though, were to no avail, Martial was afraid.

He told Robert that he would have to leave and go home.

The Germans though, had positioned themselves in between him and his family's home. He decided he would take a longer, more roundabout route outside of the town so that he would not have to go near the Germans.

It was a decision that was to save his young life.

For many others, the sight of the SS arriving in town was more of a curiosity than a concern. They continued to go about their business as before.

This was, all too shortly, about to change.

The soldiers and their officers began to emerge from the vehicles. All of them carried machine guns or pistols.

With practiced efficiency, they immediately set about the task of detaining townsfolk and steering them towards the Fairground.

More vehicles continued to arrive. They carried on past the first arrivals and continued towards the northern end of the main street, linking up with Lt Kleiss' roadblock.

The SS troops got out of their vehicles and immediately went to work. They began to bang on doors and drag people out of their homes and businesses.

These detainees were escorted under guard, to join the rapidly growing mass of captives now congregating at the Fairground.

**

Lt Barth was warming to his task. He was a believer in the Nazi creed of Aryan superiority. These were French peasants, nothing more than pathetic, inferior *untermenschen*. Their petty grievances held no interest to him.

One of the civilians sought him out as he was marched past.

"*Monsieur*, I am *Monsieur* Desourteaux. I am the Mayor of Oradour-Sur-Glane. I demand to know what is happening here! Why are you doing this?"

Barth looked at him without any sign of emotion. He spoke to the Mayor in his very good, though strongly accented, French.

"This is nothing more than an identification inspection, *Herr* Mayor. We do these all the time. If everyone in the township complies with our requests, then it can all be dealt with swiftly and everyone can go about their business again."

Desourteaux was somewhat pacified by this explanation. He set about telling anyone who approached him with concern, that it was just as Lt Barth had explained.

Once this explanation gained currency, most of the detainees began to relax. It would all be over soon. For others though, deep fears remained.

Major Diekmann patrolled the main street, checking that his men were being thorough as they went from house to house.

No one was to be missed. He wanted no witnesses.

A number of the SS soldiers were conscripts from Alsace and consequently, spoke good French. They engaged with the local residents as they shepherded them towards the Fairground. Many of them were proving affable and even joking with the townsfolk. Their seemingly easy-going attitude was further helping to put people at ease.

Monsieur Compain, the pastry baker went up to one of the German soldiers.

"May I please go back to my shop? I have an oven full of pastries. They will all be ruined if I don't get them out shortly."

The soldier said, "I am sorry, *Monsieur*. You have to stay here. I will tell my Lieutenant. He will have one of our men to go and tend to them for you."

Monsieur Compain returned to his place with the others. He had no trust that the Germans would concern themselves with the triviality of his small business.

He resigned himself to the realisation that the entire batch was destined to be ruined.

***

Many people gaped in alarm as the Germans began setting up machine-guns on tripods at several sites around the Fairground.

Machine-gun posts were also appearing in other parts of the town.

"Why do you have them? What have we done?" Worried questions came from the townsfolk.

The soldiers would simply reply that it was their standard procedure. To ensure the security of everyone, including themselves.

"Just ignore them, they don't matter."

The gathering up of the townsfolk continued.

***

The schools in Oradour-Sur-Glane, as is usual throughout France, taught lessons on Saturday mornings. Those classes were just finishing for the day as the first German vehicles began arriving in town.

The teachers kept the children with them as a precaution until they knew what was going on.

All too soon, soldiers began to call at the schools and issued instructions for the teachers to lead the children down to the Fairground and join the rest of the townsfolk.

For many of the children, this all seemed like a great adventure. Many skipped happily as they walked along. Some of the younger children though, began to cry out for their mothers. Fortunately, once they arrived at the Fairground, most found that their parents were already there waiting for them. For a while, these family reunions helped relieve the mounting anxiety of many in the crowd.

A more intrusive, house-to-house search for anyone attempting to hide was now underway.

No one was spared. Even the bed-ridden and elderly were dragged out onto the streets and forced to assemble with the others.

Some of the more resourceful had managed to hide themselves successfully in secret locations within their homes. They had resolved to wait out the hours until the Germans would depart, no doubt pleased with how clever they were.

For most, it would do them no good.

***

The afternoon was passing slowly for the townsfolk assembled in the Fairground.

As the sun continued to warm the land, the air became more humid and uncomfortable.

The time was now past three p.m.

The Germans were still checking houses, still finding more people, but they were almost done.

The number of people gathered in the Fairground was now well past six hundred. It was approaching six hundred and sixty.

Over an hour of rigorous house-to-house searching was drawing to its end.

Lt Barth went looking for Major Diekmann. "I believe we have everyone now, Herr Major."

"Excellent work, Lieutenant. Now, it's time to get to work," said Diekmann.

Chapter 15

10 June 1944: Morin Farm, 2:20 P.M.

Yvette was nearly beside herself.

"You can't be serious! You cannot possibly go there again! They nearly killed us both just now. I refuse to let you!"

Daniel stood by looking solemn but determined.

Delphine had finished tending to the bullet wound in Yvette's left shoulder. Almost miraculously, it had proven to be very clean. The bullet had gone neatly through the flesh and had done no damage to the bone.

Delphine had made clothes all her life. Those needlework skills suddenly came to the fore.

After some initial nervousness, she had little trouble in executing a couple of sutures on the entrance and exit wounds before then applying some sulphur powder.

Everything she needed, she had found in one of the British medical kits, secreted away with the weapons cache.

Yvette had resisted having any pain relief. She wanted to stay sharp. The pain of the suturing was intense but mercifully brief. She had maintained a stoic, gritty silence throughout the process.

If Yvette could now keep the wound clean, and there was no subsequent infection, she would be fine.

With her immediate injury crisis dealt with, Yvette now turned her attention to Daniel, who had just announced that he intended to go back, in another attempt to get through to Oradour-Sur-Glane.

"I'm sorry, Yvette, I'm going! You know what the SS is capable of doing. You've seen it for yourself. Someone has to try and warn the town."

"We might be too late by now. There might be no point," she said in desperation.

Daniel shook his head. "But equally, I might not be. I have to try. Perhaps we are worrying about nothing. Perhaps the Germans aren't planning anything. I don't know. But if they are, and I do nothing, I will never be able to live with myself."

He looked solemnly at all three.

"I have to go!"

There was a moment silence as they all took in his words. They all knew he was right.

Yvette spoke up again. His words had echoed the same thought she had had earlier. "In that case, I am going with you again. I'm not badly hurt. I won't let you go alone!"

Daniel smiled at her. "I knew you were going to say that. I guess it's pointless my trying to stop you?"

"It certainly is! Now let's get going, shall we?"

Bernard spoke up. "Don't you think a few bullet holes in the back of the car will attract some unwanted attention?"

Daniel thought about if a moment.

"We shall just have to take the risk. At least the front of the car is undamaged. No bullets went through the front windscreen, perhaps if we put some tape or something over the holes at the back. Is there anything here that would be quick and might work?"

"I have an idea that should work," said Bernard, "I have some pitch in a tin can. Delphine, can I have some strips of plain calico, please?"

Delphine hurried off to her sewing room. She reappeared moments later with a large piece of calico. She began to tear it into strips about five centimetres wide.

The all went out into the yard as Bernard went ahead to get the pitch and a brush from the barn.

Bernard then painted the pitch onto the cloth and stretched the lengths across the rear doors of the van, covering the couple of bullet holes but also creating a regular striped pattern. The pitch formed a very effective and strong glue. The strips would not come off easily.

It looked ugly but at least it would draw less attention from Vichy *Gendarmes* or Germans, than would the prominent appearance of fresh bullet holes.

Yvette quickly hugged her grandparents again and got back into the van. Daniel embraced them also and got back into the driver's seat. Without another word, they were on their way for the second time that day.

"Will we try the same way again?" asked Yvette with a wry smile.

"Definitely not!" replied Daniel, "I'm going to try and find a way through Limoges. It's longer but we can go along with the regular traffic. It'll be safer."

Yvette reached for the map from the van's parcel shelf. She looked over it intently.

"It shouldn't be too hard to find our way there. There is a main road heading west that starts to the south of Limoges. I think that might be faster but there are likely to be many more Germans. If we go through Limoges, there is another road leading from the north. That might be the better way to go."

"All right then," replied Daniel, "let's try that one."

10 June 1944 Oradour-Sur-Glane, 3:00 P.M.

Major Diekmann had taken several officers aside. He gave them each their own orders to separate the townspeople into groups. This was the most important part of the operation. Maintaining the calm was vital. If panic were to start, it would be difficult to control.

All the officers had done this before in Eastern Europe. An excess of compassion was a weakness from which none of them suffered.

They all knew how to show a genial face to the crowd. A smile and a pleasant voice could work wonders. It was easy.

Lieutenant Barth had perhaps, the most difficult task of all, managing the huge number of women and children. Together, they numbered more than half of all the detainees.

He selected a large group of over thirty men, and they set about separating the women and children from the men and older boys. Knowing the potential difficulty of the task, he had hand-picked as many of the French-speaking men in the battalion as he could find.

The effect that French-speaking soldiers had on the assembly, proved very calming.

Tensions occasionally arose when the soldiers tried to separate some of the larger, older boys from their mothers. Most of the teenage boys were happy to stay with the men, but occasionally, a boy who might have looked older than he was, demanded to stay with his mother.

The Germans ultimately proved amenable to allowing these boys to stay where they wanted. It eased nerves and kept the crowd from getting too restive.

The large group of women and children eventually formed up quite peacefully. Some of the Germans joked with the townspeople as they gathered. The guards told them they were going down to the church to get them out of the sun. It seemed a thoughtful gesture. The afternoon had indeed become warm and humid.

The soldiers explained that once everyone was comfortably settled in the church, then the checking of identity papers could commence.

It all sounded perfectly reasonable; no one seemed to be unduly concerned.

It proved a very large group that finally got underway to walk down to the church. Over four hundred and fifty women and children, all trusting in the good intentions of these men who led them along so confidently. At least the children would be out of the sun.

***

Back at the Fairground, once the women and children were on their way, the remaining men began to notice a change in the attitude of their SS captors.

Captain Kahn stepped forward and called out in French, "Who is the Mayor of this place? Come forward immediately!"

Monsieur Desourteaux stepped forward and approached him.

Kahn demanded he follow and led him away from the others.

Once they were out of sight of the others, Kahn turned to *Monsieur* Desourteaux.

"We know that there are weapons stored here in this town. We are going to search the entire village. You, *Monsieur* Mayor, will nominate men we will hold as hostages. In the event we find the weapons, we will then make a decision as to what to do with them."

Monsieur Desourteaux shook his head. "I am willing to put myself forward as a hostage *Monsieur* Captain, but I will not give you the name of any other. That is a choice you will have to make for yourself!"

Captain Kahn looked intently at *Monsieur* Desourteaux for a moment.

"Very well then. As you wish!"

Kahn then led *Monsieur* Desourteaux back to the men still waiting in the Fairground.

As Desourteaux took his place once more, Captain Kahn stepped forward and addressed them.

"We know there are weapons stored here. We know the Maquis operate from here. I demand you tell me what you have. We shall be lenient with anyone who is truthful and co-operative."

A couple of men spoke up, stating that they had hunting or sporting rifles. These were not of particular interest to the Germans. They would have expected to hear such a response. These kinds of weapons were common.

"Come now," continued Kahn, "anyone with nothing to hide will be released unharmed. We are going to search the town thoroughly. Is there anything any of you wish to tell me?"

No one spoke up further. All the men were confident that there were no hidden caches of weapons anywhere in the township. These Germans were wrong; Oradour-Sur-Glane was not a Maquis town.

Some of the men grew more confident. Surely then, once the Germans had completed their search and found nothing, they would realise their mistake. They would leave the town in peace.

The thought was reassuring.

By now, the gathered men had been waiting in the sun for a considerable time. Some began to grow restless and move around, looking for shady places to sit.

The machine guns pointed at them were menacing, but surely, if the Germans were going to shoot them, they would have done so by now.

Some began to relax and think of what they would go back to doing, once the SS had left and all of this had settled down.

A few noticed with concern though, that the German officers had begun talking amongst themselves and the remaining troops were breaking into smaller groups.

Kahn approached the men again.

"We are going to split you up into groups. We are going to take each group to a barn so you can be out of the sun. We will hold you under guard until the search of the town is complete. Now, get moving!"

The Germans then split the men into six broadly similar sized groups. Robert Hebras found himself in the largest of them, totalling about sixty men.

His group was led the short distance towards the far end of the Fairground, past an old well and into a large barn owned by a *Monsieur* Laudy.

The other groups were marched away in turn, their destinations being five other barns scattered around the town.

The Laudy barn was large but well filled. The Germans demanded the men move several wagons out of the building to create more space inside.

Once all of the men in Robert's group were finally able to settle down inside the barn, they set about trying to make themselves more comfortable. They could be in for a long wait.

Robert found a cosy spot, perched on some hay bales.

As the men stood around or sat, they all watched in nervous fascination as the SS guards started setting up two machine guns on tripods at the barn door.

Some men watched in growing apprehension, but most remained stoic, thinking it was just the Germans trying to be intimidating. All of them though, united in their disbelief at the events of this surreal afternoon… and their growing fear.

It was now almost four p.m.

10 June 1944: Limoges, 4:00 P.M.

Limoges was a busy city. Even on a Saturday, even with the German presence, there were many vehicles and hundreds of bicycles using its narrow, twisting medieval streets.

The map, which Bernard had given Daniel, was useless here. It was not an urban street map; it showed only the roads in the countryside. Yvette had been to Limoges many times in her life, but never had she ventured in the outer northern suburbs. She was struggling to provide Daniel with the accurate directions he needed.

Daniel could not get angry with her; he did not know the city at all. If he were on his own, the situation would have been even worse.

They were gradually making their way northward, hoping that they would encounter a main road or street sign that would point them in the right direction.

The bizarre livery at the rear of the little van had attracted no more than the most cursory attention. Bernard's impromptu bullet-hole repairs had done their job perfectly.

They had inexpertly navigated their way through the centre of the city, but now the streets were opening out, becoming wider, more modern and easier to drive.

Eventually, it was obvious they had reached the semi-rural allotments bordering the northern edge of the city.

Almost in desperation, Daniel took the first significant looking left-hand turn that they encountered. Thankfully, it turned out to be the right one.

They soon came across a road sign. It indicated the way to several nearby towns. Among them was Oradour-Sur-Glane. It said thirty-four kilometres.

Daniel and Yvette looked at each other.

They had not spoken very much since they had left the farm; each immersed in the depths of their own thoughts.

"It's not too late to turn back, you know," said Daniel.

Yvette looked at him in shock. "Why would you say that? Do you want to?"

Daniel looked determined, but pensive. "A part of me is screaming to do exactly that! I feel like we're going into battle."

Yvette nodded in agreement. "I know what you mean. I feel exactly the same way, but we can't go back. You know that."

"I know," replied Daniel, "the fact is, we're most likely to find our way into a quiet little town that is completely fine. The Germans will just leave it alone and go past."

"May it so please God. Please let it be so!" replied Yvette. "I would feel very foolish for worrying so much about nothing, but at least I'd be able to sleep."

She looked at Daniel and reached out for his hand. She pulled it towards her mouth and kissed it.

"Whatever happens, we are doing the right thing."

Daniel nodded in agreement, too deep in his thoughts to want to speak.

***

The road was empty of other vehicles and Daniel had made good time when the little van crested a hill only a few kilometres to the northeast of Oradour-Sur-Glane.

Yvette cried out in shock and Daniel pulled over to the side of the road. They both climbed out of the little Peugeot and gazed in awe towards the south-west. Their mouths gaped open in wordless horror.

Whilst they could not see the town itself from where they were, a huge column of dense smoke was arising in the distance, as well as smaller ones, too numerous to count. The faint, dull crump of heavy explosions carried across the distance.

They looked at each other, both feeling the nightmarish grasp of certainty sinking to the pit of their bellies.

They were too late!

Neither spoke. Neither was able to.

Daniel opened the van door for Yvette, then sat himself back behind the wheel, put the van into gear and drove on. Slowly and watchfully now. Who could say what they might meet just around the next corner.

Yvette studied the map carefully.

She was sure that they must be just to the east of the intersection with the road that led north from Oradour. She cautioned Daniel to drive even more slowly.

They may well run into a German presence very shortly.

The van approached a bend in the road, veering sharply towards the left. Daniel stopped the van whilst still on the blind side of the corner. He remained in the driver's seat whilst Yvette got out and surreptitiously crept towards the bend, trying to see if it was clear to proceed down the next stretch of road.

Nervously, she peeked from behind an old elm tree down the next stretch of road.

Immediately, reflexively, she pulled her head back. Bending low, she hurried back to the van.

Yvette's heart was pounding. "We must go back. They are just beyond the corner! Please hurry!"

As carefully as he could, Daniel put the Peugeot into reverse and gently eased off the clutch.

After going in reverse for over a hundred metres, he turned the car around and set off back along the road they had just travelled.

After putting enough distance between themselves and the Germans to feel safe again, he pulled the van over to the side of the road, still facing in the direction of Limoges. They both got out, desperate to escape the confinement of the van.

"Now tell me," he asked, "what did you see?"

Yvette was still high on adrenaline. The words poured out of her in a torrent.

"There is a big roadblock! Many vehicles, big ones! Many soldiers! Machine guns! Everything!"

Daniel understood.

The Germans had blockaded the town. No one could get in or out.

What must be going on there was too terrible to think about.

He turned to Yvette. "I doubt they will come up here. From what you describe, they have a defensive position only. We need to wait here. Once they are done with the town, they will move on. Then we can go in. Then…" He could not finish the sentence.

Yvette looked at him.

"What do you think they are doing there?"

Daniel swallowed hard.

"Only God can answer that question. I dare not even think!"

Yvette reached out to him and Daniel responded. They both clung to each other tightly.

Chapter 16

10 June 1944: Oradour-Sur-Glane, 4:00 P.M.

Time seemed to hang in a fragile, delicate moment.

The sullen heaviness of the humid afternoon was relieved only by the hum of insects and the songs of birds going about their busy lives in the early summer warmth.

A brief moment of bucolic peace settled, fleetingly and deceptively over the town.

That came to an abrupt, shattering end.

Major Diekmann was standing outside the Desourteaux Garage on the main road. He was content that all was in readiness.

He turned to a corporal who was holding a demolition charge. Diekmann nodded to the soldier and gestured towards the Garage.

The corporal ignited the fuse and threw the bomb deep inside the building.

Diekmann and the others then moved back as the fuse burned down.

***

The tense, uncomfortable atmosphere inside Laudy's Barn was shattered by the thunderous concussion of a huge explosion.

Those captive men who were sitting, suddenly jumped to their feet and looked at each other in shock.

A mere instant later, the German machine guns opened fire.

The explosion had been their signal.

Aiming low, the guns traversed back and forth in scything sweeps, shooting out the legs of the men crowded into the barn.

Robert Hebras was standing towards the rear of the group. A man in front of him took several bullets to his chest from some of the random shots that flew higher. The impact flung him backwards. He knocked Robert to the ground, his mortally wounded body covering and protecting the teenager.

A vicious hail of bullets continued to pour into the room. Men were collapsing after taking shots in the legs, only to have their fall present their upper bodies to the stream of low-aimed bullets.

Screams of horror and outrage quickly gave way to moans of agony. No man remained standing.

Only then did the machine guns ceased firing.

***

The same horrific scene repeated itself in each of the other five barns.

Some men, perhaps lucky, were killed out-right. Most, however, fell with multiple wounds. Lying in agony or screaming out obscenities at the SS bastards who did this.

Some still struggled to understand what was happening. Why would anyone do such a thing to them? What had they done?

Cries and groans filled the barn, cries of anguish, agony and anger. Some voices weak as death was close, others still strong in defiance or confusion.

Robert Hebras recognised the voice of a neighbour, *Monsieur* Brissaud. He was a middle-aged man. A veteran of the last war. That war had cost him a leg.

Now he cried out in rage and agony, "The bastards have shot off my other leg!"

Some men called to God, some for their mothers or other loved ones.

Others simply wailed in despair, knowing that it was not yet over.

Once the machine guns fell silent, the SS troops began to pick their way around inside the barns, looking for anyone still alive. Their pistols or rifles cocked and at the ready.

Soon enough, the sounds of single gunshots began to ring out around the village. Hundreds of them.

Depending on the caprice of the individual soldiers, some of the wounded townsmen had the mercy of a clean *coup de grace*. Others though, were shot again or bayonetted, simply to cause additional suffering.

There was a reason the SS had selected barns for the shootings. They were full of timber and hay. The soldiers now began to spread large bundles of both across the dead or helpless, damaged men sprawled across the floors of each one.

Burning the bodies was the easiest way of disposing of them.

***

Up until now, Robert Hebras had remained miraculously unhurt.

Several men had fallen on top of him. He was scarcely visible underneath their bodies.

As the Germans made their way through the barn, shooting anyone that showed any sign of life, somehow, they missed seeing him.

His luck was not destined to last though.

A man, heavily wounded and groaning in agony, lay with his upper body across Robert's legs. A soldier came up and shot him in the head. The bullet passed completely through his skull, striking Robert in the leg. Despite the pain, he did not flinch. To do so would mean instant death.

He lay there in mute stillness, aware that the Germans were now starting to spread piles of hay over the mass of bodies littering the floor of the Laudy barn. Hay and pieces of timber.

My God! he thought, *they're going to burn us alive!*

After a few minutes, the troops left the barn, pulling closed the large timber doors behind them.

A moment later though, one of those doors opened again. A soldier tossed an incendiary grenade into the barn and closed the doors for good.

Sealed inside the building, the explosion was deafening, but more terrifying still was the sudden rush of acrid, billowing smoke and flames that found immediate purchase in the piles of hay and wood.

Other voices began to call out again.

Robert was not the only one still left alive. He was though, the only one still capable of moving. He could not do anything for the others. For the more desperately wounded men that the SS had not yet finished off, their awful fate lay in the flames.

Those flames were spreading rapidly now. If Robert were to stay where was, he too would surely burn to death.

Despite the tumult and chaos within the barn, he was suddenly shocked to hear the incongruous sound of music coming from beyond the locked barn door. The Germans outside had cranked up an old gramophone. They were killing an entire town to the accompaniment of grand opera.

Clambering out from underneath the bodies of men whose own deaths had saved his life, he quickly spied a door along a rear wall of the barn. He could stand the flames no longer. He had to try to get out. Surely, a bullet would be preferable to being burned alive.

Despite the fresh wound in his leg, he quickly picked his way around the mass of bodies and soon stood with a hand pressed against the door, ready to open it. Possible salvation or certain death most likely lay beyond it. He had no idea which, but he knew he had no choice.

Mustering his courage, he pushed it open and stepped outside, fully expecting to find SS soldiers there with their weapons ready to turn on him.

There was no one. The door had only led him into a small open courtyard with no other exit.

He hurried back inside the barn and looked around desperately. He spied a second door, one that he had not seen earlier.

Opening it, it led him into a stable, which adjoined the barn.

He heard other voices, speaking softly, but urgently. The language was French, not German, so he chanced his luck and sought them out.

To his amazement, he found four of his young friends; two of them, like him, carrying bullet wounds. They had also managed to escape, and find their way into the stables.

They were now all trapped, however, by the inferno in the barn behind them and by armed Germans waiting beyond the stable doors. Now, most pressingly, the fire from the barn was spreading into the stables.

Looking around desperately, one of the boys noticed that an old brick wall at the rear of the stables was starting to crumble.

They quickly got to work, knocking and kicking out bricks. Soon, they had created a hole large enough for each of them to squeeze through.

They found themselves now, in yet another, much smaller barn. This one though, as yet untouched by fire.

The five teenagers quickly sought out places to hide themselves, hoping that they might be able to wait out the remaining hours until the SS left.

They finished hiding just in time. The barn door opened and two SS soldiers came in.

They looked around briefly and saw nobody.

Then one of them lit a match and dropped it into a pile of straw. It ignited immediately. The other soldier had his rifle loaded with incendiary bullets. He fired a few into the timber ceiling of the old barn.

It caught alight as well.

The Germans then left and closed the barn doors behind them.

Once again, the boys found themselves trapped by fire.

There was one door, at the rear, that they could try. The found it opened onto a small lane that led straight towards the Fairground.

There was a German machine gun set up right at the end of the lane. Fortunately, for the moment, it was unattended.

The boys resisted leaving the burning barn as long as they could. In the end though, the fire, growing more intense by the second, left them with no choice.

If they chanced their luck in the Fairground, they would, almost certainly be seen. There was too much open ground to have to cover. There was no doubt they would be spotted and gunned down.

In the other direction though, the short lane led back into a large, enclosed yard, accessible only by this narrow lane and a second one that ran down to the main street. It was formed by the rear walls of buildings running along the street and the Fairground, on two sides. The barns and stables they had just escaped from completed the enclosure.

The SS seemed to have been unaware that this sheltered space existed. The yard itself though, offered no shelter or cover. That is, until one of the boys spotted some large stone rabbit hutches against one wall.

They quickly crossed the open ground to the hutches, unseen. Cramming themselves into the first one, they pulled the doors shut behind them.

The Germans would be unlikely to have any interest in these old, dilapidated hutches. The boys finally felt some sense of safety; at least for the time being.

***

The women and children, under guard in the church, heard the first explosion and the sound of many machine guns opening up. An awful realisation ran through them; it could only mean one thing, their men, their fathers, husbands and sons were being slaughtered.

Where moments earlier, the interior of the church offered reassurance and security, now it felt like a prison, or worse. The sacred interior was soon echoing to their screams and sobs.

Soon enough, the smell of smoke, burnt cordite and gunpowder from the burning village so close by, reached them. There were further explosions, more machine gun fire. The sounds were unending.

With the men now dealt with and dead, the SS turned their attention to the task of blowing up and burning every building in the town.

Diekmann ordered that the town be razed.

The women and children, crammed into the church, could only hold each other for comfort and listen on, as the utter destruction of their world continued outside.

***

The flames and explosions began flushing out people who had thought themselves securely hidden.

All too quickly, they joined their fellow villagers in death. A bullet to the brain.

The SS left most bodies where they fell. A few though, were disposed of with a more insidious cruelty.

The Germans found one of their victims hiding in a bakery. After promptly shooting him, they set about stuffing him into the still-operating oven. Only his upper body would fit, so there they left him; head, shoulders and torso to cook on until the fire eventually died. Still other victims had their bodies thrown down the well at the far end of the Fairground, only metres from Laudy's barn.

The orgy of killing and destruction was continuing unchecked as the SS, helping themselves liberally to any alcohol they came across, cast off the last vestiges of their humanity.

Diekmann now turned his attention to the only remaining group of captives.

The women and children held, under guard, in the church.

There was a plan to deal with them also.

Diekmann called for Lt Barth. "Lieutenant, you know what to do. I want incendiaries and plenty of them. Now get moving!"

Barth ran over to his platoon. They began preparing the explosives.

***

Inside the church, many of the women were kneeling in prayer. Desperately trying to invoke the assistance of the Almighty in this, the gravest hour of their lives.

Others sat with their backs against the wall, listening to the sounds of the nightmare unfolding outside, unable to comprehend why this was happening.

Those with children, clung desperately to them; as much for their own comfort as that of the child.

Surely, it must be over soon. The gunfire and explosions had been going on for over an hour.

Then, suddenly, the door of the church was flung wide open. Several young troops carrying a large, obviously heavy wooden box entered the building.

They set it down in the middle of the church and the stepped well back.

There were a number of thick, black cords hanging from the box. One of the soldiers stepped forward and began to light them.

The women closest started screaming in terror as it dawned on them what was happening. The box was a huge incendiary bomb. The fuses burning, the soldiers hurriedly retreated to the doorway, waiting for the explosion.

It detonated with a loud 'crump', expelling a torrent of flammable chemicals and sending a choking plume of dense, billowing black smoke roiling through the church.

As the flames quickly took hold, some women rushed to a door within a little alcove to the side of the church's main chamber. The door led into the Sacristy, a small room that they hoped in their desperation, might afford some shelter from the inferno now taking hold.

The sheer weight of their numbers broke the locked door down. Watching this from the main entrance, several soldiers went back into the church and opened fire on these women. There was no way out for those that had sought shelter in the Sacristy. The troops stood in the doorway and machine-gunned them all.

Meanwhile, the flames had flashed through the huge internal cavity of the church. Timber pews, pulpits, beams and fittings all caught alight in moments.

Those women and children, closest to the incendiary as it exploded, were showered in the flaming chemicals as they erupted from the device. They were the first burned alive, shrieking in writhing, contorted agony as they died.

The fire established itself with terrifying speed. Within bare minutes, even the roof of the old church, more than twenty metres above their heads, was completely ablaze.

Metal fittings on the ceiling began to melt, dripping molten metal onto the women and children trapped below.

The last SS soldiers had now backed out of the church. Others had grabbed anything wooden they could find outside; chairs, loose timber, firewood, anything that would burn. They hurled this into the church also, as additional fuel.

Finally, they closed, locked and barricaded the doors. They would now leave the fire inside to run its course.

The main door was at the rear of the church. The troops stationed there, stood by without emotion, as the frantic pounding coming from the inside grew more desperate by the second.

The heat inside was now intense. The lead of the stained-glass windows was beginning to melt.

For one woman, however, desperation lent her strength.

Marguerite Rouffanche had just watched as her daughter was shot dead in front of her eyes. They would have killed her also, had she not collapsed and pretended to be dead herself.

Now, almost overwhelmed by the smoke, she had found a small pocket of breathable air towards the front of the church, behind the main altar.

There were three stained glass windows in the wall above. The centre one could be opened and it was larger than the other two. It would be big enough for her to squeeze through if she could only get up to it.

Grabbing a stool that had somehow, thus far escaped the fire, she positioned it under the window and climbed onto it, just managing to reach up, undo the latch and open the window.

Somehow, she then found the strength to pull herself up and scramble through the opening, dropping down over three metres to the sloping, rocky ground outside. The open window would normally have been clearly visible to anyone on the main road as it ran past the church, but the thick, swirling smoke lent her an almost miraculous cover. That, and the fact that the SS were fully occupied at the opposite end of the church, near the main door.

As she struggled back to her feet, a voice called to her from the window above. Another woman had followed her up and was holding a baby, imploring Marguerite to catch it.

How could she say no?

The woman dropped the baby down to her, and scrambled through the window herself.

Picking herself up after the heavy fall, the other woman took back the now screaming infant. They both began to run down towards the Glane River, barely one hundred metres away.

The screams of the distressed baby had attracted the attention of two German soldiers. They came around the side of the church and saw the two women running for their lives.

Raising their machine guns, they cut them both down in a hail of bullets.

The soldiers did not even bother to go over to check on them. They just turned and re-joined the others at the main entrance.

Marguerite lay as still as she could. She had been struck five times but, although serious, none of the wounds would prove to be mortal. She carefully looked over towards the other woman and the baby.

They were both dead. They had taken the full force of the fusillade, partly shielding her in the process.

She continued to lie there, motionless, until she was certain the Germans were not going to come over and check on her.

Then she struggled back to her feet and hobbled on, this time looking for cover behind the rear of the church. She crawled into a large, communal vegetable garden and there, she finally found safety. The garden was healthy and lush enough to conceal her, once she had laid down in a furrow, between the rows.

From there, where she lay hidden, she watched the terrifying blaze that had, by now, completely engulfed the church.

The ancient house of God was like a scene from hell.

Flames leapt high into the afternoon air, twisting and dancing between dense, coiling plumes of smoke that stretched all the way to the heavens. The roof and everything inside was now totally consumed by the inferno.

Then, with a terrible roar, the roof itself collapsed into the shell of the devastated building.

Marguerite could no longer hear any more screaming above the din of the collapsing roof. It was obvious though that, by now, there could not have been many left alive inside still able to scream.

There were further loud, concussive crashes as still more remnants of the roof continued to fall into the flaming charnel house below.

Most of the soldiers stood frozen, unmoving with mouths agape, gazing in rapt awe at the spectacle unfolding before them. The newer recruits amongst them, seemingly dumbstruck by the magnitude of what they had done.

There had been over four hundred and fifty women and children inside the church.

Only Marguerite Rouffanche had made it out alive.

***

A tram approached on the track from Limoges. It was undertaking a test run, after major servicing.

Five men were on board, all employees of the tram company.

It crossed the Glane River Bridge as it made its way into Oradour from the south. Seeing it coming across the bridge, a group of SS troops hurried down to intercept it. Guns levelled at the railway workers; the troops immediately ordered them off the tram.

The men gaped in incredulous awe at the sights in front of them.

The church in its blazing death throes, the terrifying destruction going on in the town beyond, these frightening SS troops levelling guns at them. They could only wait, trembling in fear for their lives, whilst one of the soldiers hurried off to find an officer.

A heated argument now broke out amongst the remaining soldiers. Some unmistakeably wanting to shoot them on the spot, whilst others demanded they wait for an officer to arrive. Noticing the guards were distracted, one of the railway men decided to act for himself. He turned away from his colleagues and started hurrying back towards the bridge.

It was a futile and fatal mistake. He had only made it a few metres before the troops saw him running. They calmly shot him dead, as if it were a simple, everyday act. The other captives froze, not daring to breathe. Were they going to be next?

The troops turned their guns back onto the others, now clearly moments away from ending their lives with as little fuss as they did their colleague.

Bare seconds later, the timely arrival of a Lieutenant, making his way down from the church, restored calm. Under his orders, the guards lowered their weapons while he demanded to be told what was going on.

In the minutes that followed, the Lieutenant, his name unrecorded to history, showed the only hint of mercy seen in Oradour-Sur-Glane that day. He ordered the remaining railway workers back onto the tram and sent it on its way, back to Limoges.

Two soldiers then picked up the body of the dead tramway employee, and unceremoniously threw it over the bridge into the Glane River below. It floated a little way downstream before finally coming to rest against the riverbank.

The tram set off on the journey back to Limoges, taking with it the first news of the horror, still in full flow, happening in Oradour-Sur-Glane.

***

Robert Hebras and his four companions were still not safe. The flames that consumed the adjacent barns were now closing on their refuge in the rabbit hutch.

The row of hutches was in clear sight, should any passing soldier pause to look up the short, narrow laneway leading straight from the main street. Trying to find any other cover was not an option. There was no other cover to find.

The hutch they were crammed into was the largest of the three. It was also the rear-most, closest to the fire. With the flames now too close for comfort, they had no alternative. They slipped out of the hutch and into the next one along. It was not much, but it gave them a little bit of respite from the encroaching flames.

The regular deep 'crump' of exploding demolition charges and the still-frequent sound of gunshots continued unabated. The methodical destruction of the town now had a life of its own.

To the five young boys crammed into the unlikely haven of their rabbit hutch, what was happening, just metres beyond, seemed surreal. The savagery was just too enormous for their young minds to grasp.

Another hour passed and the flames were creeping closer once again. The second hutch was now under immediate threat. The fires progress was slowing now as it consumed the last of the fuel it craved, but it was still frighteningly close.

A quick check that the coast was clear and they all hurried into the third, and last of the hutches.

There was nothing after this. If they had to leave this one, it would mean crossing a large area of open ground. That thought was just too terrifying to contemplate.

10 June 1944: Oradour-Sur-Glane. Approaching 7:40 P.M.

Major Diekmann had been pressing his men hard to finish the task.

One thought struck him, if only briefly. They had found no weapons cache in Oradour-Sur-Glane.

Despite the systematic checking and destruction of every building, only the occasional light-calibre hunting rifle had turned up. Clearly, the town was not a Maquis centre after all.

It doesn't matter, he thought, *the lesson is the same, regardless.*

He had long since learned to rationalise away the occasional naggings of his conscience, as it retreated into the atrophied confines of his soul.

It was now starting to get late and he was keen to get his battalion away and on to a new bivouac for the night.

He stood, perched on a half-track, calling out loudly to attract the attention of any subordinate officers within hearing.

Only Captain Kahn and a couple of sergeants heard him and they came at his beckon.

He ordered them to search the town for all officers. He told them to have those officers assemble their men and prepare to get underway immediately.

The orders travelled quickly around the now shattered remains of the town.

Men soon began to appear from all parts of the village. With little prompting, they began to load their equipment back into the half-tracks and lorries, parked the length of the main street.

Major Diekmann finally spotted Lt Barth.

Calling him over, he said, "I want you to go up the road and notify Lieutenant Kleiss that we are preparing to move out. He is to join us at once. Tell him we are heading on to the town of Nieul. Not very far, I believe, about ten kilometres to the east. He is to follow us. The road leads out from the southern end of town."

Barth promptly got into a half-track that already had its motor running and ordered the driver to head north.

The evening light was fading now as the soldiers continued to straggle back to their vehicles.

There were large supplies of alcohol found amongst the homes and businesses, as they ransacked their way through the town.

Not just alcohol. Oradour-Sur-Glane was a wealthy town. The SS had helped themselves to anything of value they could carry. Jewels, silver, artwork; all became booty.

They had completely emptied the wine and spirit shop of *Monsieur* Deny before blowing it up. There was plenty of alcohol to go around, even for so large a group as the 1st Battalion.

The men were now in high spirits, fuelled by adrenalin, alcohol and the rapacious, bestial camaraderie they had shared. They came from all parts of the town in their scattered groups laden with their booty, and began to climb back aboard the vehicles that had brought them to this place.

Major Diekmann had kept a couple of cases of wine and Cognac aside for himself.

As the officer in charge, responsibility dictated that he had to restrain himself for the moment, but he had every intention of enjoying his share of the booty once they were underway.

The first vehicle began to move out shortly before eight p.m.

They drove through a scene of otherworldly devastation. Not a single building remained as it was.

Almost nothing, be it a business, school, post office or home had escaped either demolition charge, grenade or fire. Most were still burning fiercely.

Only the over-head electricity cables for the tram service and the telephone lines, suspended from their tall concrete and iron pillars, remained recognisably intact.

Even as the vehicles were moving out, many of the troops continued tossing grenades into the remains of houses they had already destroyed. Laughter and cheering accompanied the sound of each new explosion.

They had surrendered all control of their rational selves. Their animal instincts were in full flow.

As they crossed the bridge over the River Glane, one of the troops unpacked an accordion, which he had brought with him.

The happy music and singing which thus accompanied the withdrawal seemed to provide the final, bizarre touch of tragic irony to the day.

With Lt Kleiss' detachment bringing up the rear, the last of the SS vehicles finally left Oradour-Sur Glane.

Only a few brief hours previously, it had been a beautiful, peaceful and content village, doing its best to see out the war with as little involvement as possible.

Now it lay, a smoking, flaming, shattered ruin. Almost all human life within, had been ruthlessly extinguished.

A tragically few survivors somehow remained. They were all that were left to keep the memory of the old town alive.

The old town. The one before the SS arrived.

Chapter 17

10 June 1944: Oradour-Sur-Glane, 8:45 P.M.

Nearly an hour had passed since the last of the German vehicles had left.

Marguerite Rouffanche had kept her head down for as long as she could. She had seen the column of vehicles leaving. Surely, they were gone now! Surely, it was safe now.

She finally raised her head and looked out towards the vision of horror that lay before her.

Her family was in there… somewhere.

She had seen her eldest daughter killed in front of her inside the church. What of her husband, her son, yet another daughter and her infant grandson?

She was too numb to take in the enormity of it all. Soon, the loss of blood from her wounds would see her lose consciousness. At least for now, there would be no dreams. They would come later.

***

Robert Hebras and his friends finally summoned the courage to emerge from the third rabbit hutch. The fire had not reached them. It had been quiet for a while. The Germans had left.

Somehow, they had all survived.

A faint and piteous cry carried to them from beyond the smoking, devastated remains of Mayor Desourteaux's Garage.

The five teenagers began to walk towards the sound.

A young boy emerged through billowing clouds of smoke that still choked the remains of the town.

He saw the group of older boys and ran to them in tears.

One of Robert's friends recognised him. "It is Roger Godfrin," he told the others.

"How did you escape, Roger?" he asked of the lad.

"I hid behind some trees at the back of the school. Where is my mother? Do you know?"

Robert and his friends could only look at each other. They did not know; they could only hope.

Each of the teenagers gathered around young Roger and hugged him, offering him what little comfort they could.

Then another voice called out to them.

Robert's friend Martial had spotted them as he cautiously made his way back through the town.

He and Robert embraced each other in desperate relief. Martial explained that he had gone and hidden in a secluded spot he knew, near the river.

The small group of young men all looked at each other. Were they all that remained?

***

Incredibly, a small Peugeot van slowly appeared out of the swirling smoke. The man and the woman in the vehicle looked in open-mouthed horror at the nightmare vision before them.

Never in their worst imaginings could Daniel and Yvette have believed that such a sight could exist.

Fires still raged everywhere. No building remained intact.

There were no birds, no animals anywhere to be seen.

Above all, there were no people.

***

Daniel and Yvette had stayed by the car on the side of the road for hours.

Several other vehicles had also come along the road during that time. Daniel had waved them down and told them what lay ahead. All of them had turned around and headed back towards Limoges. Several of them with the intention of notifying the civilian authorities there.

As the afternoon blended into evening, Daniel checked his watch. It was after eight o'clock. They got back into the Peugeot and, leaving the lights off, slowly began to drive back towards the roadblock they had encountered earlier.

Daniel stopped in the same place as before and Yvette got out and looked once more to see if the Germans were still there.

There was no sign of the roadblock. The Germans had gone.

Driving slowly and watchfully, they continued on, towards the intersection where the SS roadblock had been. The way now looked completely clear.

Daniel and Yvette turned and looked at each other. They knew they had to go into the town to see. Neither of them had ever felt such apprehension.

Letting out the clutch, Daniel steered the vehicle towards the town. Within seconds, as it moved cautiously down the road, it had vanished into the choking swirls of smoke.

Short moments after that, they entered a scene from another world. A world of fire and total destruction. It was as though they had crossed the very portals of hell itself.

After driving deep into the town, they saw a parkland opening out on their left. They had reached the Fairground. Daniel parked the car on the grass, close to the road and they both slowly got out.

A burning car sat there in front of them, flames blistering the paintwork as it consumed the interior.

At first, there appeared to be no one alive. Daniel walked up to a body, lying on the roadside, with a bullet wound to the head.

Then, to their amazement, a small group of teenaged boys appeared out of the swirling smoke. As soon as she saw the boys, Yvette ran over to them.

Realising she was not an SS soldier, the boys desperately embraced her. All of them dissolving into unstoppable tears. The youngest one did not want to let her go.

Daniel hurried over and joined them. He waited until the boys had recovered enough to control their tears.

"What happened here?" he asked, knowing, full well, the answer.

"The Germans, *Monsieur*! The SS! They came here and did this!" said one of them.

"Where are all the other people?" asked Daniel, looking around.

The boys stood silently and just stared at him.

The same boy spoke again. "I think they are all dead, *Monsieur*. I think the Germans have killed everyone. They machine-gunned all the men who were with me. There were over sixty of us. There were other groups as well…"

The boy was starting to shake badly. The shock was beginning to have its effect on him.

Daniel reached out and hugged the boy closely. "Tell me your name please, young man," he asked.

"My name is Robert, *Monsieur*," he replied.

"My name is Daniel. I thank God that I am able to meet you and your friends. This lady's name is Yvette."

The five older boys looked at her and nodded but did not say anything. The youngest lad though, still clung to her.

She knelt down beside him. "Are you able to tell me your name, please?"

The boy took a moment to compose himself before he spoke. "My name is Roger, *Madame*."

Yvette patted his shoulder and stood up again.

Daniel looked around the Fairground and then turned his attention back to the boys. "Have you seen anyone else? Surely there must be others."

The boys all looked at each other and shook their heads.

Robert spoke up again. "We haven't seen anyone else yet, *Monsieur*. We haven't looked around much though. We were hiding until just a few minutes ago. There might be others."

Before they had the chance to consider any further action, the faint sound of laughter and drunken revelry hit them like a bolt of electricity.

There were still Germans, somehow left behind, in the town. They had not all gone.

The colour seemed to drain away from the boy's faces in an instant.

The sound came from towards the southern end of the town. The direction of the river. It did not sound very close but there was no time to wait and make sure.

"We have to go immediately," said Daniel. "You boys should come with us now!"

Martial spoke up first. "No *Monsieur*. I will show my friends where we can hide. We have to stay here. For our families…"

Robert Hebras joined him. "He is right, *Monsieur*. We have to stay. Please, you two go and tell everyone what has happened. We will be all right now. We will hide."

Yvette looked at Daniel and nodded. She turned to the boys. "We understand. Then go now and hide well. We'll try to get help. Good luck."

The boys ran off, following Martial as he led them out of the village, away from the drunken voices.

Yvette and Daniel quickly got back into the Peugeot. Daniel winced at the noise as the engine started. He wasted no time in putting it into gear and turning around, to head back the way they had come.

No shots followed them. The Germans were either too drunk, or too occupied to notice.

Daniel took the roads they had followed earlier, to get back into Limoges.

They made their way to the centre of the city, looking for a *Gendarmerie* or a civilian Police Station.

They finally found a Police Station and hurried inside.

Even though it was now approaching ten p.m., the reception area was a hive of activity.

Yvette looked at Daniel. "This can't be normal. Not at this time of night. They must have heard something."

Daniel nodded in agreement.

They went up to the front desk and tried to get the attention of the duty sergeant who was deep in conversation with a group of police officers.

"Excuse me, *Monsieur*," said Daniel in a loud voice.

The sergeant looked towards him and said, "In a moment, *Monsieur*. Please, be patient."

The sergeant turned back to his conclave.

"Are you talking about Oradour-Sur-Glane?" asked Daniel pointedly.

The police all stopped instantly, turned and stared at him. The sergeant's demeanour changed drastically. "What do you know? Have you heard something?"

Daniel looked at Yvette and then turned back towards the police who were now looking intently at the two of them.

"We've just come from there. We left less than an hour ago."

The sergeant's eyebrows nearly disappeared up under his hat brim.

"Please *Monsieur*, come this way." He led Daniel and Yvette into a small interview room. All of the other officers who had been with the sergeant came in as well.

Daniel, Yvette and the sergeant sat down. The other police officers stood crowded around the walls, desperate to hear the news.

"Now *Monsieur*," said the sergeant, "we have heard some reports starting to come through. Some tramway people are saying that there is something terrible going on. The Germans apparently shot one of their number. They say the town is in ruins. Is any of this true?"

The police officers and the sergeant looked intently at Daniel and Yvette.

Yvette spoke first, "It is far worse than that. There seems to have been a massacre. The whole town is on fire. Every building seems to have been destroyed."

One of the officers, wide eyed, spoke to Daniel. "Is this true, *Monsieur*?"

Daniel nodded. "Yes, it is. Every word. There are still German troops in the town. How many, I don't know. We got out as soon as we heard their voices. I don't think they saw us. There are some survivors though; we met some teenage boys. They are in hiding somewhere now."

"Did you see any bodies, *Monsieur*?"

"There was one that I saw, Sergeant. Lying in the open on the street."

"Only one? So you can't be certain about a massacre then?" said the sergeant.

"I believe it has happened, *Monsieur*," said Daniel emphatically, "one of the boys told me that he was with a large group of men and the Germans machine gunned all of them."

The sergeant inhaled deeply and most of the officers around the room just stood in horrified silence.

"How is it that you survived, *Monsieur*?" asked the sergeant.

Daniel chose his words carefully. "We weren't there at the time, *Monsieur*. We just happened to drive into the town from the north, apparently shortly after the Germans left. We were stunned by what we saw. We encountered these boys and they told us what had happened. Then, as I said, we heard some German voices in the distance and we got out as fast as we could."

Daniel did not have to stray too far from the truth. He just made sure to leave out the part about why they were there in the first place. He wanted it to sound as though they happened upon the event by accident, and then came running straight to the police.

For their part, the police had no reason to disbelieve him.

The sergeant looked around the room at his colleagues.

Daniel asked, "Well, are you able to do anything, *Monsieur*? Can you arrange for assistance? There must be ambulances that can be sent, or something?"

The sergeant looked very uncomfortable. "Please *Monsieur*, leave the matter with us. I believe that those in control of this Department will have a response underway shortly."

"But are you sure? We need to get help to this town immediately!" demanded Daniel.

"Please, *Monsieur*! We are civilian police. We have no authority here. Those who need to know will have been told by now. Something will be happening soon, I'm sure."

He looked at Daniel who was staring at him in disbelief. He had realised the police were going to do nothing!

The sergeant looked at Daniel and Yvette and his shoulders slumped. He let out a long sigh.

"You must understand, *Monsieur*. I cannot take my men up against an SS Battalion. The SS will not even listen to Vichy, let alone us. If what you say is true, they would just as happily machine-gun all of us as well if we try to get involved. You have done the right thing, *Monsieur*. You have come to the police, but in this matter, right now, we are as powerless to act as you are yourself."

Daniel could see the anguish in the sergeant's eyes. He understood. This was far beyond the power of the police. He nodded slowly.

"What should we do then?" asked Daniel, looking at Yvette.

"Go home, *Monsieur*," replied the sergeant. "Go home and let the powers that be deal with this. We cannot get involved."

Daniel, Yvette and the sergeant got up and slowly left the room.

"Do you want our names, our address? Do you want us to make a deposition?" asked Daniel.

"Ordinarily, I would say 'yes' *Monsieur*, but something tells me that it might be in everyone's best interests if there is no formal record of your having been here tonight. I have not asked you both why you went to Oradour-Sur-Glane tonight. In truth, I don't want to know. Please understand though, that I am very grateful for what you have told us tonight.

All of us here yearn for France to be rid of the Boche. More than ever, now!"

The sergeant walked them both towards the front door of the Police Station.

"Now, I would like you both to get in your car and take yourselves back to your home. Do not stop and talk to anyone else. This is not a good night to bring yourselves to the attention of either Vichy or the SS. Go straight home please."

Daniel put his arm around Yvette. He understood the sergeant's message.

The sergeant put out his hand. Daniel shook it and nodded his thanks.

Yvette smiled at him wearily. They turned and left the Police Station.

They sat in defeated silence in the car for several minutes. Daniel had not yet started the engine.

Yvette said, "So that's it? We can do nothing more?"

"That sergeant was right. This is too big. It will all come out over the next few days. If we try and do anything now, we'll probably just end up as two more murdered victims."

"So these monsters will get away with it then?" demanded Yvette.

"No they won't," replied Daniel, "I'm certain of that, but it might be a while in coming. They can lose themselves in the war. No doubt, they'll be posted up to Normandy to face the Allies. The Germans will try to get them away from here as quickly as they can."

"I hope the Allies kill them all!" said Yvette. "First Tulle, and now this. I saw these things with my own eyes, and I still can't believe it."

Daniel reached for her hand, drew it towards his mouth and kissed it.

"We need to go back to Flavignac. We can think more clearly there. Let's go home."

Daniel started the engine and pulled away from the kerb.

As they drove in silence, Yvette found some comfort in the fact that Daniel had just referred to Flavignac as 'home'.

10 June 1944: 11:15 P.M.

In a small, abandoned farm shed, nearly six kilometres north of the now shattered town of Oradour-Sur-Glane, SS Major Helmut Kampfe sat, bound and gagged, on a simple wooden chair. The previous morning, he had made the uncharacteristic mistake of going for a drive to familiarise himself with the local area. Apart from the driver, he had been alone in the vehicle. He had just disobeyed one of his own most important rules.

He had ventured out into unknown territory with insufficient force to protect himself.

In truth, he had been deeply unlucky. The ambush they drove into had been entirely opportunistic. A small Maquis group had just set themselves up, hidden alongside the road, with the singular purpose of observing and gaining intelligence on the rapidly increasing level of German troop movements in the area.

To their amazement, they suddenly saw a *Kubelwagen* with only a driver and an officer aboard approaching, it was too good an opportunity to let pass.

There had been three Maquis operatives, all armed with machine guns. The *Kubelwagen* had to slow to take a sharp corner, and it was then that the Maquis struck.

The ambush was sudden and savage. The driver was killed in a hail of well-directed bullets.

Kampfe, in the back seat, was physically unhurt but badly shaken after the car crashed into the thick hedges along the side of the road.

His Maquis captors had secured him as a prisoner before he had even regained his seat, after the crash.

Trussed up and with a gun at his head, Kampfe was quickly spirited away in an old farm cart, towed by a tractor.

The Resistance fighters took him to a remote, dilapidated stone farm shed, well away from anywhere they thought the SS might look. They had not yet decided quite what to do with him. He was not so senior an officer that he was a guaranteed mine of useful intelligence, but he was certainly still a good catch.

After the initial capture, the Maquis were making plans to move him further away still and undertake a thorough interrogation of him.

There had never been any serious intention to burn him alive, as the Milice informers had told Diekmann. It was just one of the many impulsive ideas thrown around, in the hours after his capture.

That was until the first news of the massacre at Oradour-Sur-Glane reached them! Nothing official, just the shocking reports from the first escaping survivors.

From that moment, Kampfe's fate was sealed.

Guy Rochefort, before the war a middle-aged goat cheese maker, but now the leader of a small local Maquis group, gathered up two of his men. They set off on their way to the small shed where Kampfe was being held.

They followed a careful route through a network of small lanes and fields, thus avoiding any Germans who would likely be using the larger, more direct roads.

Kampfe could tell from the looks on their faces as they entered that something was terribly wrong.

He had never seen such naked, unbridled hate on display before. At least, not from the perspective of the victim.

Rochefort strode over to him and spoke in a soft voice, fighting hard to control the rage that was burning within him.

"We have just heard your SS friends have just destroyed a town a short way from here. First reports are they have killed every man, woman and child in that town. WHY?" he suddenly shouted directly into Kampfe's ear.

Kampfe strained against his bonds.

"Were they looking for me? For us? For the Maquis?" He gestured towards his comrades.

"The town they have destroyed had nothing to do with us. It was a comfortable, bourgeois town. No friendly place for communists I can assure you. SO WHY?" he screamed again at Kampfe.

Kampfe now knew what was about to happen. His heart was racing. He lost control of his bladder and a stream of urine flowed down his leg.

Rochefort saw it.

"Good! Piss yourself! Die like the fucking vermin you are!"

He produced Kampfe's own luger pistol. He had kept it as a trophy after they captured the SS Major. He flicked off the safety catch.

"Rot in hell, Major." He put the gun to Kampfe's temple and pulled the trigger.

***

Kampfe's body was smuggled away from the shed via the same circuitous route that Rochefort and his comrades had taken to get there.

They dumped his body into the boot of their car and then drove to a spot just alongside the main road, about eight kilometres north of Oradour-

Sur-Glane. It was a quiet spot, off the road and well hidden by a dense hedgerow.

The road was only a few metres away, but the car was thoroughly obscured by this high, convenient barrier. It was very late at night now, but they were taking no chances. When they were content it was quiet enough, two men carried his body out and dumped it in the middle of the road.

The men quickly snuck back to the car and drove away again, unseen.

They knew the Germans would find the body soon enough.

The Maquis realised that after the massacre, the killing of just one man, a mere Major, would hardly balance the ledger, but at least it was a statement.

11 June 1944: Morin Farm, Outside Flavignac, 7:55 A.M.

Daniel and Yvette had no choice but to take a very wide detour to get home safely. The more direct route south from Limoges was a constant flow of Waffen-SS vehicles. If they were seen driving at such a late hour, they were certain to be stopped. To avoid this, they headed eastwards and then circled back towards the south-west, taking only small rural roads and lanes. They drove without headlamps as much as possible.

Finally, they arrived back home shortly after two a.m.

It was far too late to disturb Bernard and Delphine, so they went straight on to Yvette and Lucien's own farm.

Such was their exhaustion, they fell asleep as soon as their heads touched the pillows.

***

Delphine, knocking on the bedroom door, awakened them. She had brought some food down with her for their breakfast.

"How did you know we were here, *Mamie*?" asked Yvette.

"We heard a car go past in the night. We knew it would be you."

Daniel felt deeply self-conscious at Delphine finding him asleep in the bed that had been Lucien's for so long. At least, both he and Yvette had lain down and fallen asleep fully dressed.

Delphine, however, showed no sign of caring. She came in and sat beside Yvette on the edge of the bed. "Can you tell me what happened? Is everything all right up there?"

Having to face her grandmother and relive the events of the last twenty four hours was simply too much. She rolled over and buried her face in the pillow as she sobbed her heart out.

Delphine gently rubbed Yvette's back to try to comfort her, as it fell to Daniel to tell of what they had witnessed the previous day.

After he had finished, Delphine remained, still quietly sitting on the edge of the bed, unable to say a word.

"So we don't really know how bad it is," concluded Daniel, "it may be in the several hundreds of dead. Perhaps more. I just don't know. Certainly though, the town itself seems to have been utterly razed."

"Dear God in heaven!" said Delphine softly, "how can this be true? How can people do such things?"

"I don't know how they do it, *Mamie*," said Yvette, her voice muffled by the pillow, "but I've seen it with my own eyes. They truly are that cruel."

Chapter 18

13 June 1944: Field Marshal Erwin Rommel's Head Quarters

The Field Marshal had instructed his secretary that he was not to be disturbed in his office for a few minutes.

He had received the preliminary report on the massacre at Oradour-Sur-Glane less than an hour earlier. The report was far from comprehensive but left no doubt as to the magnitude of the events.

The report stated that an armoured column of Waffen-SS troops from a battalion in the '*Das Reich*' Division had been attacked by units of the French Resistance, within the limits of the town of Oradour-sur-Glane.

The ambush had led directly to the SS having to fight a major battle, which had resulted in extensive damage to the town and serious loss of life amongst the local civilians.

The report was thorough, and Rommel did not believe a single word of it.

The SS had committed an atrocity as barbarous as any he had heard of from the Russian Front. There had been far too many of those for the chivalrous Field Marshal to reconcile with his conscience.

This time, however, it was in the middle of France! Not just one atrocity in fact, but two!

The first one in Tulle was bad enough. That had deeply troubled him, but the second one in Oradour-Sur-Glane…!

He had needed some minutes alone in order to clarify his thinking.

The contents of the report had left him horrified. *How would the rest of the world react when the news got out?*

The divisional commanding officer responsible for the battalion, this General Heinz Lammerding, he had some serious explaining to do. Someone had to be held to account.

Much that had happened in the war had left Rommel with moments of profound disquiet. Excesses by the SS were nothing new. This, however, was something far more sinister, far more disgusting.

Rommel left his office and went out to speak with his secretary.

He issued an order, summoning this General Lammerding to his office immediately.

Briand Farm, Outside Flavignac. Mid-Day

Nothing official had yet been released concerning the massacre at Oradour-Sur-Glane, but word was spreading around the country like a wildfire.

Even Daniel and Yvette, who had seen it with their own eyes, were shocked when they heard of the true enormity.

Reports were coming through from the Resistance that the SS had been back there on the 11th and the 12th to finish off the destruction and remove as much evidence as possible as to their involvement in the crime.

Yvette sat in an armchair in her grandparent's lounge room, rubbing her forehead. The events of the last week had taken a toll on her that was worrying her grandparents and Daniel.

She had been sleeping badly and such sleep, when it did come, was punctuated by nightmares.

Daniel himself was still struggling with what he had seen, but he also recognised that he did not have to deal with the horror Yvette had experienced in Tulle on top of it.

She was going to need time, rest and a great deal of love to help her come to terms with the events of the last few days.

That at least, was one commodity that Yvette had in abundance. Between Daniel and her grandparents, she would be amply cared for and loved unconditionally.

***

Delphine had been preparing lunch for the four of them. She had just finished laying the table.

Daniel stood up from his seat on the lounge and reached out for Yvette's hand. She grasped it and stood up. Together, they made their way over to the table.

Bernard had just uncorked a bottle of wine and was arranging a glass for each of them.

He suddenly paused and stood up, turning his head towards the front door. The unexpected sound of a car coming up the driveway interrupted the lunchtime ritual.

They all looked at each other with some concern. The unexpected arrival of a car in wartime France seldom brought good news.

Daniel hurriedly crossed the room and carefully peeked out of the window. It was a small Renault sedan.

An attractive woman in her early middle age was getting out of the car. Somehow, she seemed familiar to him. Then he remembered; he had met her once before, right here, in this house, in this room.

She was at the Maquis meeting shortly after he had first arrived.

Daniel nodded to Bernard and the women to put them at ease. The caller was a friend.

Bernard crossed the room and opened the door, just as the woman was approaching.

"Angeline! This is most unexpected. What on earth brings you to our little home?"

"*Bonjour* Bernard. I'm so sorry to trouble you both, but there is something that I simply have to discuss. Do you mind?" The tone in her voice suggested she was troubled.

"Not at all," replied Bernard, "please come in. Have you eaten? You are most welcome to join us for lunch."

"That is very kind of you. I haven't eaten a thing all day," said Angeline as she entered the house.

She halted suddenly and drew in a sharp breath as she saw both Daniel and Yvette in the room with Bernard and Delphine. She had not expected to either of them.

"Oh! I am so sorry. I didn't mean to intrude," she said.

"Not at all!" replied Daniel, "please forgive me, I know we've met once before, but I can't remember your name."

"My name is Angeline, *Monsieur*. It's a pleasure to meet you again."

They embraced each other with the traditional kisses on the cheeks.

Delphine spoke, "Have you travelled down here from Limoges, Angeline? What is so important that it could have brought you all this way to see us?"

Angeline tried to compose herself.

"There is a matter… a personal matter, which I had wanted to tell you about. I had hoped to discuss it with you first before I went to see… the person that it most involves." She cast an involuntary glance at Yvette.

She now had everyone's attention.

"But it appears that person is here with us now. Would you all please forgive me if I took a few moments of Yvette's time?"

Yvette stepped forward. "What is it that could possibly concern me, *Madame*?"

Angeline steeled herself. "I have heard the news from Tulle. I know of what has happened to Lucien." She steadied herself before continuing.

"There is something which I need to tell you. It concerns Lucien and myself. Please forgive me if it comes as a bit of a shock to you. It is my earnest hope that it may ultimately be of some comfort. Would you mind if we were to step outside so that I may speak freely to you?"

Yvette looked at Daniel. He shrugged and then nodded in agreement.

Thoughts of food temporarily forgotten; Angeline led Yvette out through the door. They wandered across the yard and found a quiet, shady spot, away from the humid warmth of the early summer's day.

Inside the house, Delphine and Bernard both looked at Daniel. He could only shrug his shoulders once again.

Both of them were beginning to develop a deep regard for Daniel. It was clear the he was very much in love with their beloved granddaughter. They could also see that, despite her current troubled mind, she was equally in love with him.

In their way, they had loved Lucien too. He was a kind, good-hearted and ultimately, very brave man, but they had never reconciled themselves to his being an appropriate husband for Yvette. Now he was gone and Yvette's future clearly centred around Daniel.

The three of them sat down at the table. Daniel picked up his wine glass and held it up.

"May it please God, to better days ahead!" he said.

Both Delphine and Bernard responded. They each took a sip of the wine.

None of them, however, began to eat. Nervous apprehension dulled their appetites. They would wait for Yvette and Angeline to return.

***

Half an hour passed. The occasional peek through the window showed that Yvette and Angeline were still deep in conversation outside.

Delphine had taken the cooked food and placed it back in the oven to keep it warm.

Then Bernard, who was keeping a keen eye on the conversation in the distance, spoke up.

"They are standing up!" he said, as though a momentous event was happening.

Delphine and Daniel came over to join him.

They watched from behind the curtains as Yvette and Angeline hugged each other for a long time.

The two women finally drew apart and began to walk back towards the house.

Daniel, Bernard and Delphine quickly ran back to their chairs and tried to pretend they had been talking the whole time.

As they entered the house, Angeline and Yvette smiled at each other as they looked at the other three. They had noticed the occasional movement of the curtains. They guessed they were being keenly observed from across the yard.

Yvette looked at the three people she loved most, sitting together at the table. She was feeling a kind of euphoria, as if a terrible burden had been lifted from her.

She knew now that Lucien would have let her go to be with Daniel. He had found new love himself.

Her grief for Lucien had somehow changed in its form. She now grieved for the love denied to him and Angeline. He had so deserved to find his own happiness.

At least now, though, she could see a future with Daniel untroubled by her own unsettled conscience.

She smiled at Daniel again. This time it came from her soul.

"Well *Mamie*, I thought lunch was supposed to be ready!"

Delphine marvelled at this sudden change in her granddaughter. This was the most alive she had seen her in days.

"It is ready, my darling. And there is plenty for five!"

Yvette and Angeline joined the others at the table. Delphine and Bernard had set an extra place whilst the two women were talking outside.

As everyone found their places, Delphine set about retrieving the food from the oven and placing it back on the table.

Everyone, except Angeline. "Perhaps I should be going. I never meant to intrude upon you at a meal."

Yvette reached out and took her hand. "No! Stay please, Angeline. I want you to be a part of my family now."

Angeline immediately broke down in tears.

Yvette continued to hold her hand as the others looked at each other in wonderment.

As Angeline continued to sob, Yvette related the details of their conversation.

After she had finished, everyone sat quietly, each picking at their meals in contemplative silence. There was so much to have to process; so much news, so much emotion, so much change.

Daniel and Yvette's eyes met across the table. He could now understand and share the sense the relief that had lifted her mood so dramatically.

There was still a war raging, however. The success of the Allied invasion was far from assured. The Germans were now fighting back desperately in Normandy and France was not yet certain of regaining her freedom.

Their love might be secure, but nothing else could be, until after the conflict was finally settled.

14 June 1944: Field Marshal Erwin Rommel's Head Quarters

General Heinz Lammerding had been kept waiting, he believed deliberately, by Rommel for nearly two hours. He was angry and frustrated.

Even though Field Marshal Rommel considerably out-ranked him, the SS held themselves to be innately superior to the mere 'career soldiers' of the Wehrmacht.

Furthermore, he did not intend to be lectured to, by the man who had lost the North African campaign. A man who was widely known to have little regard for Nazism.

The telephone on the secretary's desk rang.

She picked it and listened briefly. "At once, sir!" she said and put the handset down.

"The Field Marshal will see you now, sir," she said in an emotionless voice to General Lammerding.

"Very accommodating of him," replied Lammerding, his voice heavily laced with sarcasm.

He got up and went to the door, letting himself into Rommel's office.

Rommel was standing with his back to the window as Lammerding entered the room.

"Good morning, General," he said.

"Good morning, *Herr* Field Marshal," replied Lammerding coolly.

"I'm sorry for keeping you so long, General. The fighting in Normandy is taking most of my time now. I had to put off seeing you until I could be sure we wouldn't be disturbed."

"I appreciate your consideration, *Herr* Field Marshal," said Lammerding with terse irony.

Lammerding's obvious impertinence was not lost on Rommel, but he let it wash past him. He did not want to give Lammerding the satisfaction of seeing his rudeness draw a response.

Rommel sat down at his desk and indicated Lammerding to the leather bound chair opposite.

"Please have a seat, General. I have sent for you because I wish to discuss two extremely disturbing events from recent days. One in particular, I find to be particularly incredible."

"There is, or perhaps I should say there was, a town near Limoges that has been completely destroyed. The last count I heard is that over six hundred civilians have been massacred. I believe this was carried out under your orders, General."

Lammerding haughty demeanour swiftly evaporated. He fidgeted in his seat. Rommel's eyes were locked on his. He felt his tension levels rising under the Field Marshal's intense stare.

Rommel continued, his voice was controlled, but his stare was locked on Lammerding's eyes. "Before I pass judgement, General, I would like to hear what you have to say on this matter. Did you give the order for that town to be razed?"

Lammerding swallowed and looked squarely back at the Field Marshal.

"No sir, I did not! I gave the officer commanding the battalion orders to respond in force to any Maquis activity they encountered but I did not authorise this attack."

His response gave Rommel pause. He had not expected such a meek denial.

"Then who did? Had you been advised of it in advance? Did you have the opportunity to step in and order that the attack not be carried out?"

Lammerding spoke again. His earlier impertinence forgotten under Rommel's intense barrage of questions.

"I was only told that the battalion was entering the town to look for a Maquis weapons cache. We had received some intelligence that the town was a Maquis centre. I did not learn of the... events there, until late that night. The battalion had already left the town by that stage."

Rommel continued to hold his gaze. "Who was the officer in charge? What was his name?"

"He is Major Adolf Diekmann, *Herr* Field Marshal."

"Major Diekmann? A mere Major ordered this massacre? He must have believed that his orders gave him latitude for such behaviour. Did he have that latitude, General? Could there have been anything in his orders that led him believe he was acting under the authority of yourself?"

Lammerding instantly bristled at the implication.

"No, *Herr* Field Marshal! Not at all. I believe he acted on his own impulse. He went far beyond the authority I gave him in his orders."

Rommel sat thinking for a few moments. "Just to be clear, General, you are telling me that this Major Diekmann, on his own recognisance, ordered this massacre. That he alone is responsible. Is that right?"

Lammerding nodded. "Yes, *Herr* Field Marshal. That is correct."

Rommel sat back in his chair and let out a long sigh.

"I cannot stress how important it is that SS Regiments in the field realise that this is not the Russian Front. You cannot act as you did when you were there. If the Americans and the British, not to mention the so-called Free French, were to break through in Normandy, they could be here in a matter of days. What will happen when they hear word of this massacre? Or the other one for that matter."

"Anyone taken prisoner in a German uniform, especially an SS uniform, might find themselves being shot out of hand. And frankly, who could blame them?"

Rommel paused and massaged his temples.

"Once I have more detail, I am going to order a Court-Marshall of this officer. I want to find out precisely what went on. I refuse to allow this crime to go unpunished."

Lammerding sat uncomfortably in his chair. There were other officers present who heard him rail against the Maquis on the night he ordered Diekmann up to Oradour-Sur-Glane. He knew there were others still, who could testify that he had ordered Diekmann to create a demonstration the local populace would not forget.

He had no idea Diekmann would go as far as he did, nor would he have authorised it if he had, but he could certainly be implicated as being behind Diekmann's actions.

He was now a worried man.

Rommel continued, "Where is this Major Diekmann at the moment, General? Is he still in the area?"

"No, *Herr* Field Marshal. His battalion is currently deploying north towards Normandy. They left two days ago."

Rommel nodded. "I would be loath to recall an entire battalion at this stage. We need all available men up there. General, I would like you to monitor the whereabouts of his battalion closely. Once the Court-Martial has been convened, I will wish to have Major Diekmann and his subordinate officers brought out of the line to face the charges."

Rommel had to be careful with his language. He only had limited authority over the Waffen-SS. They had their own hierarchy that stretched all the way up to Hitler himself. He could order, but it was better to ask.

Rommel got to his feet. General Lammerding knew the meeting was at an end. He stood up also.

Field Marshal Rommel came around his desk and extended his hand towards Lammerding.

"Thank you for your time, *Herr* General. It's a great pity that we meet under such circumstances."

Lammerding shook Rommel's hand. "A pity indeed, *Herr* Field Marshal. *Auf weidersehn!*"

Lammerding stepped back and stood at attention. He gave Rommel the Nazi salute. "Heil Hitler!"

Rommel only responded with a nod and a half-hearted raised arm. "Thank you General, you are dismissed."

Lammerding spun on his heel and left the room.

He was furious at what he took to be an act of disrespect to the Fuhrer in the Field Marshal's last act. As he saw it, Rommel's position was due entirely to the benevolent indulgence of the Fuhrer.

Rommel is the one who should be Court-Martialled, he thought.

Even so, he now saw his own position as being under examination and threat. He would have to call an immediate meeting of his officers.

If a scapegoat was called for to pacify the Field Marshal, then Major Diekmann it was going to be.

Diekmann's military career could end in front of a firing squad, but not that of General Heinz Lammerding.

15 June 1944: South of Poitiers, 5:30 P.M.

A full battalion on the move is a slow and ponderous beast, and Diekmann's was a large battalion.

Frequent short, sharp engagements with Maquis fighters had further hampered the speed of the redeployment.

Two days of travel through these savage, hit and run engagements saw them now approaching the medieval city of Poitiers.

There was still a long way to go. Over two hundred kilometres still separated them from deployment along the front lines. Diekmann and the men of the 1st Battalion were almost desperate to be rid of these mosquito-like annoyances from the Maquis. They wanted to be part of the real action.

They had set up a large bivouac in picturesque pastureland, just outside Poitiers, alongside the Claine River. This meant that there would be plenty of fresh water for the men to bathe, shave and fill their canteens.

The events of just five days ago no longer featured in the men's conversations. Many of them had been willing participants in such acts in the past. They did not dwell on the morality of what they had done. There were new challenges now; they had moved on.

Diekmann, Kahn and Barth were settling down to enjoy their evening meal and more of the wine from the stock they had appropriated in Oradour-Sur-Glane. Between the three of them, they had acquired a large haul of excellent wines from Deny's shop before the other troops got to it. They had drunk a great deal of it over the subsequent five days and now the supply was beginning to run low.

Soon they would need to find another source to raid.

Vehicles had been arriving constantly over the last two hours, so the approach of a single motorcycle did not arouse their interest at first.

Shortly after though, their happy conviviality was shattered.

The despatch rider had finally caught up with the column and had promptly requested directions to Major Diekmann's Head Quarters.

The three officers were sitting and watching as the rider stopped his machine outside Diekmann's tent.

The rider set the bike on its side-stand and opened up one of the leather panniers at the rear. He removed an envelope and marched over to the group of officers.

He saluted and stood rigidly to attention.

"I have a delivery for Major Diekmann, direct from General Lammerding."

Diekmann extended his hand and took the envelope. "Thank you corporal, you are dismissed."

The rider returned to his bike and set off on his way to look for a meal. He had been riding for hours.

Diekmann slit open the envelope and took out the two typed pages.

As he read the lines, his eyes began to grow wide in horror and rage.

"This cannot be! Rommel is calling for me to be Court Martialled for the action in that town the other day! What nonsense is this?"

Kahn and Barth looked on in concern. If Major Diekmann were to be Court Martialled for the massacre, then they would surely follow.

Diekmann finished reading the letter and then passed it over to Kahn.

He reached for his wine glass and sat back into his chair, deep in thought. He waited until the other two had both read it before he spoke again.

"I think it might all blow over. Apparently, Rommel has had his romantic sensibilities upset by our cleansing of that pathetic little ghetto the other day. He does not control the SS! I have no doubt that General Lammerding will go all the way up to Himmler if need be. This will be dropped."

Kahn and Barth listened, nodding intently in agreement.

"Anyway, the letter is not recalling any of us yet. We can continue travelling to Normandy. By the time Rommel might be ready to proceed, we will be in action. High Command will not pull their best fighting units out of the line to suit the whims of Field Marshal Rommel."

Diekmann slowly sighed and took another sip of wine. He was regaining his composure.

"Yes indeed, gentlemen. I believe this will pass. I shall write back to General Lammerding this evening. I shall point out that he had given me explicit orders to act as we did. He said that we were to follow the same tactics we had used against the Ukrainians. We both knew what that meant."

The three of them returned to their wine glasses again as a group of orderlies approached with their evening meals.

They each ate in pensive silence. The flatness of the mood in stark contrast to the earlier jocularity of the evening.

All three of them hoped that Major Diekmann's analysis of the situation was correct. None of them, more so than Diekmann himself.

16 June 1944: Limoges, Late-Afternoon

General Lammerding sat, deep in thought, at his new desk in his new Head Quarters.

Open in front of him lay a letter from Major Diekmann, responding to the one he had sent the previous day. Diekmann had obviously stayed up late into the evening writing his response, so that the motorcycle courier could deliver it back to Limoges promptly.

Clearly, the Major was concerned. He did not want to be made a scapegoat, to be convicted at a show trial.

In his letter, he made the point several times that he was acting under the orders of General Lammerding when he carried out the 'demonstration' at Oradour-Sur-Glane.

Lammerding was well aware of the orders he had given to Diekmann. He had told him to *make it hurt*, but what did that really mean?

Lammerding could argue that he meant something proportional. He could point to the mass hangings in Tulle and say that was the example he wanted followed. Something that would hurt, but not the mass extermination of an entire town.

He would argue that Diekmann had taken it upon himself to enact a retribution so extreme. He had far exceeded the remit of his orders.

There were other officers present at the meeting outside Tulle that afternoon. Officers who had heard Lammerding give Diekmann his orders.

Those same officers then witnessed the events in Tulle. They would understand the meaning of a proportional response. Furthermore, they would be far more likely to stand behind their most senior officer, than fall in beside a mere Major.

They would know where their best interests lay.

If Diekmann wanted to try to shift the blame back onto Lammerding, no one would support him. The ultimate blame would rest entirely with him.

Suddenly, Lammerding sat bolt upright at his desk.

A powerful idea had occurred to him. He would not wait idly for Field Marshal Rommel to call for a court martial; he would do it himself.

He, Heinz Lammerding would become the aggrieved party.

He had issued the orders, Diekmann had disobeyed them.

He got up from his desk and went out to see his secretary. He asked her to come into his office and take dictation.

There was work to do.

Chapter 19

21 June 1944: Argentan, Normandy, 9:00 A.M.

Despite almost daily attacks by disparate bands of Maquis resistance fighters, the 1st Battalion had covered many kilometres over the last week and now it was closing in on the combat zone.

They were now on the northern side of what had once been the beautiful medieval city of Argentan. Allied bombing, prior to D-Day and since, had caused catastrophic destruction. Much of its historic beauty was now in ruins, lost forever.

Diekmann had led the battalion to its latest bivouac. They were now preparing to break camp and get underway once again.

Today, they would be heading up through the so-called Falaise Gap and then on into the combat zone. Once they were past Falaise, they would receive instructions as to where they had to deploy before going into action.

From here on, they could start to expect to receive the attention of allied aircraft. American and British fighters and bombers controlled these skies now.

They were about to be at war again.

Major Diekmann was speaking to a group of junior officers, outlining final arrangements for the day, when a corporal approached carrying a telegram.

"Excuse me *Herr Major*, this is for you. It is marked urgent!" said the corporal.

Diekmann excused himself from the meeting and ripped open the envelope.

The colour drained away from his face as he read the contents.

"Oh, my God!" he said aloud, not even realising he had spoken.

Captain Kahn noticed his reaction and came over immediately.

"Is everything all right, *Herr* Major?" he asked with concern.

Diekmann did not speak, he just handed the telegram to Kahn to read.

Diekmann was being recalled to Limoges immediately. He was to be Court Martialled for the massacre at Oradour-Sur-Glane!

The battalion was to proceed on without him. They were still needed at the front.

The two men just looked at each other in shock. Finally, Diekmann spoke.

"That bastard Lammerding, he is behind this. He is throwing me to the wolves to keep his own neck safe. Well, at least I will get to say my piece. Give me back the telegram please, captain."

Kahn handed it over and Diekmann resumed reading. "I am to go down to a place called Sees immediately. There is an airfield there. An aeroplane will be waiting to fly me back to Limoges. Clearly, they don't intend to waste any time!"

Diekmann smiled, rueful and humourless. "Well then Kahn, I must leave the battalion in your care. I hope to re-join you all soon. I have no idea how this will all play out."

The other officers came over to find out what was happening. Diekmann explained the sudden change in his fortunes.

Lt Barth in particular looked furious at the news. "They would have expected no less of us in the Ukraine! What makes these damn French so special? There is the stench of hypocrisy about all this!"

Diekmann smiled and patted him on the shoulder. "It is all right, Heinz. I will get my chance to speak. I will tell the Court Marshall that we were following, precisely, the orders, as they were given. Anyway, it appears I must be going. Captain Kahn, can you arrange a car for me, please? I have to see to my packing."

***

Sure enough, when the car carrying Major Diekmann arrived at the civilian airfield, south of the city of Sees, there was a small Fieseler Storch aircraft waiting for him.

He placed his bag in behind the seats and took his place alongside the pilot.

Diekmann was no lover of air travel and flying in such a small aircraft as the Storch would normally have unnerved him. This time though, his mind was too preoccupied for such concerns. In the event, the flight proved a welcome distraction. He enjoyed the superb glory of the central French countryside as the little aeroplane flew at only a thousand metres altitude, in order to avoid the unwanted attentions of possible Allied fighters.

Once on the ground at the Limoges aerodrome, a car and a haughty SS Captain were there to greet him. The Captain was keen to let a superior officer know that he was not here for pleasure.

The vehicle took him to a hotel in the centre of Limoges where he checked into a surprisingly comfortable room that had already been booked for him. He had expected something more spartan, as befitting a man soon to be on trial.

The Captain left him with instructions that the court martial was scheduled for the following morning. He was not under arrest and was thus at liberty to wander around the city of Limoges. However, the captain added that he should be back at the hotel for dinner and not go out again that night.

A car would arrive to pick him up at ten o'clock in the morning.

The Captain left, and Diekmann was suddenly on his own. He had spent so much of his life since the war began, in the company of others, or at least so close that their presence was inescapable. This was the first time he could remember being in a room by himself in years. He could not hear the sound of another human being.

The silence, the sudden solitude and being alone with his thoughts, quickly became oppressive.

He took the Captain at his word and decided to go out into the city. He needed to walk off this growing sense of dread that was unexpectedly threatening to consume him. He was under no illusions that he had been singled out as the guilty party. He was to be the one held to account in the eyes of the world.

He walked the ancient streets for several hours, seeing little, trying to clear his mind and decide what he would say in the morning.

He ate an uninspiring evening meal in the hotel restaurant before returning to his room. He took a seat at a small table with the intention of writing to his wife. He had not written home since the massacre. He sat there for an hour, but the words would not come.

Thoughts of his own wife and children jarred powerfully as he contemplated what he had seen in Oradour. Nightmares, made real under his orders.

Eventually, he put paper and pen aside and gave up.

A myriad of contradictory thoughts were now crashing around inside his head. Emotions he was unable to control were welling up inside of him, stifling his ability to reach out to those he loved most. What was happening to him?

The silence and solitude of this lonely room began to beat on him, as though he was inside a drum.

***

Before he had gone to bed, Diekmann had left his uniform with the concierge to be cleaned and pressed, and his boots to be polished.

He had a small breakfast, then washed and shaved, before dressing in his now perfect uniform.

He was ready for them. He had not slept well, but he was ready.

The car came for him promptly at ten a.m. He was already in the lobby, impeccably presented and awaiting its arrival.

Taking a seat in the back, he made himself comfortable as the vehicle drove off towards the Limoges Head Quarters of the Waffen-SS.

Once they arrived, Diekmann was swiftly ushered into a waiting room and offered an armchair, where he sat, waiting to be summoned.

He helped himself to a glass of water from a nearby cut-crystal pitcher.

He had anticipated that they would leave him on his own for a considerable length of time. A practice intended to increase the mental pressure on the accused. The long wait in nervous apprehension.

The wait turned out to be no more than fifteen minutes. It appeared everything was in readiness.

An immaculately dressed sergeant came into the waiting room and spoke to no one in particular, seeming to address the empty air.

"Major Adolf Diekmann, will you please follow me!"

Diekmann stood up and pulled at the lower hem of his uniform jacket, straightening it after being seated. He adjusted his cap and marched off, in perfect step with the sergeant as they entered the large, ornate room that was the theatre for the court martial hearing.

The doors closed behind him as he approached the seat set for him in front of the assembled senior officers.

The central figure in the assembly was General Lammerding. Sat on his right was Diekmann's own Regimental commander, Lt Colonel Stadtler. It was to Stadtler he had first reported, after the action in Oradour-sur-Glane. Stadtler had not been happy.

"Thank you for coming, Major Diekmann," said General Lammerding. "Please take your seat. Now, let us get underway."

26 June 1944: Normandy, Outside Caen. Early Afternoon

The car carrying Major Adolf Diekmann arrived at the command post controlling the defences to the west of the city of Caen.

The city was one of the principal objectives of the allies as they pushed hard to build upon the bridgehead they had established in Normandy.

The allies had expected Caen to be one of the first large cities liberated after the invasion. However, the German resistance stiffened and prevented the allied forces from gaining the quick victory that they had planned for and anticipated.

The liberation of Caen had now become a major battle in its own right.

The allies were winning, but it was vicious fighting, suburb to suburb.

Diekmann was held in detention for nearly three days in Limoges following the Court Martial.

That it had found him guilty was no more than he had expected.

Initially, he was confined to his lonely and oppressive hotel room, before Lammerding relented and allowed him a certain latitude to wander about the city.

He had ample time alone in his room to dwell on the events of the previous two weeks. His head resonated with visions of the town of Oradour-Sur-Glane.

Things he had not intended, but that had happened because of the orders he had given.

The sight of a dead baby, crucified upon a tree.

The sight of helpless people being dragged from their homes, shot in the knees and then thrown back into the buildings to burn along with their homes.

The sight of his troops, drunk and out of control, looting homes that had been quiet, safe and secure havens only hours before.

Adolf Diekmann had been given too much time alone. Time to think was the last thing he needed.

That was behind him, now he was back at the Front. It was time to reunite with his battalion.

A battalion commander with as much experience as him was far too valuable a commodity to leave languishing deep behind the lines.

The next link in the chain after the court martial was an actual criminal trial.

In the interim though, Diekmann, a proven fighter, was ordered to rejoin his battalion. Further investigation was still going on and a criminal case was not yet prepared.

So then, here he was.

He found the regiment deployed along a front to the south-west of Caen.

The region was characterised by small farm lots, separated from each other by dense hedges. Most rural roads ran in between low earthen embankments, making the roads appear to be sunken below the level of the land. Atop these embankments would be still more of the dense hedging.

The French name for this man-made landscape is '*bocage*'.

The German armies were using the *bocage* to telling effect as they fought a desperate defensive campaign against the relentless push of the allies.

For the Americans and the British, every hedge could be hiding a German position. All too often, they were.

The Germans could not have hoped for a better defensive landscape in which to fight. However, as hard as it was for the allies to advance through it, and as bad as their losses were becoming, their forward momentum was building inexorably.

The *bocage* did not extend forever. Soon, the Allies hoped to break through into a more open landscape beyond. The advantage would then swing heavily in their favour, with their lighter, more manoeuvrable tanks and total command of the air.

Meanwhile though, the German-held city of Caen still stood in their way.

Diekmann had travelled most of the way back to Normandy by car. Allied air cover now made it far too dangerous to fly into the combat region, especially in a slow, unarmed aircraft.

He waited in the vehicle whilst the driver went into the command post, looking for directions to the battalion.

He returned shortly after and they set off again, heading further west before then veering north.

Finally, the car passed some soldiers that Diekmann recognised. He was back with his men.

Getting out of the vehicle, Diekmann looked around for an officer. Lt Barth spotted him first and came hurrying over.

"Major! Welcome back!" he said smiling, temporarily forgetting the formalities of military protocol. He quickly remembered and stood to attention, saluting.

Returning his salute, Diekmann said "Thank you, Lieutenant. It is good to be back. Now, how is the unit? What is the situation?"

Straight back to business.

"Strong sir," Barth replied, "performing well. Different kind of enemy to the Russians. Much less keen to throw their men against our machine guns, than they were. They seem to rely more on artillery, armour and air power here. Makes it more difficult to get to grips with them."

Diekmann nodded. "That is no surprise. That is their great strength. Can you please send for Captain Kahn at once? I need a full briefing."

"Of course, sir!" replied Barth and he set off.

Diekmann spied an orderly and set him the task of preparing a tent. The battalion commander was back and needed accommodation.

28 June 1944: Normandy, South-West of Caen, Late Afternoon

The American barrage had been going on for over two hours. The battalion's entire world was a mind-shattering realm of screeching shells and cataclysmic explosions as the allied artillery found the range on their positions.

"It's just like being back in Russia!" shouted Lt Barth from the fragile safety of his foxhole.

"It's nothing like Russia," replied Captain Kahn, crouched next to him. "The weather here is much warmer!"

Barth managed a forced smile. Both of them knew two officers should not be sharing the same foxhole. A direct hit would kill too many experienced leaders. The barrage had commenced so suddenly, however, that they had no choice. They both leapt into the nearest foxhole.

They had been quietly discussing the situation concerning Major Diekmann between themselves. Both were deeply aware of the change in him.

Since re-joining the battalion, he had become increasingly withdrawn and non-communicative. His drinking was noticeably heavier.

His tactical commands though, were still astute and his personal bravery undiminished, but something had changed.

As suddenly as it began, the American artillery barrage ceased.

Kahn patted Barth on the shoulder. "You keep a watch here. It may mean tanks. Get the men ready. I'll head over to the right flank."

Kahn scrambled out of the foxhole and began to head over towards the opposite end of their defensive line.

Diekmann spotted him as he ran. "Captain, where have you been?"

Kahn changed direction and came over towards where the Major was standing. He was out in the open, looking over the defensive deployments.

"I was over on the left, sir. The artillery bombardment forced me to shelter there. I was just going over now, to check on the right. There may be tanks coming through shortly."

"Yes Kahn, I agree. Make sure that there are plenty of anti-tank and mortar rounds. We will need them. The artillery took out one of our 88s. The infantry will have to fill that gap."

"Yes sir, I'll see to it," said Kahn as he hurried off.

Diekmann watched him depart. He turned and walked back towards the artillery emplacements, further to the rear. The loss of one their 88 mm's was significant. It was a fearsome anti-tank gun. An American shell had scored a direct hit. The gun was totally destroyed, three of its crew had been killed instantly.

Diekmann reached the spot and gazed silently at the shattered gun and the mangled remains of what were, only minutes earlier, three men who served under him. Men he all knew by name.

Now, all that was left of them would fit in a couple of buckets.

He stood, staring silently at the gore until a voice calling his name filtered through, catching his attention.

It was Captain Kahn. "There doesn't appear to be any enemy tank movement, sir. It looks like this was purely an artillery strike only."

Diekmann looked at him without responding. Eventually, he nodded and began to walk back towards the forward infantry lines. Kahn accompanied him.

"Have you had anything to eat yet today, sir?" he asked. "You don't seem to have eaten very much at all lately."

"I've had a bit, thank you, Kahn," he replied. "I might have something more, later."

Kahn steeled himself to ask the next question. Now seemed as good a time as ever. "*Herr* Major, is everything all right, sir? You haven't really spoken much since you got back. We know about the outcome of the Court Martial. Is there anything that you need from me? From any of us?"

Diekmann stopped walking and turned to Kahn. "I don't really care about the outcome of the Court Martial, or what will follow on from now. What is done is done. That is all out of my hands, and I'm glad for that. Others can judge what I have done. I will just continue to do my duty."

He stood looking at Kahn, saying no more.

Kahn tried to steer him back to the present. "Do you have any orders, sir? Anything more that needs to be done here?"

Diekmann hauled himself out of his dark reverie. It needed an almost physical effort of will.

The merest flicker of a smile briefly toyed with his face and he said, "We are as prepared as we can be. Just stay alert. They might not be advancing this time, but it may be that they are trying to get us used to a pattern of shelling with no follow up, and then spring an assault on us. We must stay alert."

Kahn nodded and saluted. For a brief moment, the Major had seemed almost back to his old self. Clearly, the court martial had affected him more than he had realised. That must be what it was.

***

That evening, Kahn and Barth stopped by the Major's small tent, which had been set up towards the rear of the battalion positions.

They had a bottle of cognac with them.

"Would you care to share a few drops with us, *Herr* Major?" asked Barth from outside the tent.

"Actually, gentlemen, I was hoping you would call by. Thank you," came the reply.

Diekmann's tent was too small for guests, so he came out and the three of them found chairs and a small table.

Major Diekmann almost seemed back to his old self. Perhaps a bit more withdrawn than usual, but wanting to talk again.

For a time, they spoke about the war and about the movements of the battalion after Diekmann had gone back to Limoges. After the alcohol had begun to loosen their tongues, the conversation began to drift back towards what had happened at the court martial. The Major had not spoken of it since he had returned.

"It went exactly as I expected," said Diekmann. "It was set up to find me responsible for what they are calling 'the massacre' and to keep General Lammerding in the clear."

"Did you get a chance to speak in your own defence, *Herr* Major?" asked Kahn.

"I was given that opportunity, yes," replied Diekmann, "but I chose not to push it too much. I said that I believed that I was acting under orders. That we did nothing we hadn't done before, in the Ukraine."

"And how did they respond, *Herr* Major?" asked Barth.

"Well, they were clearly very well prepared for me to say that!" said Diekmann with a wry smile.

"They pointed out that we were not in the Ukraine; that we were in France, and a very different set of guidelines now applied. Strange, I have no recollection of receiving these so-called new guidelines. Anyway, I kept my counsel from there on and let it all flow as they intended. I really didn't care too much after that."

"So, what happens now, *Herr* Major?" asked Barth. "Does this mean that a trial is to be held? That means we will all get a chance to speak in your defence. We can all point out that we had never been told that France was to be different than the Ukraine."

"That is quite all right, Heinz. I really do appreciate you saying that, but I do not believe it will ever come to a trial. We are at war, and war has a way of changing even the best of plans."

Diekmann took this cryptic point no further. Both Barth and Kahn looked at each other quizzically.

Major Diekmann continued with a sigh, "I miss my family, you know. I miss my children. I have been thinking about them a lot lately. I wonder if I did let things go too far in Oradour-Sur-Glane."

He paused for a moment, deep in thought.

"I wonder what kind of a father I can be to them, after all that I have seen in this war. After what I have done in this war. There are some things that I would change…"

Once again, he left the point hanging, unable to finish the sentence.

The three men sat in silence for a few minutes, sipping their drinks.

It was now getting late in the evening. For once, there was no shelling going on in their sector. Neither side seemed to wish death upon the other this night.

Diekmann leaned forward in his chair. "Well, gentlemen, we know our dear friends, the Americans will no doubt be knocking at our door first thing in the morning. We should get such sleep as we can and be ready to face them. I shall bid you both good night."

He got up and without another word, retreated into his tent.

Kahn and Barth continued to sit for a few minutes more, as they finished their drinks.

The bottle emptied, they quietly got up from their chairs, about to walk back to their bivouacs, when an unexpected sound caught their attention.

The sound of muffled sobbing was coming from Diekmann's tent.

29 June 1944: Normandy, South-West of Caen, Mid-Morning

It was the German's turn to commence the barrage today. At least, they started first.

The Americans were quick to accept the challenge, and soon the air was rent with the soul crushing thunder of countless artillery shells exploding on both sides of the line.

The Americans had the greater resources, and soon the German guns began to fall silent. Partly to conserve their ammunition, but in several cases, because they had been damaged or destroyed by the allied guns.

The troops of the 1st Battalion were huddled as low as they could manage in their foxholes. This was a heavy bombardment. Far heavier than the day before.

The Americans must have brought up more guns in the night.

To the huddled troops and their commanders, this must surely be the prelude to a major advance. They struggled hard to steel their nerves, knowing that once the artillery stopped, the real fighting would begin.

Diekmann had been huddled in a foxhole along with two privates. He did not attempt to speak to either of them, nor they to him.

There was a look in his eye that told them he wished to have no part of human company. The two soldiers looked at each other and shrugged. Then they huddled down deeply in the foxhole, intent only on surviving this cataclysmic barrage.

Captain Kahn and Lieutenant Barth had also found shelter in foxholes. Each either side of the one that the Major occupied, each about forty metres distant from it.

Occasionally, someone would quickly raise his head above the earthen parapet to check the state of their situation. So far, everything was holding well.

In his hole, Diekmann suddenly began to rock back and forward. His companions turned towards him with concern. Was the Major starting to lose his mind? They had never imagined seeing him like this. He had been as steadfast as a rock for years. What was happening?

Barth lifted his head once more for a brief look around.

His mouth fell open as he watched Major Diekmann emerging from the foxhole. He screamed at him to get back into the shelter. His efforts were futile, his voice drowned out by the mind-numbing cacophony of uncountable artillery explosions.

Barth could only watch in horror as the Major stood up straight and began to walk along the line. He was moving away from Barth, heading in the direction of Kahn's foxhole.

Two helmeted heads appeared from the foxhole that Diekmann had just left. They were frantically waving for the Major to come back.

Diekmann seemed oblivious to them. To Barth, he seemed to be strolling, almost casually.

Barth reflexively pulled his head back down as an American shell burst in the air above their positions.

He waited a few seconds for any shrapnel to fall and then he looked up again.

Diekmann was lying on the ground. He was not moving.

It was still too dangerous to leave the foxhole and go to his aid.

The two privates in their foxhole, and Barth in his, had no choice but to wait for the shelling to subside before they could go and find out Diekmann's fate.

After another twenty minutes, the barrage finally ceased. Barth clambered out of his foxhole and hurried over to the stricken Diekmann.

The two privates also emerged from their foxhole when they saw Barth go past. Captain Kahn emerged from his, just as Barth reached Diekmann. It was clearly far too late to render any assistance.

A razor sharp sliver of shrapnel had all but taken Diekmann's head completely off.

There was no time for emotion or sadness. They could hear the distant sound of American armour on the move. They were advancing.

Captain Kahn quickly ordered the two privates to find a stretcher and remove Major Diekmann's body from sight.

He and Barth then turned their minds back to the approaching fight. They were seasoned fighters. There was work to be done, and pity was for the weak.

Chapter 20

5 September 1944: Limoges, Liberation Day

The streets of Limoges seemed like rivers of joyous, jubilant colour. Women in their thousands, gaily dressed for the first time in years. Men also trying their hardest, by adding a coloured scarf or hat to their usual drab street clothes. Children excitedly playing and chattering and everywhere, the tri-colour of France waved enthusiastically in what was now the free air of a beautiful early autumn day.

Enormous crowds lined the streets as, from the north-west, an American armoured column under the command of General George S. Patton began to make its way through the city.

The day had finally come. Tears were as common as laughter, but now at last, they were tears of unbridled joy.

After four terrible years, the Germans were gone.

The joy, however, was not for all. Many in the city had prospered under the occupation. Many women had entered into relationships with soldiers of the occupying army. Many others were active agents of the occupation.

These *collaborateurs* now lived in fear.

The first to be singled out and persecuted, were those women known to have had physical relationships with the German invaders. The nature of the relationship did not matter. Whether it was for love, or merely sex, the outcome was the same.

Their vengeful fellow citizens herded these women, like cattle, into the streets. Once there, they were held down whilst their hair was shaved or clipped off. Close-cropped hair was to become the instantly recognisable badge of dishonour for women all across France. Those who, willingly or otherwise, had dallied unwisely with the Germans.

These celebrations and reprisals were all happening at once. It was a day for those most deeply contrasting of emotions: jubilation and vengeance.

Daniel, Yvette, Bernard and Delphine had driven to Limoges from Flavignac. They were but four amongst the many thousands who had arrived for the Liberation parade. The last of the Germans had left over twenty four hours earlier, and it was now safe to travel on any roads they chose.

They had been keeping their eyes out for anyone they knew from the Maquis cells they had worked with. Yvette was particularly hoping to see Angeline, but amongst the thousands of faces lining the streets, there was little chance of recognising anyone.

None of them knew Martine, the young seamstress who worked for Angeline. To them, she was just another of the distraught, screaming women who were having their hair brutally cut off by the vengeful crowd. This was her price for having had a German boyfriend.

***

Daniel and Yvette held each other tightly. There was a chance this might be the last time they saw each other for a while.

Daniel's convalescence, following the pneumonia, was over. He felt well and keen to re-join the army of which he was a part.

Yvette had been distraught when Daniel told her that he was going. It had been the hardest conversation they had ever had. For Daniel though, there was no alternative.

He had found two strong allies in Bernard and Delphine. They completely understood and supported him. It was their resolution that had finally helped Yvette come to terms with his leaving. They would stand by her.

The armoured column had been filing past for nearly two hours when the last of the tanks had finally cleared the streets. The vehicles following were mostly lorries carrying the vast array of supplies that a mobile armoured force needed to stay on the move. General Patton clearly did not intend to pause his pursuit of the retreating German armies.

He was in a race with his despised rival, the British General Montgomery, to reach the German homeland first.

For these two highly egotistical Generals, bragging rights mattered deeply.

Once the tanks had passed, several of the support vehicles began to pull up and park around the centre of the city, wherever they could find an unoccupied space.

American officers, NCO's and privates in their dozens began to emerge, only to find themselves engulfed by an irresistible wave of joyous well-wishers.

Daniel was desperate to catch the attention of any one of these officers. They might be able to advise him how to get in touch with the Free French forces under General Charles De Gaulle. Daniel was sure that they would not be too far behind.

Finally, he got his chance. A number of the vehicles the Americans called Jeeps, pulled up close to where he and the others were standing. He kissed Yvette's hand and pushed his way through the crowd until he reached the vehicles.

He found himself face to face with a Lt. Colonel. Daniel spoke English well enough to be able to explain his situation to the American.

The Colonel explained that the Free French were still well over two hundred kilometres behind them, but if Daniel could wait a while for the American's to set up an administration centre and begin to get themselves sorted, they might be able to arrange transport to get him back to their positions.

It would not be today though, or tomorrow. There was too much traffic, all heading in their direction, for any vehicle to go back the other way.

Daniel smiled gratefully and saluted. The American saluted in return and promptly went back to his previous business.

He made his way back to the others and let them know the news.

"It looks like you have to put up with me for another two or three days. They can get me back to the Free French, but they need to wait for the roads to clear."

"How far away are they?" asked Bernard.

"Over two hundred kilometres apparently. That would have them somewhere up near Tours," replied Daniel.

"So, shall we go home then?" asked Yvette.

"That sounds like a wonderful idea," replied Daniel.

"Well, I think we should find a market first," suggested Delphine. "This is a famous day. Let us have a decent meal tonight."

"And some decent wine!" added Daniel. "I still have several francs left. Let's spend it on something good, shall we?"

It felt good to be able to laugh aloud in public again. They set off on the way home.

9 September 1944 North of Poitiers, Late Morning

Daniel had finally managed to secure a ride in a jeep heading back up the road from Limoges.

He and Yvette had three more days together before he returned to Limoges on the 8th. The Americans were able to find him a lift on the following day.

They left early. The car was on the road before five a.m. but could only make slow progress. They found themselves frequently pulling over to let vehicles bound for the front have right of way.

Daniel was conscious of the fact that he had no uniform. He was confident though, that his presence in France as an SOE agent would be all the explanation he would need.

They were given directions to a large private estate outside the city of Poitiers. The tri-colour was flying prominently from a masthead. He had reached the local HQ of the Free French army. The months of frustration were behind him. It was time to re-join the fight.

Signs directed him towards the most prominent building. It was the main administration centre.

Letting himself in, he approached a sergeant sitting, clacking away at a typewriter on a large desk.

"What do you want?" asked the sergeant without looking up.

"I am Lt Daniel Martin of the Free French army, sergeant. I am reporting for duty. Is there a Duty Officer I may speak to?"

The sergeant looked up in surprise. This man was dressed like a peasant.

"You don't look like a Lieutenant to me," said the sergeant.

"Then you will have to take my word for it, sergeant. Now is there a Duty Officer available please?"

A door opened behind them and a captain entered the room.

"Did I hear someone asking to speak to the Duty Officer?" he said.

Daniel came to attention and saluted. "I did, sir. My name is Lt Daniel Martin. Free French army. I have been in France since early May. I have been working as an operative of the British SOE. I have been assisting the Resistance up until now."

The captain looked surprised. He looked over Daniel with obvious suspicion.

"And just how can I be of assistance to you now, Lieutenant?"

This was not the welcome Daniel was expecting. "Well sir, I would like to be de-briefed and then be allowed to re-join my Regiment. I assume they will be here in France by now."

"If what you say is true, Lieutenant, then I shall be only too happy to get you back to your Regiment. First, however, we shall need to confirm your story. There have been a number of instances of German agents trying to infiltrate the French army with stories similar to yours. I shall have to ask you to allow yourself to be held in custody until we are able to have your story confirmed."

Daniel was aghast. "You can't be serious! I have travelled for days to get here. I can tell you anything you need to know about my service and my Regiment."

"I have no doubt about that, Lieutenant, but please understand, the German agents that have been apprehended so far were all very well briefed. If your story is true, then I will be the first to apologise and wish you well, but in the meantime, you must remain under guard."

Daniel unhappily resigned himself the process. It took over a week for his file to arrive from the SOE in England, but eventually it did, and his identity was confirmed.

True to his word, the Duty Officer came to his room and, with a huge smile, shook Daniel's hand.

The two of them had become quite close whilst Daniel waited out the detention. The captain's name was Yannick Lefebvre. He was a Parisian. He was delighted when confirmation of Daniel's identity came through. He went over and advised him immediately.

They had used the time of Daniel's incarceration to have the sergeant, who was a trained stenographer, transcribe in detail the events of his deployment in the Limousin.

Captain Lefebvre put the transcription into a confidential report and had it forwarded to the headquarters of the Free French Army. There, it was brought to the personal attention of General Charles De Gaulle.

The French senior command had heard stories of the massacres in Tulle and Oradour-Sur-Glane. They now had an eyewitness account. The General would be most keen to see it.

Captain Lefebvre had been content as to Daniel's legitimacy long before the file arrived from England. An SOE Major delivered it in person. He was to be present at Daniel's de-briefing.

Lefebvre had taken steps to arrange new uniforms for Daniel. He would need them now that he was back in the fold.

After a haircut, bath and shave, a very different looking Lt Daniel Martin presented himself to the senior staff for his formal de-briefing.

The officers had all read the report prepared by Captain Lefebvre. Now they wanted to hear it directly from Daniel himself.

They questioned him in detail for several hours.

His story chilled them to the bone. France was now being set free of these monsters, but an adequate reckoning still awaited those who did this.

Daniel had asked earlier to re-join his Regiment, which was operating to the north, alongside the British forces. Now that all the formalities were dealt with, he asked the question again.

He was deeply conscious that the pneumonia had prevented him from playing the active role for which he had volunteered. He was desperate now to take on serious active duty.

The assembled officers looked around at each other. No one raised the slightest objection.

The following day, Daniel was on a light aeroplane heading north to re-join his Regiment.

17 February 1945: Briand Farm, near Flavignac, Mid-Morning

Bernard and Delphine had been waiting patiently for Yvette to arrive.

They knew that she would come up to visit. She had not called in yesterday and she never missed seeing them more than two days in a row.

They had been keeping company with an unexpected guest for over an hour.

A captain of the Army of France had called in. He had let them know he would like to speak to their granddaughter.

He had important news.

Eventually, they saw Yvette coming up the laneway that led down to her farm.

They waited in the house for her to knock at the back door, which she always did before entering. Just to let them know it was she.

As she entered the old house, Bernard and Delphine came into the kitchen to greet her.

They looked serious.

"Yvette, there is a captain from the Army here to speak to you," said Bernard. "He says he has very important news."

Yvette suddenly looked concerned. Had something happened to Daniel? Not now! Not this close to the end of the war!

She looked at them with concern briefly until they both started to smile.

Looking resplendent in his new uniform, with its captain's markings on the shoulder, Daniel appeared from behind the door that led into the lounge room.

Yvette squealed with joy and raced into his arms.

After she regained her composure, she asked with a smirk, "Now what was this important news I heard about, *Monsieur*?"

"Oh, nothing that important really," replied Daniel, "just something to do with a marriage."

Epilogue.
5 March 1945: Oradour-Sur-Glane

A tall, lean figure with a prominent, hawkish nose, led a group of invited dignitaries and survivors of the massacre on a long walk through the remains of the town.

The war was not yet over but France itself had been free of the German occupation for most of the last two months.

General Charles De Gaulle had wanted to visit the town since he had learned of the calamity, the previous year. The ongoing war and the desperate need to rebuild the governance of France had kept him completely occupied in the months since, however.

Now though, almost nine months after the events, he was finally able to come and see the remains of the town for himself.

The sight of the shattered township, even after many months in which the streets had been cleared of rubble and much of the destruction had been tidied up, was still a profound shock to him.

The final death toll from the frenzied and savage assault by the SS had ultimately been calculated at six hundred and forty two.

Innocent townsfolk. Fathers, Mothers, children. Shop owners, employees, teachers and their charges, elderly and infants. All had perished.

As he walked along the main street, *Rue* Emile Desourteaux, De Gaulle came to a realisation. This had to stay as it was. He would not allow it be cleared further and rebuilt.

He would have it declared a national monument. A permanent memorial to the tragic cost of freedom. A freedom paid for in full, by France.

Oradour-Sur-Glane would become a permanent symbol of lost innocence and lost humanity.

A reminder to the world, of the depths of evil for which man is capable. It would be left as it was, to remain as a lesson to all, for all time.

De Gaulle nodded silently to himself. He had the authority to decree this, so decree it he would.

***

After the walk through the shattered remains of the town, the General was finally led back to the large, open green space that used to be known as the Fairground.

Once there, he went over to an assembled group of special guests. He was introduced to those few survivors of the massacre who were able to attend.

He met little Roger Godfrin, the youngest to survive. He met some of the boys who had hidden with Robert Hebras in the old, stone rabbit hutches. He met others who had somehow managed to find a way to escape the villainy of the SS, and of the flames that followed so close behind them.

Robert Hebras himself, after being reunited with his father who, almost miraculously, had not been in Oradour-Sur-Glane that day, was not able to attend.

After meeting the survivors, De Gaulle was then introduced to a few additional guests, who had other roles to play in the aftermath of the disaster.

He moved along the line slowly, speaking to those whose names he recalled from briefing notes.

He stopped when he came to a handsome French army captain and the lovely, young woman who stood beside him.

"I believe you must be Captain Daniel Martin, *Monsieur*," he said.

"*Oui, Mon General!*" replied Daniel.

Daniel turned towards Yvette. "May I introduce you to my fiancée, Yvette, *Mon General?*"

"*Enchantee, Madame*," said General De Gaulle, kissing the back of her hand.

Yvette blushed.

De Gaulle turned back to Daniel. "I have read your report, captain. Several times in fact. It makes for sobering reading."

Daniel nodded. "I understand, *Mon General*."

Daniel then pointed over towards the place where he and Yvette had stopped their car when they first came into the town.

"We pulled up, not far from here, *Mon General*. Just over there, in fact. That burnt out car there," Daniel pointed to the shell of what used to be a Peugeot, "was still burning when we arrived. We met the group of boys almost where we are standing now."

De Gaulle looked over the scene Daniel was describing.

"I believe it was your hope to get here in time to warn the town of the imminent threat?"

Daniel nodded. "It was never to be, *Mon General*. We were always going to be too late."

De Gaulle nodded in sympathy.

"Be that as it may captain, you tried. In fact, you tried several times I believe. Most would not have been so persistent. You bring honour to your uniform, captain. It is my great pleasure to shake your hand."

Daniel reached out towards the general's offered hand and shook it gratefully.

The general turned towards Yvette and took her hand, kissing it once again.

"I am aware that you were present here as well, *Madame*. In fact, I believe that you were also in attendance at the other tragic event, in Tulle."

Yvette nodded silently.

De Gaulle took off his cap and tucked it under his left arm. He paused before speaking again.

"I'm not sure who I should be saluting, Madame, you or your husband. May God bring his blessings upon you both."

The general came to attention and saluted. Daniel instantly followed him, and returned the honour.

General De Gaulle smiled at them and shook Daniel's hand once more.

Then he moved on to the next in the line of guests.

THE END

Author's Afterword

This book is a novel. Principally, it is a work of fiction.

However, the events of June 1944 in the City of Tulle and the town of Oradour-Sur-Glane were all too real.

With the exception of the fictitious character of Major Krebbs, all the German protagonists in this story are the real people who undertook these massacres.

My telling of the uprising in Tulle is highly fictionalised. The actual events were spontaneous and largely driven by the dominant communist faction within the local Maquis. The totality of the events there were complicated, and far beyond the scope of what I intended for my story. I chose to simplify the action into a single fictitious event in the lead up to the brutality of the SS response. The character of Paul Launay – in my narrative, the final victim hanged in Tulle – is also fictitious.

The characters of the victims of the town of Oradour-Sur-Glane are the real people.

My telling of the events as they un-folded, is based in no small part on a narrative written by the Oradour-Sur-Glane survivor, Robert Hebras in the years after the massacre.

He wrote an hour-by-hour account of the events as they unfolded; from before the Germans arrived in the town, up until their eventual departure. His narrative is, by necessity, based around and limited to his own experiences of that awful day. It tells of what he witnessed, as well as his part in avoiding capture and resulting survival.

In my narrative, I have allowed the young boy Roger Godfrin to be reunited with Robert Hebras and his friends after the SS left the town in the evening. In reality, Roger survived by running away from the town before the SS had completed setting up their perimeter around the village. He was found, distressed and wandering, in a nearby town the following day.

His story is the only major liberty I have taken regarding the authentic townsfolk of Oradour-Sur-Glane.

Other survivors had their own stories to tell. I have drawn on some of these accounts to help offer a fuller picture of the horrors of that day. In particular, of the appalling events that occurred at the church.

I have tried as best I can, to present these events as honestly as my writing skills will allow. It was always my prime consideration to show the utmost respect to the memory of the victims.

Roger Godfrin aside, I have ventured into the purely fictitious only regarding the meeting between Robert Hebras, his co-survivors and my fictitious characters, Daniel and Yvette.

I felt compelled and inspired to write this story as a direct consequence of having visited Oradour-Sur-Glane in October, 2019. I saw first-hand the scale of the destruction and fury visited upon that innocent town by the SS.

The passage of the years has softened the appearance of the ruins. Plants have overgrown much of the damage. Rust has helped render twisted and flayed metals into more organic tones.

The church has been scrubbed clean of the worst of its scars; initially by teams of workers, but ever since, by the gentle action of the French climate as weathering slowly erases the scorch marks left by the inferno of 10 June 1944.

Perhaps though, the greatest tragedy of the razing of Oradour-Sur-Glane is not that it happened at all, but that it still happens so regularly.

The history of our species shows such barbarity being a common and recurring theme. We can be a truly brutal animal.

From the most ancient times, up to the most modern, we continue to do these things.

There are some lessons, it seems, we are incapable of learning.

For Marguerite Rouffanche, the events of 10 June, 1944 left permanent and deep emotional scars. She experienced horrifying flashbacks, nightmares and abiding grief over her lost family for the rest of her life. She was able to give evidence in 1953, at the only trials to be held in France relating to the Oradour-Sur-Glane atrocities. The defendants were few in number and comprised only lower ranking SS troops.

47 years old at the time of the massacre, she lived a long life, dying in 1988 at the age of 91. She is buried in the cemetery in Oradour-Sur-Glane.

Robert Hebras himself also lived a long and full life, dying only in February of this year (2023) at the age of 97. After the war, he returned to his trade of automobile mechanic, repairing and selling cars in the new village of Oradour-Sur-Glane, built alongside the shattered remains of the old. Later, he moved his business to the larger town of St. Junien. He dedicated his life to the preservation of the remains of the martyred village and the memory of those who died there. France awarded him the Legion of Honour in 2010.

As for the SS perpetrators of these crimes in Oradour-Sur-Glane, justice ultimately proved itself both elusive and inadequate.

After the war, General Heinrich (Heinz) Lammerding was arrested in West Germany and brought to trial there, for his role in the two massacres. He received only a short sentence and returned to civilian life afterwards, eventually becoming a successful civil engineer.

The French government tried many times to have him extradited to face justice in their own courts. The West German government refused, saying he had already been found guilty and punished for these crimes. He lived out the remainder of his life in Dusseldorf, dying of cancer in 1971.

Lt Colonel Sylvester Stadtler played, perhaps, the most active role within the coterie of principal SS protagonists, in bringing charges against Diekmann. He was reportedly horrified when Diekmann advised him of the massacre, only an hour or two after the events. Noticeably though, he did not relieve Diekmann from duty.

An Allied captive during the closing stages of the conflict, his American captors held him in high regard. His well-documented, humane treatment of Allied prisoners captured in Normandy and subsequent battles, ensured their respect for him.

After the war, in the new West Germany, he returned to university and earned a degree in business management. He built a career in management, eventually dying in 1995. He is buried just south of Augsburg in Germany.

In the opinions of many historians who have studied the events of the day, Lt Heinz Barth was one of the most deeply involved in the enthusiastic prosecuting of the Oradour-Sur-Glane atrocity.

He returned to (what became) West Germany after losing a leg in the latter part of the war. He managed to stay 'under the radar' for many years, even being awarded a "War Victim" pension in 1981. An extraordinary irony.

He was finally identified for his role in the massacre. After many years of freedom, he was tried in West Germany in 1983. At the trial, he showed no remorse and stated, in effect, that what happened in Oradour was simply what they, as SS soldiers, did.

There are some terrible stories that have emerged from their time on the Eastern Front in Ukraine that would add credence to that point.

He was released from prison in 1997 due to poor health and after finally admitting remorse for his actions so many years earlier. He lived another decade, dying in 2007.

Adolf Diekmann died under circumstances much as I described in my narrative.

His comrades had noted how moody and depressed he seemed after his return to the battalion following the court martial. He took himself out from under cover during an artillery bombardment and was all but decapitated by a shell fragment. Coincidentally, the date of his death, 29 July, 1944 was also Robert Hebras' 19th birthday.

It is difficult to say whether his actions amounted to suicide; we can never know. All we can do is try to infer a motive from his actions, and the observations of those who were with him.

They were aware of his state of mind, and several indeed believed he had deliberately set out to get himself killed that day.

Based upon what I have read of him as the better man he was before the war, I can only hope that it was in part, a rekindling of some part his atrophied humanity that compelled him to take that final, short walk.

If that were the case, perhaps it might have been the most sincere apology he could have offered to the citizens of Oradour-Sur-Glane.

Or perhaps that's just me, trying hard to look for some good in him.